Sarah Goodwin completed the BA and MA in Creative Writing at Bath Spa University. *The Alpine Retreat* is her eighth novel to be published with Avon, following several years as a self-published author. She lives in Cornwall with her family and a very spoiled dog.

Also by Sarah Goodwin:

Stranded
The Thirteenth Girl
The Resort
The Blackout
The Yacht
The Island
The Private Jet

THE ALPINE RETREAT

SARAH GOODWIN

avon.

Published by AVON
A division of HarperCollins*Publishers* Ltd
1 London Bridge Street
London SE1 9GF

www.harpercollins.co.uk

HarperCollins*Publishers*
Macken House, 39/40 Mayor Street Upper
Dublin 1, D01 C9W8, Ireland

A Paperback Original 2026
25 26 27 28 29 LBC 6 5 4 3 2

First published in Great Britain by HarperCollins*Publishers* 2026

A catalogue record for this book is available from the British Library.

ISBN: 978-0-00-873282-0

Set in Sabon LT Std by HarperCollins*Publishers* India

Printed and Bound in the United States of America

This book is dedicated to everyone who had an awful time working in hospitality. Including myself.

Chapter 1

The takeaway cup of coffee was burning my fingers, but I wasn't going to set it down for anything less than a third-degree burn. Doing so might have taken even more urgency out of the actions of the woman behind the tobacco kiosk in the remote ASDA I was unlucky enough to find myself in on that particular Friday morning. As I watched her laboriously unlock every single sliding door to the tobacco products I wondered if there'd ever been a study on how many hours of a smoker's life are wasted waiting for their fucking cigarettes.

I was tapping my foot on the linoleum, the £450 leather of my Weitzman pumps meeting the scuffed plastic floor. I shouldn't have had to be there, not in person. I should have been in London at that moment, where you could get a coffee and a cigarette on the go instead of having to wait for the poxy supermarket to open. My Costa triple-shot Americano had come out of a vending machine, for Christ's sake. I was in the Boonies.

But that was the job. You had to go to the clients most if not all of the time. Usually because they couldn't set foot outside their country house in the middle of nowhere without being papped or giving an unfortunate soundbite. Or because they were locked up in a police station, hiding out at a luxury hotel or staying with their mistress in a modestly priced two-bed love nest in the middle of nowhere. It took all sorts.

There was sweat prickling under my Yves Salomon cashmere coat, cold sweat, because in a minute my phone was going to ring. I could almost feel the crackle of data streaming through the air, coming at me like a swarm of angry wasps. It was like waiting for the starting pistol at the race of my career. Only I had no idea how long the track was or how many hurdles would be in my way. I just knew I had to get to the end as quickly and cleanly as possible.

My heart was beating faster now and I inhaled, trying for a moment of calm, eyes narrowing on the woman in the green tabard, who was, thankfully, finally, opening one of the doors and taking out the pack of cigarettes I had asked her for ten minutes ago. Twenty. It felt like forever.

'There you are, love, that's £18.80.'

I slapped the twenty-pound note down and was already leaving before she could finish her sentence. I didn't care what she did with the change – it wasn't worth my time to hang around for it. Not at my rates.

My phone rang as I was stepping through the automatic doors into the bracing January air. It stung my cheeks and made me regret putting my hair up, leaving my ears to the mercy of the icy breeze.

'Wallace Consulting – you've reached Chloe,' I said, because there was no time to check the caller ID. I was striding towards my car, one of only two in the entire car park at that early hour. The other was a white transit van with a man sleeping inside it, his vending-machine coffee fogging up the windows.

'Chloe? It's worse than we thought. Something else happened with M. Shale Limited overnight.' My assistant-slash-underling Brie sounded particularly rattled today. A bad sign, and worse news, given that we'd already thought it was going to be an absolute shitshow with M. Shale. But then again clients didn't ask for me because they had 'little mistakes' to fix, they came in demanding Chloe Wallace because their worlds were ending, and they needed a miracle. Or a devil's bargain.

Which I suppose made me the devil. Not entirely inaccurate. I certainly felt like it most days.

'How bad is it – what's he done now?' I asked, elbowing the car door open and throwing my bag at the passenger seat as I juggled coffee and cigarettes – the wine and wafers of my personal communion. The bag tilted and spilled into the footwell, littering the floor with face wipes, MAC lipsticks, vodka miniatures and pocket mouthwash. For the clients, you understand. There was nothing worse than wheeling a disgraced CEO out in front of the cameras only to discover he had the shakes. All my clients went on stage with fresh breath, industrial deodorant and a slight buzz to take the edge off. Nothing said 'guilt' like stress lines and a stiff posture.

'I've sent you the video – but Montgomery's gone and put a video on Twitter and it's blowing up.'

Brie, like everyone else in the world, still hadn't got the hang of saying 'X' when referring to Twitter. Mostly because, like everyone else – including me – she thought 'X' sounded stupid. I stuck my coffee into the cup holder, found my phone and opened the app. A quick search for Montgomery Shale and his account popped up. I tapped 'play' over the image of his florid face and my car filled with the sound of his voice. The homophobic slurs jumped out at me like fruit machine tumblers. When he hit triple cherries I stopped the video. It wasn't getting worse than that. They didn't hurt me personally – I was used to it by now. Thick skin didn't cover it, I was a bloody rhino. I'd had to be.

'Christ, who let him have his phone back?' I muttered, scrolling. The number of shares and comments made me wince. It was going nuclear. Nip-slip-at-the-Oscars nuclear.

'Should we take them down?' Brie asked.

If I ever asked Brie to put out a fire, she'd probably throw petrol on it. 'That's the last thing we want to do. No, there's already screenshots of them everywhere. Nothing looks worse than trying to hide the undeniable. No, we need some radical intervention if we want to save this . . . Can we get Mandy on the phone?'

'Sure, give me a second.'

While she dialled Amanda Shale, Monty's daughter, I ripped into the cellophane on the cigarettes like a starving animal and pulled one out. Victory. My lighter – an S.T. Dupont I'd received for covering up a 'minor' car crash involving the unlicensed son of a bank's managing director (not to mention the Smirnoff and molly found in the 'borrowed' Bentley along with the two underage passengers). The lighter really was gorgeous: red lacquer and yellow gold, with a snake etched into it. That was me, I reflected – an expensive little snake. He'd even given me the matching pen.

I lit the cigarette and tossed the lighter at my bag, watching as over a grand's worth of luxury tobacciana bounced around the footwell like a pinball. Christ, what was the point in something like that if every time you looked at it, you thought about paying off two sobbing sixteen-year-olds, one of whom had to have a metal rod put in her arm?

'Chloe? It's Mandy here.' Her voice came down the line, sharp and quick as a razor. Albeit one that went to public school. 'I've seen Daddy's little . . . stunt. And I'm not happy. First the discrimination claims and the incident with his chiropractor, now this? I've got London Pride on the phone wanting a statement and three separate investors threatening to pull out of the Scottish expansion. What the fuck am I paying you for?'

I took a drag on my cigarette and shut my eyes. 'You're paying me to fix it, which is exactly what I'm going to do.' The 'if you shut up and let me get a word in' was implied. She duly shut up and let me speak. Which was good of her especially seeing as how I'd left her in charge of his phone.

'OK, so the former strategy is not going to work now he's doubled down. An apology and a few photo ops aren't going to gloss this over. There's two main avenues we can explore – or three, if we go for a dementia angle—'

'He's only sixty-five,' Mandy interjected.

'Which is why that's on the back burner for now,' I said, already feeling exhausted by this whole affair. 'We can always claim it's early onset if it comes to that. But the two main options are either we get him to come out – say it was all self-loathing and he's a late-in-life gay man who struggled through the stigma of the times, blah blah. Plus, we can probably get him a boyfriend, lots of out-of-work actors about who'd jump at the publicity.' I took another drag and let the delicious poison circulate my veins. 'Option two is . . . we crucify him. You're already planning to take over in a few months, but we can move it up. It'll make the apology easier to swallow if it's delivered by a young woman, signals that the company is entering an era that's more tolerant and accepting. Good optics. That plus a massive charity donation and taking his name off the new building might just sell it. But that means he's on his own with the backlash and he can't receive a penny from the company on paper.'

I waited while Mandy chewed over her options – get her mid-sixties dyed-in-the-wool homophobe of a father to pretend to be gay, or, throw him to the wolves. She'd need a minute I thought, glancing at the clock in my car, waiting for the numbers to change. Before they had a chance, Mandy spoke up.

'Get me a list of potential boyfriends by the end of the day,' she said, voice just as clipped as it had been since the start of the call. 'If he wants to keep his villa in Tuscany, he can play ball until after the expansion, then retire with a bit of grace.'

'Great.' I tossed my cigarette out into the car park and watched it hiss on the wet tarmac. 'Just keep the idiot off Twitter and any other socials until then. I can get someone lined up to manage them for him, write all the content and get some staged photos of him and his partner. Should be sorted in time for the Sunday papers. I'm about an hour away from your head office and I'll break it to him personally. If you could pop in towards the end to smooth over his ruffled ego, that'd be wonderful.'

Mandy hung up and I heard Brie still breathing on the

line, waiting for her orders like an eager gun dog panting at my feet. I shut my eyes and reeled off the names of a few likely looking actors – the kind that couldn't even get booked for *Strictly* or a panto in Luton. Then I added in the names of a few creators we had on the payroll who could get some posts together and reminded her to pick up my dry-cleaning, water my plants and make sure my office coffee bar was fully stocked. Then I hung up.

It had started to rain, that grim drizzle that seems to billow over towns in the north-east. A sort of airborne gruel of water and misery. I wound up my window and took a sip of my coffee. It had gone cold, sometime between asking for cigarettes and ending that phone call. I took a few greedy gulps anyway. I needed the caffeine, and something sweet to wash away the bitter lies furring my tongue.

I was good at my job, that was the worst thing. I was a good liar and a great manipulator and God knows I'd had to be. It wasn't as if anyone else had been watching my back after Mum binned me off on social services and clattered off into the sunset with whichever bloke was covering her pub tab that month. I'd created myself from nothing and now I had my own company and I was sitting in a Mercedes, in cashmere, at a fucking ASDA trying to save some bigot's reputation. It was funny how life worked out.

I lit another cigarette. I'd come so far and, really, the perks of my job far outweighed the griminess. I often reminded myself of that. What was the harm in wading through muck if you got to wash it off in a rainfall shower in a chic London flat that cost half a million pounds?

Yet I was still all alone, no friends – I wasn't sure Brie

counted, because I paid her – and certainly no girlfriend. I hadn't the time, really, with work calling me to action at all hours. When and where was I ever going to meet someone decent? I wasn't going to Pride this year, that was for certain. How could I? Montgomery wasn't even my first homophobe triage of the year and it was still January. I didn't belong in a big parade with the rest of my community, marching with pride and in solidarity.

As good a living as I made, as secure as working hard made me feel, it didn't give me much time to make friends. Most days I just wanted to leave work and crash at home in blessed silence. My last girlfriend had broken up with me via Brie, because we hadn't seen each other in weeks and I never had time for her calls.

Looking at the tiny bottles of vodka littering the floor of my car I contemplated having a little drink before the meeting. Just something to make me feel less brittle. Less like I was about to snap under the strain. Monty was going to go off on me, I knew that. He was going to call me every name under the sun, spittle flying all over my face. I'd be lucky if he didn't throw something at me when I brought up the boyfriend plan. When I'd taken his phone away to give it to Amanda he'd lobbed a decanter at my head and only just missed. He'd also called me a slur I'd had to google.

I was fiddling with the lighter, listening to the '*cling*' as it flipped open again and again. I didn't need a drink. Or I did, but that wouldn't fix anything. I knew that. My entire career was built on hosing off minor and major celebs and politicos who'd tried and failed to find answers in a bottle, a syringe or a woman with her eyes on a pay cheque. No, I had to be smarter than them. That was how this worked. Smarter than my clients and the press and sometimes even the police. Or, at least, prepared to go lower than they'd ever suspect another human being of being capable of going.

Starting the car, I roared out of the supermarket car park, manicured fingers clenched around the heated steering wheel. I didn't need a drink, or another cigarette or even a few days back in the civilised world of London. I was never going to quit my job, but I did need a fucking break. From the clients and work and the constant scrolling of social feeds to find new and even more morally bankrupt people to add to my roster. I'd used up everything I had in the tank and the year was barely new. A rest, a break from my phone going off every five minutes and some pampering. Then I'd be back like a bat out of hell, ready to claw my way to better things.

Fortunately, and ironically, I had a good number of options if I wanted to disappear for a while. All thanks to my job. Because what self-respecting PR crisis manager doesn't know of at least six or seven tech-free, exclusive hideaways, where you can get a dozen fresh oysters and a hot stone massage around the clock, but won't be bothered by a single outside soul? The perfect place to stash even the most rambunctious client away from every temptation.

I instructed my phone to call Brie back, and had her make my reservation at a brand new wellness retreat. The ideal spot, really, as I'd never sent anyone there and so the staff wouldn't connect my name to a TV being thrown out of a window, or a drunken bender that required new carpets to be fitted. One of my most recent clients was on the board of their parent company and he'd talked endlessly about the place while I'd driven him home from the police station. Even at the time I'd thought it sounded like just what I needed. He owed me a favour, and I'd gladly use it to get a room there last minute. I needed to get out of Dodge as soon as possible. Before I keeled over from a heart attack at a cigarette counter.

The knot of tension under my breastbone started to ease as I drove through the January drizzle. I just had to hold out until Shale's snafu was sorted, and it was off to The Sorgente, in Switzerland.

With any luck, I'd spend a fortnight there and leave with my soul just a little cleaner, aired out in the alpine atmosphere.

Chapter 2

Despite my best intentions, I wasn't able to set my phone aside while I was on the plane. For one thing, I'd spent so long with it permanently glued to my hand that not checking it every fifteen seconds stressed me out as much as looking at the bloody thing. Besides, I like to do my research and I didn't yet know much about The Sorgente, just my client's connection to it. Frustratingly even he didn't know much about the place – it was just an investment made by a company his company owned. It also had almost no social media presence. He'd talked it up but must have cribbed most of the info from the investor's brochure. There was nothing much online. No pictures or videos or vlogs from the wellbeing retreat itself. Hardly any posts even mentioning it. Like it was even more of a secret than the most discreet rehab places.

That was interesting. Either they hadn't had many customers yet or the ones they had hosted wanted to keep their time there as their little secret. Still, it didn't seem to be affecting business. An idle check of their website gave me no info about how busy it might be – bookings had to be requested and there was no indication of room availability. I wasn't sure if that was just coy hype-building, or if my client had pulled some serious strings to accommodate me. Almost as many strings as I'd pulled to keep his involvement in that yacht orgy quiet. (Who hosts a yacht orgy on the Thames during the London Marathon? Hello, media coverage. Even if you aren't dumb enough to run the thing aground.)

So although I'd shelled out for business class, downloaded a white-noise playlist and spent fifty pounds on a lavender-stuffed eye mask with supposedly massaging and spiritually cleansing properties, I was awake and glued to my phone for the entire flight. I couldn't seem to stop myself from scrolling socials and watching as scandals bloomed, died and rotted on the vine. Endlessly fascinating to me, all the grotesque permutations as the A-list to C-tier wriggled on the hook, waiting to be chewed up alive by the previously adoring public.

Still, at least it wasn't a long flight. Switzerland wasn't the other side of the world, though I was hoping it would feel like it once I was there. Up in the Alps at The Sorgente, going from steam room to ice-cold plunge pool to five-star dining room and bed.

I was in my own little bubble until we landed, only surfacing for a cup of weak coffee and wishing we'd never disallowed smoking on planes. God knows what I was going to do at the retreat itself; I couldn't imagine smoking would be allowed between spa treatments and hikes. I'd brought a few vapes to tide me over. Though I wasn't too keen on them they were better than nothing.

I collected my luggage, the two matching TUMI suitcases piled with casual clothes I'd not even taken the tags off, and about twelve books I'd been planning to read for the past two years. This break was going to be serious business. I planned to go home having read every book and truly maxed out on wellness and self-improvement. I'd brought deep-conditioning masks for my hair, face, body and feet, a jade gua sha still in its gift box and a whole folder on my laptop with films I'd missed at the cinema. In short I was planning to catch myself up on everything I'd missed during the past few years while work took over my life like a cancer. Albeit one that paid me very well. I'd be enjoying it all with a few glasses of the artisanal gin and tonic stashed between the layers of jumpers and jeans. I was all for rest and relaxation but I wasn't about to go full wheatgrass for the duration if I could help it.

Outside in the diabolically cold air, I hugged my coat around myself. Turning to my left I spotted a line of cars that stood out from the rest of the airport traffic. They clearly weren't taxis, despite sharing their bay, and they were all motionless in the seething hustle of cars. As I got closer I saw that each one had a logo on the side, a light teal wellspring in the centre of some ripples. The Sorgente logo, with the name below in indigo.

I'd been told there would be a car waiting for me and had expected a taxi or something, but it appeared that The Sorgente had their own fleet. I also apparently wasn't the only guest arriving today. From the lack of social media action and the lack of transparency on how booked up it was, I'd hoped to have it mostly to myself, but there were eight cars there and another pulled up as I found the driver holding a teal placard with my name on it. My heart sank. I'd thought my connections had put me ahead of the game but it appeared not. Even without online buzz, word had still spread somehow. Probably through whispers and PAs gossiping over their rushed lunches about how their boss had jetted off for a little bit of secret rehab or to recover from a facelift.

'Miss Wallace?' the driver, a medium-height unassuming man with a light French accent, confirmed with me. I nodded and abandoned my cases by the boot for him to load.

'Welcome to Switzerland,' he said, depositing the placard on the front passenger seat. He was wearing a chic uniform, pale grey with dark blue piping, complete with leather gloves and a scarf that looked like cashmere. The Sorgente apparently spared no expense in outfitting its employees. 'I'm Michel, please make yourself comfortable and I will have you at The Sorgente within the hour. Help yourself to refreshments.'

He opened the rear door for me and I climbed inside. The upholstery was custom white leather to match the exterior of the car and the centre console boasted a glass-and-chrome setup with carafes of water bursting with mint, cucumber and lemons. Each with a chunk of clear quartz inside for some reason that was no doubt highly spurious, as well as gleaming silver thermal jugs of herbal tea and lion's-mane-infused hot chocolate. No coffee, I noticed, glad I'd thought to pack a few bags of French roast and my Georg Jensen Bernadotte coffee press. As much as I was going to enjoy the peace and quiet I had no intention whatsoever of giving up my creature comforts. Not on my first holiday in five years.

God, five years. I really had been working too hard. No wonder I felt like shit. It wasn't the job, it was me. My mind and body were obviously exhausted.

I helped myself to a cup of chocolate, only to find it was completely unsweetened and quite bitter despite being creamy and rich. I pulled a face, thankful I was cut off from the driver by a privacy screen, and dumped in some cream from a miniature glass bottle. According to the label it was from the retreat's own pasture-raised dairy herd. At least it diluted the bitter chocolate.

As we drove out into the country I started to unwind a little. The views really were stunning – the road meandering like a river through wide plains between the impressive mountains. Although it was January and quite bleak, it was bleak in a beautiful way. The same way London looks in a grey morning mist, the sky like sealskin and a hundred thousand chimneys exhaling wisps of white smoke. If I believed in auras I'd imagine those roads were what mine might look like – patchy snow, grey rocks and dead yellow grass waiting for spring and for the thaw.

We followed a wide river for a while, rimmed with ice, each of its slick black rocks topped with a white hat of snow. I sipped my chocolate and shivered with the enjoyment of being warm and snug in the plush car interior. This was what I needed. This was what my mind and body had been crying out for.

I was enjoying the drive so much that, even though it was quite long, I was still a little disappointed when we arrived at the gates to The Sorgente. It appeared that the road we were on was private as I hadn't seen any buildings or junctions or even a road sign for a while. Just the rolling valley we were in and the stream alongside the road.

The gates we stopped at were in a tall stone wall that flowed across the road and vanished in either direction.

Though the raw stone was studded with succulents and small rock-garden plants to soften their appearance, they still gave off a feeling of high security. Beside the entrance was a little office with mirrored windows. I guessed whoever was in there operated the secure entry and made sure no outside nuisances could get in. After a brief pause the gates opened, splitting the chrome wellspring logo in half as we were admitted. Glancing back, I saw them close. If the other cars from the airport were on their way, they weren't on the stretch of road behind us. Maybe they'd been dropping guests off instead of picking up? I could only hope.

Beyond the gate the landscape was more of the same, albeit studded with cows. That dairy-herd thing hadn't just been a marketing gimmick. The road also had the occasional cattle grid in it, which did somewhat ruin the smooth drive. The only sign of an actual farm I could see was a timber barn in the far distance. The cows themselves steamed in the chilly air and I realised that I'd never actually seen one in real life before. It wasn't as if they hung around at Fortnum's.

I could also now see the retreat itself, above the bucolic fields. It was nestled into the side of the mountain, far above me, standing out from the craggy rocks with its stark, straight lines. Behind it a fringe of pines pointed at the sky. The glass shone as the sun came out from behind the cloud and reflected off the snow and ice. The wood siding hadn't yet weathered enough to blend in completely with the rocks and the bright birch planks were still blond and new. Below it, at ground level, was a smaller version of the same type of building, and outside it two white cars were already parked. The whole thing was very impressive; I couldn't understand why they hadn't put any pictures up online. It would have really been a draw. Perhaps they were waiting for spring to get better images.

How I was going to reach it remained a mystery until I noticed the cables in the air between the upper and lower buildings, some sort of cable car or lift that would take me the rest of the way up to paradise. Though I could see the road continued beyond the building, it probably took a long, circuitous route up the mountain and why would guests want to wait for that when they could enjoy the sweeping views that the direct route was sure to offer?

The car pulled up under a stone shelter attached to the building and when Michel opened the door for me I felt the blast of concealed heaters warming the little carport. He unloaded my luggage as the doors to the retreat opened and a staff member in a reverse of his uniform – dark blue with grey piping – hustled out to take custody of my bags. A second employee, a blonde woman in a navy sheath dress, floated towards me on matching court shoes. She was incredibly beautiful, down to a cute mole on her cheek and the faint French accent that curled around her words like a lazy cat as she welcomed me.

'Welcome to The Sorgente, Ms Wallace – I'm Silvie, please, come with me.' She wafted me through the doors and showed me into the lobby, which was large and sparsely decorated – an enormous curved desk with the front upholstered in brown leather was the focal point and she stepped behind its sculptural shape, indicating a matching leather chair for me. The other staff member and my bags had already vanished from view, presumably on their way to be loaded onto whatever contraption would take me up the mountain.

'I hope your journey was comfortable,' Silvie said, flashing her perfect teeth at me. They were so white they matched her pearl earrings. I was envious. Even with bleaching to compensate for the coffee and cigarettes, mine weren't that perfect. I wondered if I could get whatever treatment she'd had on-site.

'It was fine, thank you,' I said. 'I'm looking forward to getting settled in for a rest though.'

'Understandable,' Silvie said, smiling again as she took out a small pile of creamy papers held together with a silver clip. 'The full programme of treatments and experiences will be available to you tomorrow. For today, you're free to familiarise yourself with the retreat and relax, go for a walk – enjoy the fresh air before the welcome dinner. If you'd like to read and sign here—' she indicated the paperwork '—I can show you to the aerial tramway.'

Her perfect smile became a little frozen, I noticed, as I started to actually read the paperwork. It was quite possible I was the first person to ever do so and the awkwardness of not getting an immediate signature was something she wasn't prepared for. I wouldn't have been surprised to find that out. Not after years of thrusting non-disclosure agreements at people and watching them scribble on them with their eyes still on the fat cheque my client was cutting them. On this occasion I wasn't looking for anything in particular. But first rule of business – read the damn document. Especially if you're a crisis manager looking for a loophole.

'Would you like a drink, while you read?' Silvie asked, eventually. 'I can direct you to a more comfortable seat in the waiting area?'

'Oh no, I'm fine thank you,' I said, still reading. It was a fairly standard document, just confirming the charges for my stay (exorbitant and paid in full before my arrival, I had plenty of savings to cover it), a waiver to say that I understood all activities and treatments were to be undertaken at my own risk (presumably in case I accidentally roasted alive in the sauna, or the 'aerial tramway' plummeted into the valley) and finally a neat paragraph that forbade me from taking or posting any and all images, video or audio from anywhere on The Sorgente's property. That one explained the lack of presence on socials. But it was to be expected if the clientele were paying top rate for anonymity and discretion. Most A-listers didn't want leaked pics of them in seaweed wraps with every wrinkle and inch of cellulite ruthlessly unfiltered.

I signed with a flourish and Silvie looked slightly relieved. I imagined she was worried I might kick off or cause a scene over the social media thing. Many would, especially the media personalities who would be flocking to this place for its exclusivity and expense. But it was ideal for anyone looking to lose a few pounds and heal from their first facelifts and scandals. I'm only on social media to watch, never to post, anyway. My life is private, because all your social media footprint is, at the end of the day, is evidence.

'Allow me to show you to the lounge,' Silvie said, standing and smoothing her crease-free sheath dress in one practised movement. She gave the impression of having been raised in the kind of environment where even the napkins at dinner were ironed with starch. I wondered if she was working here to learn the ropes before she inherited some part of the business or was ushered into a management role. Though a waft of cheap vanilla body spray suggested that maybe she was just acting the part, just like me.

Silvie led me across the foyer and through a set of gleaming wood double doors, which opened automatically to reveal the tramway waiting area. There were already two guests in there, but I took my time admiring the room itself. When around celebrities, or even wannabe celebrities, staring is discouraged. Mostly because if you look at them too long the real deals will get annoyed and the wannabes will try and talk to you.

Three of the walls were made of glass and showed a view of the mountain and a stream running down it, presumably the wellspring for which The Sorgente was named. I took a seat on a midnight-blue velvet sofa and cast an eye over the carafe of lemon water on the white marble pedestal before me. This place was really keen on hydration. I was already dying for a double-shot hazelnut latte.

It was only as Silvie inclined her head politely and left me to it that I turned my attention to the two other guests already in the room. They'd taken seats against the wall, out of the bright light reflecting from all that snow and ice. Hungover? Possibly. The dark glasses on the woman were another piece of evidence, and were preventing me from recognising her, though a faint bell was ringing. I'd seen her recently, in a still image on grainy newspaper. As for the words around that picture, I was drawing an unfortunate blank.

She was in maybe her mid-fifties, but well preserved from what I could see. I imagined her suitcase, wherever it was at the moment, was laden with Clinique and La Mer. Judging by the value of what else she had on, I'd even expect a cheeky pot of the Crème Merveilleuse I'd been eyeing online – at a breathtaking £915 a pop.

Her chin-length ash-blonde hair framed her slightly jowly face and her lips were painted frosted pink, matching the blouse under her greige blazer. Fashion that wasn't lighting the world on fire but was obviously expensive and possibly hand-tailored. I quickly assessed that her shoes were both sensible and expensive, and that the charm bracelet on her wrist was real, solid gold. Someone's wife, that was for sure, that or she'd invented some kind of kitchen gadget in the mid-eighties – an automatic cocktail shaker or something suitably pointless yet chic for its time. She had that Martha Stewart vibe, though I doubted she'd ever prepared anything more strenuous than a martini.

The man sitting a few seats apart from her was someone I recognised. Though if I'd had any other job I wouldn't have. I couldn't quite remember the name of the band; it definitely had a number in it but I was blanking. But then again they'd broken up before I'd left school. The wrinkles on his leathery skin spoke to a lifetime of tanning and the sallowness around his eyes suggested he'd only recently started spending a lot of time indoors. I was betting on rehab, judging from the evidence of nervous cuticle-picking on his fingers and the vacant way he was looking out of the window, anxiety pinching at his face.

As if he could feel my covert gaze, he shifted uncomfortably and his Hugo Boss leather jacket flopped open a little more. The vinyl lettering was cracked from age but I could still make out the logo on his shirt – NW1, for the Camden-based emo boyband that had topped the charts exactly once in my teens. By the late-2010s they had been just noteworthy enough for their break-up to lodge in my consciousness. Mostly because of the news coverage of the hotel fire that followed. What was his name? Emmery? Emil? Something like that. Last I'd seen of him he had a full black fringe and snake-bite piercings. Now he had that slightly balding mala-and-braided-bracelet look of many a central London barista. Probably something he'd picked up in rehab or therapy. I hoped it was working for him this time. It was a sad reality that fifteen minutes of fame could all too often buy you a lifetime of substance abuse.

I got my phone out to see if I could find anything on the mystery woman or remind myself of the boyband member's name. Not because I was really interested. It was more the kind of idle curiosity I'd feel when I vaguely recognised the face of someone in a not particularly gripping film. One quick IMDb visit and my interest would be gone, satisfied as easily as tossing back a handful of bar snacks.

Emmitt. That was it. Emmitt McDonald. Lead singer on the hit 'Razorblade Bae'. The woman took a little more effort but I proved myself right about her after a few scrolls through my favourite gossip accounts. Olivia Prior – wife of disgraced MP Martin Prior and the mastermind behind a range of 'hand-painted' mugs at Waitrose – whose hubby had recently been caught with his hand in public funds and his penis in a mistress thirty years younger than him. Never a good look. No wonder his wife (possibly soon to be ex-wife) was hiding out here. Probably already sick of having cameras thrust into her face for the behaviour of her useless fucking husband.

I'd just finished scrolling when a third guest entered. I knew her right away and felt a sting of pity. Jade Sutton – fitness influencer, brand ambassador, Commonwealth

Games medallist and, most recently, cancer survivor. I actually followed her on TikTok and regularly made her protein coffees in lieu of breakfast. To be honest, I had a slight crush on her and had done ever since I'd seen her sportswear adverts on the Underground.

She was just as pretty in real life as she was under a ring light. Her hair had been buzzed off and was just growing back as glossy black baby curls but it suited her gorgeous bone structure no end. She was dressed in Calvin Klein sweats and if you didn't already know, you'd never have noticed that her chest was completely flat. Double mastectomy – prophylactic, in case her cancer returned – that was what I'd heard. The things people were writing about her online were fucking vile. Between the men lamenting the 'waste' of perfectly good fun bags, like she was a theme park they'd wanted a chance to visit, and the brain-rotted bigots who couldn't tell a cancer survivor with mastectomy scars from a trans man, and were attacking her accordingly. I could see why she'd want a tech-free break.

As usual she looked perfectly composed and elegant, the sweats augmented with a pair of statement cubist Fendi earrings and an understated Moncler mini tote. She was as cool as Olivia was classic – both of them equally decked out in designer, but Jade made it look effortless, like she'd have picked the exact same things from a pile of Topshop tat.

Having looked over all the other guests I made an effort to turn my working brain off and just tried to focus on my phone, blocking everyone else out. We were waiting a while and I heard the others moving around and going in and out of the waiting room to ask the woman who'd greeted us when we'd be leaving and to use the small powder room after sipping too much lemon water.

By the time the smooth chrome tram came sliding down the cables towards us, another three guests were waiting. I'd given them all the once-over and was already praying that none of them would be in a chatty mood on the way up. I wasn't here to work and without a cash incentive I had no desire to listen to anyone's woes. For once, the problems of the famous and (sometimes) wealthy, weren't mine to try and solve. I was the posh client here, and I planned to enjoy myself.

Chapter 3

I let everyone else get on the aerial tram ahead of me so I could be the first one off once we arrived. All I wanted was to get to my room, make a cup of illicit coffee and have a few puffs on my vape out of a window. Then I could start to relax properly.

Of the two late arrivals I only recognised one: Patrick Keegan, an actor. Your run-of-the-mill 'that guy from that thing' sort of English character actor, cropping up in everything from ITV crime dramas to BBC period piece as filler, a cadaver or someone's creepy uncle.

Patrick had been trending on Twitter for over a week now for all the wrong reasons. He'd turned up to an interview semi-plastered, unsuccessfully come on to the interviewer (a lovely girl called Steph, who I'd met a few times professionally – also we'd dated the same *Metro* journalist at different points so we were practically exes once removed) and then unleashed a torrent of racial abuse on the driver who was taking him back to his hotel. Not a good look. The double whammy of sexism and racism had got him fired from an upcoming project – though, reading between the lines, his drinking was the main reason they ditched him. But you wouldn't have known it to look at him. He was standing with his hands clasped on his stomach, showing off a Rolex as he leaned against the tram wall. His hair was just taking on a whisper of grey. Every inch of him screamed 'I'm the most famous person in this place', even though it wasn't true – not with Jade there.

The mousy woman who had arrived with him was probably his PA, and she wouldn't be for long if she kept dressing in discounted Berkertex and crusty Skechers slip-ons. She looked like she ought to have been managing a rural post office, or a library, with those glasses.

Facing the window I shut my eyes for a second, trying to turn off the part of my brain that was constantly assessing people and shuffling them like cards in a hand. It wasn't just my job; it was something I'd learned to do before I could even remember. It was part of learning to survive – being able to work people out, to assign a type to them in an effort to predict their behaviour. But it was exhausting too and it left me feeling like a mean-spirited bitch.

This break was a chance to knock that off, to just exist without constantly making judgements and calculations. Easier said than done, of course, but I'd give it my best.

I enjoyed the aerial ride, despite my longing for a cigarette and the overpowering wafts of cologne from Patrick battling the Chanel No. 5 cloud emanating from Olivia. The building we'd waited in slowly shrank to the size of a shoebox and the snow-covered landscape seemed to stretch out in all directions. I couldn't see a single other building or even a road that wasn't the one we'd come in on. The sheer amount of space was almost as dizzying as the heights we were ascending to. I could feel my chest relaxing, my breathing becoming more even and deeper. Nowhere in London felt like this. I was used to being hemmed in by impossibly tall buildings, packed into Tube carriages and weaving through shops crammed with people. But here my eyes feasted on the nothingness, the empty space, and I felt relieved.

Patrick's irritated sigh impinged on my enjoyment of the scenery. 'Could this thing be taking any longer?' he hissed through his teeth at his assistant. 'I could have stayed in the bloody car. At least it had drinks.'

His PA squeaked something conciliatory and he rolled his eyes at her. I shot him a sideways look of annoyance and caught Jade doing the same. Our eyes met briefly in a moment of familiarity and she looked away. Unfortunately as she did so she ended up catching Patrick's attention.

'Aren't you that gymnast?' he said, leaning against the glass wall and eying her up and down, shifting his wrist as if to draw attention to his expensive watch. Or to blind her with its reflection.

'Sprinter,' she corrected flatly, but more nicely than I would have in her shoes.

'I bet you're still very flexible though,' he said, and his PA's mouth pursed up so hard that her lips vanished. I pulled a face. Apparently being a massive racist wasn't going to stop him from shooting his shot. He was doing some mental gymnastics of his own.

Jade raised her eyebrows and smiled without teeth, the universal sign for 'leave me alone'. But he wasn't getting it.

'So, are you here to rest up for the Olympics or . . . what?' he continued.

'Something like that.' She took her AirPods out of

her pocket and held them ready for deployment the way someone else might have held mace.

'Very exciting – an athlete in our midst. I'm Patrick, by the way.'

'Jade,' Jade said, and put her headphones in as punctuation. I watched Patrick register the rejection and saw the ugly pink flush it brought to his neck and face. Thankfully we had reached the end of the cable and were arriving at a similar station to the one we'd just left behind, complete with smiling staff members, there to unload the luggage from some hidden compartment on the tram.

My hopes of being first off the tram were dashed when Patrick rudely elbowed past me. His PA scuttled after him, whimpering apologies. I felt bad for her and made a mental note to give Brie a nice gift on my return to show how much I valued her.

I walked behind them as we were herded into an identical lobby to where I'd signed my papers with Silvie – the same sculptural white desk with leather panels, the same ultra-modern chrome statement light and a similarly uniformed blonde – though he was a man and equally as beautiful. The pair of them together would have given definite Von Trapp vibes. Like a pair of blond, blue-eyed china dolls. The dent of a healed piercing in his ear and nose was the only sign that he'd had a life before becoming a perfect, smiling employee at The Sorgente. I wondered if the recruitment process involved a makeover. On the desk in front of him were velvet lined boxes, one for each guest – open and empty.

'Welcome to The Sorgente – if you would please deposit any personal electronics and any valuables, they will be transferred to our vault for the duration of your stay with us,' the smiling blond man explained. His name tag said Renard and I wondered how many times he'd gone through this spiel and if the reaction was always the same. If so, I felt sorry for him, what a shit job.

'No fucking way,' Emmitt scoffed, as if Renard had just suggested he take his testicles and put those in the box for safekeeping – a combination of disbelief and offence.

'I'm afraid it is our policy,' Renard said smoothly. 'As is detailed in the booking forms you have all signed. This is to ensure that your time here is spent as restfully as possible, free from the distraction of material possessions.'

Judging from the shuffles and sighs of annoyance, I was the only one who had read the documents and seen this coming. Not that I really cared. I had a laptop in my luggage as well as my backup phone. That was how I always travelled – backups for my backups. I'd be a terrible crisis manager if I was ever truly incommunicado, even on holiday.

Emmitt scoffed but tossed his phone into a box, followed by a moderately expensive but fucking hideous sports watch. His surrender prompted everyone else to slowly empty their possessions into their boxes – phones, obviously, but also expensive watches, jewellery, headphones. Everything. Olivia was separated from her designer sunglasses and, amusingly, Patrick had to surrender his silver hipflask – which he drained before throwing in the box.

That done, Renard closed each box and another member of staff began to move them to a chrome trolley to take to this vault of theirs. Through the glass doors I saw uniformed staff waiting to escort us to our rooms –

welcoming smiles pasted on their faces. A beautiful olive-skinned woman in a white suit was standing unobtrusively to one side and I wondered what she was waiting for. Judging by the lack of uniform she was management but I couldn't read the gold name tag on her suit; it was reflecting the sun too brightly.

'Patrick and Roberta Keegan.' Renard graced them with a bright smile. 'If you'd come this way.'

He led them away and I watched them go. That was his wife? The poor woman. Judging from the surprised flickers I saw on a few other faces, I wasn't the only one who'd assumed she was his personal assistant. What sort of successful actor wore a Rolex while his wife went around in over-washed acrylic knitwear? And why was she allowing that?

'Chloe Wallace?'

I realised Renard had returned after handing the Keegans off to their guide. I marshalled a smile for him, glad to finally be on my way to my room. He showed me out of the little tramway 'station' and passed me on to a woman with dark, silky braids coiled on the back of her head, who introduced herself as Nina. Thankfully she took her lead from me conversation-wise and so we walked in easy silence as I soaked up the atmosphere at The Sorgente.

A winding path led from the aerial tramway towards the main building. Large, smooth stones marked the edges of the pathway and between the patches of snow an ocean of low, dense plants lapped at the rock barrier – presumably in spring these would be more colourful as alpine flowers opened up, but even with snow between them they were lovely. The air was almost aggressively clean and I felt as if it was hurting my lungs, as used as they were to smog.

In front of the main building was a stylised stainless steel statue, shaped like the abstract fountain in the retreat's logo. An actual icicle hung from one end of it. I'd never seen a clear one before – it wasn't even grey but pure as glass.

Then the enormous glass doors of The Sorgente were sighing open and I was inside. The foyer was high-ceilinged and as bright as an airport lounge, with a roaring fire in a giant modernist fireplace right at the centre. Beyond it was half a white marble hexagonal desk with a concierge standing ready. To my right were the lifts, two gleaming gold doors on each side of a corridor sporting a sign for the spa. On my left, another discreet birch-wood plaque showed the way to the grand dining room. The floor was an intricate wooden block design spiralling out from the fireplace and overhead a huge glass-and-chrome chandelier like a vast snowflake lit the room.

The guest rooms were on the second floor and we took the lift up to a mezzanine that ran almost the entire way around the foyer below. I was staying in 204 and when Nina opened the door for me and showed me inside, I knew that every penny I'd spent was worth it.

The suite was spacious and modern as everything else at the retreat, but with an added level of comfort as expected from a living space. From the king-size bed to the Eames lounge chairs and footstools in light brown leather, everything looked both stylish and comfortable. An Innes table in the shape of a rounded-off triangle atop sculptural wooden supports held yet another water carafe, which was full of fresh ice and must have been put there while I was on the tram up the mountain. A set of three leatherbound books was laid out with an array of writing implements in a leather roll left open for inspection – all of it monogrammed with my initials.

Nina must have seen me looking at them. 'Journaling is encouraged and you'll find everything you need here. No one else will ever see what you write, so feel free to be as open and honest as the mood takes you.'

I nodded and moved around the room, taking in the various features. It had a sheltered balcony with a rattan chair topped with plump cushions and a throw for warmth. An integrated wooden sideboard in the main room had a few jars of artisanal tea, handmade ceramic cups and a gold tap for boiling water. Beside this was a room service menu detailing the array of fresh juices and snacks that could be ordered – everything from sushi to chia pudding.

The whole room was decorated in off-white shades from ecru and fawn to oatmeal and tan. Very different from the harsh whites and greys of the offices I spent most of my time in. This actually felt restful and natural as opposed to fascistically minimal.

'Would you like me to unpack and arrange your things?' Nina asked as I returned to the bedside where my luggage sat, having been brought up while I was handing over my valuables to Renard, no doubt.

'Oh, thank you, but there's no need,' I said, thinking of the contraband I had squirrelled away. 'Thank you so much for showing me up. I think I can manage from here.'

Nina left after inviting me to ring down to the concierge for anything I needed and I breathed a sigh of relief once the door was closed. I had no desire to be walked through the operation of every blind, window and thermostat in the place. I was an adult, I'd figure it out or ask if it became necessary.

I did a quick walkthrough of the rest of the room's features. The en suite boasted both bath and shower. The tub and sink were both made of hammered copper and beautifully polished. Instead of a bath mat there was a slatted pine board and all the bathing accoutrements were natural – sea and konjac sponges, loofahs and salts in glass jars. A bundle of eucalyptus leaves hung in the shower, making the air smell clean without being overpowering. The floor of said shower was made of moss, fresh and neatly laid, apparently grown to size. It accented the walls, which were 'tiled' in smooth round river stones. They'd really thought of everything. Not one object in the entire suite was mundane or simply functional – everything had clearly been chosen with the utmost care and an eye for style.

Returning to the main part of the suite I noticed the absence of a television in the lounge area between the bed and the bathroom. There obviously also wasn't any normal tea or coffee by the on-tap boiling water, though I did find the latch for a silently opening drawer filled with simple snacks – nuts, seaweed crisps, oatcakes, berries, and a small refrigerated section with individual cheeses in wax and paper wrappings.

I checked the wardrobe and found it was already stocked with undyed linen tunics and drawstring trousers paired with raw wool cardigans and cashmere shawls. God knows why, as I'd obviously packed my own clothes. Below, pairs of sheepskin slippers, shearling booties and soft leather clogs. All in my size. I took out the silk robe and matching navy pyjamas. They were a little more luxurious than mine. It was clear from the clothing provided that comfort was one of the hallmarks of The Sorgente. I could see the intention was to have me sitting on my balcony with an earthenware cup of elderberry tea, journaling my cares away in a hand-dyed shawl. I wasn't opposed to most of that, but the tea was out.

My suitcases were on luggage holders by the bed and I unzipped them to start unpacking. Inside, rows of neatly folded clothes looked up at me, surrounded by balled-up socks and paired shoes. But on top was a dark blue envelope that I hadn't put there. I picked it up, noted the fountain logo and frowned. Someone at the retreat had been through my things. I didn't like that. Thinking back to the wording of the document I'd signed, though, I realised that when it said we'd be asked to surrender any valuables for safekeeping, that could be interpreted as applying to my luggage, as well as to my person. Damn it. Always the fine print.

I took the card from the envelope and read a polite but firm message that my belongings had been checked for any 'inappropriate items that might impede my enjoyment of the retreat or encourage self-sabotage of my wellness experience' and that these had been removed to the vault for safety. I dropped the card on the bed and riffled through my suitcase. My clothes were still there, obviously, though my more showy items and designer heels had been confiscated. Ditto my leather jewellery box and make-up bag. Obviously my coffee, alcohol and vapes had not passed inspection and my extra phone and laptop were gone as well.

Damn it. They were really taking this whole 'wellness

retreat' thing disappointingly seriously. Now the wardrobe full of clothes made sense. Some of the other guests would likely be opening mostly empty cases given the designer clobber they'd shown up in. I wondered if someone would be by later to collect the fancy clothes they'd arrived wearing, or if they'd be allowed to keep those.

When had they even had time to do this? It must have been while we were all waiting for the aerial tram, I realised. They'd probably gone through it and bagged our contraband separately to be taken straight to the vault. Perhaps that's what the white suit woman had been there to oversee. Clever.

I threw the lid of my suitcase back over its contents in annoyance, not just at the fact that my things had been taken but that I'd been beaten. I'd only been at The Sorgente for an hour and already they'd got the best of me. Never a feeling I enjoyed. I'd apparently have to be a lot sneakier if I wanted to slip something by them.

My only solace was that the others I'd arrived with were probably having just as bad a time of it, if not more so, than me. Jade being the possible exception. She was likely already a bit of a health freak, given her profession. Though I'd been wrong about athletes before. Still, at least if I was going to be boozeless and caffeine free, so would everyone else. That had the potential to be quite entertaining.

Chapter 4

With coffee and nicotine out of my grasp for now at least, I decided to take Silvie at her word and 'enjoy the retreat' before the welcome dinner. After all there wasn't much else to do now I had no phone, no laptop and not even any of my books to entertain myself with. What did this place have against reading, for God's sake? Though, granted, maybe a slew of erotic romance and bloodcurdling thrillers weren't exactly on brand for The Sorgente's commitment to rest and relaxation. They probably wanted me to lower my blood pressure with something thoughtful and introspective. I'd already clocked the clothbound volumes of nature writing on a shelf near the bed. Those were staying exactly where they were, unless I discovered a wonky table.

After changing out of my travel clothes and into some clean but still comfortable leggings, a jumper under my suede jacket and some trainers, I went back downstairs. Even before the lift doors opened I could hear someone remonstrating loudly with the concierge. It turned out to be Emmitt, no longer looking as zen as Sting.

'Just who do you people think you are, huh? Going

through my stuff, *taking* my stuff?? You're lucky I haven't called the police on you for holding my things hostage! I want that shit back, right now. Right. Fucking. Now!' He was working himself up, turning a painful-looking puce.

I paused by the lifts and glanced at the concierge, a young dark-haired guy with thick fluffy eyebrows that he'd definitely laminated. Model-handsome and sporting a small, benign smile, he looked as unruffled as Emmitt was angry. 'I'm sorry for any inconvenience, however, as per our policy . . .'

'I don't care about your *policy*!' Emmitt thundered, spittle spraying over the white marble. 'I want my stuff. Now!'

A door hidden in the wood panelling behind the desk opened and two men stepped out, flanking the concierge. One tall and blond, who wouldn't have looked out of place clutching a beer stein and singing rude songs, the other short and dark in colouring, a scarf and a cigarette short of being a poetry student on a summer in Europe. They were unarmed and unobtrusive, wearing the same sort of spa-like dark blue uniforms. However those uniforms bulged a little with muscle on the tall blond, while his wiry colleague looked like he had the deceptive strength of a Russian gymnast. They had less of a customer service vibe than that of a pair of bouncers at a rowdy club. I recognised security when I saw it, even if it was smiling and not wearing a stab vest.

Emmitt didn't seem to care that he was now outnumbered and kept barking orders and demanding his things. About as scary as a small yappy dog fogging up the glass as it snarled at the postman, and just as effective. Given my earlier assessment that he was fresh out of rehab, it didn't take a genius to work out what he had hidden in his luggage. I wondered what it was, specifically – alcohol, pills, maybe heroin? Could have been anything, really. But my money was on the hard stuff – he was too keyed up to be angsting over a bottle of vodka. I'd once had a client jump from a third-floor window while I and the rest of his management team tried to help him ride out detoxing from oxy. He'd ended up in traction, having his meds prescribed. But such is life, often corpulent with irony.

I left Emmitt to either calm down or be bundled back to his room and made my way towards the spa. I knew it wasn't open yet and wouldn't be until tomorrow but I could still have a little look around. It was that or get sucked into the foyer drama and I didn't fancy that in the least.

The corridor to the spa was cool and clear of clutter, the walls tiled in large natural-stone pieces. Woven lotus mats dulled the sound of my shoes and the air was lightly perfumed with something woodsy and subtle.

Inside the spa I found a reception area with neatly rolled towels tied with jute and pine sprigs piled into pyramids on the counter behind the reception desk. The air held a hint of essential oils still and concealed speakers were playing barely audible flute tracks. On the desk itself, a large blue glass vase displayed a selection of dried seedpods and flowers.

The hallway beyond was short and seemed to lead to treatment rooms, though a door at the end had a keypad beside it. Some sort of staff only area.

A sliding door to the left of me led to an outdoor terrace with sunken hot tubs, a cold plunge pool, and what I assumed were traditional saunas beyond – small wooden buildings with turf roofs. It was deserted, cakes of snow on the surrounding benches and tables. I realised that what I'd taken for modernist lights out there were actually heaters, though obviously they weren't yet on. I walked over to the door and wrapped my jacket tighter around myself. The wind shivered through the stainless steel stair rails by each pool. It looked very lonely out there, but at the same time I was craving another breath of fresh air.

Turning away I noticed a door on the opposite side of the room with signage indicating hiking routes and Nordic skiing as possible activities. My experience of skiing was limited to some downhill practice at an indoor centre my school had taken us to. Once. That and the machines at my overpriced gym. But I was in the Alps, so why not give it a try? At the very least it would keep me away from the other guests until they calmed down following the confiscation of their things.

The door was unlocked and beyond it was a little wood-panelled room with outdoor jackets, boots, hiking poles and cross-country skis all neatly arranged. A set for each guest in grey and teal, the hooks hung with monogrammed gold charms. I found mine and put the coat on over my light jacket, then slipped the waterproof trousers on over my leggings before putting on the boots. In the pocket of the coat I found a beanie and gloves, wrapped around a pair of mirrored shades. Everything looked and smelled new. They'd really thought of everything and it all fit perfectly. I wondered if they'd checked the sizes on my clothes when they looked in my suitcase and radioed up to the retreat for them to pick this stuff from a warehouse full of items.

I certainly hadn't given them my measurements. It was somehow both conscientious and creepy.

Thankfully this level of thoughtfulness extended to a simple set of instructions for getting into the skis. It prompted my memories of taking our school's one dented minibus out for that trip and I smiled to myself as I stood up and carefully opened the outer door.

Outside, the snow was clean and unmarked, but a depression showed where a trail was and a wooden marker pointed the way. I slid one ski forward, then the other, trying to work out how to do this on flat ground. Maybe this had been a terrible idea after all. But after a few awkward minutes I settled into it – much like using the elliptical machine it was easy once you got the rhythm right and stopped worrying about face planting. Not that there was anyone around to care if I did.

Sliding forwards, one foot after the other I finally dared to look up. Another path crossed the ski route, which was served by two low wooden gates. That path was cleared of snow and led down a slope towards some pines and what looked like another building. I ignored it and took the snow-covered path intended for skiing guests.

The ski route flowed ahead with rocky slopes on either side, topped with dark pines. They were like a break for the eyes, little patches of darkness in all that white. I was regretting not putting the glasses on, but I didn't trust my balance enough to stop and go through my pockets for them. I'd just have to squint; it wasn't as if I'd be out long. Just a short jaunt to blow away the cobwebs and wake me up – no caffeine required.

The route slowly climbed but in gentle rolling slopes. After cresting a small rise and skimming down the other side, I slowed to get my breath back. I was not as fit as I thought going into this. OK, so I went to the gym five days a week but I mostly walked on the treadmill while working or ran until I felt like throwing up. My diet was coffee, cigarettes and the occasional midnight cheesecake binge. By the time I reached the next rise my lungs felt like they were stuffed full of wire wool. My mouth filled with a sour taste and I spat onto the snow. To be honest, I wouldn't have been surprised to see blood. Maybe I ought to ski every day that I was at The Sorgente and keep up more of a rigorous routine when I got home? But when would I fit it in? I couldn't exactly pound the elliptical and answer work emails. Maybe I'd leave with a better grasp on my work–life balance, wasn't that what I was here for? To change my life a little and make space for new things, new friends?

Suddenly, over my own harsh breathing, I heard the *shush* of skis coming towards me and looked back to see Jade coming up the slope. She was doing a lot better than I was and soon she'd catch me up. She made it look easy and stopped a few feet behind me, leaning on her poles and admiring the view, barely breathing harder than normal.

'Gorgeous place, isn't it?' she said. 'The air's so bloody clean.'

'Yeah, it's lovely,' I agreed, though my lungs were aching as if I was breathing in ice water.

Jade gave me an assessing look. 'Are you not joining the mob to get your stuff back?'

I shrugged as nonchalantly as I could. 'I knew it was coming. There was something about it in those forms we signed.' I wasn't about to admit that I'd misread them and had been surprised. It's never a good idea to put your ignorance on display – something more people should learn, in my opinion.

'Same.' She nodded. 'But only because I've been here before. A few months ago. But that was for rest after my treatment . . . this time I just wanted a break.'

She didn't need to say from what. I'd seen the comment sections on her Insta and TikTok; they were putrid. I could see why she'd want to come back to the last place she'd been that let her ignore the internet for a while.

'Don't suppose you were really up for skiing last time?' I said, gently.

'Nah . . . I was pretty sick still.' Her mouth twisted down at the unpleasant memory, and I saw her make a conscious effort to shake it off. 'Not now, though. I'm back and ready to take this place on, head first.'

'Amen to that,' I raised a pole in a sort of toast. 'Got to make the most of it.'

We ended up falling into line – which must have required Jade to hold back, even though she was in the lead. It felt nice that she wanted to stay in my orbit enough to do that.

We reached the top of the gentle incline we'd been slowly climbing and I slid over the flat summit, enjoying the view of distant smoky blurs of pines and black rock against bright white snow. Also, covertly getting my breath back. It was like a Christmas card, or a Coors Light advert. The nearest visible building outside The Sorgente's walls was in the far distance, practically a mirage. There were no cars moving so it was hard to tell if there were any other roads down there other than the one we'd come in on. Everything was very still and quiet. Serene.

‘Fuck me, do you see that?’

I jerked my head around to find Jade pointing at a sign on a fence further down from where we stood. Alarmed by her sudden outburst, I followed her gaze. The fence was unlike all the other man-made structures at the retreat, really quite ugly. Which, I supposed, meant it actually did something important. I shuffled closer to the edge of the plateau, looking down.

The sign was red and had warnings on it about electrocution. But below, on a bright yellow hazard sign, was a picture of a wolf in profile. Even under all my layers, I felt a shiver run down my back. Were there really wolves here?

‘Must be an electric fence,’ Jade said, softly. ‘Hope it works.’

I didn’t have a response for that, but we were in complete agreement. I tried to reassure myself that a place like this would have taken every precaution against having its rich and famous clientele eaten by the wildlife. But, even so, that fence didn’t look that strong. Electrified or not.

The thing was, dogs terrified me. And what were wolves if not exceptionally aggressive dogs with more hunting instincts and bigger teeth?

With my face burning from the cold and my feet going numb, we turned and headed back down towards where we’d come from. The route continued but this felt like a good stopping point – my thighs were already burning from the exertion. Jade was fit enough that she could definitely have carried on but she turned back with me. I wondered if she was worried about the wolves or if she’d just had a change of heart about going on a long cross-country ski.

On the way back down one of my skis hit a patch of compacted ice and I fell backwards, hard. I landed on my arse and hissed as a flash of pain went right up my tailbone. I have never been blessed in the butt department even before I adopted a strict diet, so it hurt quite a lot with nothing to cushion the blow. A throbbing ache soon spread out through my back and hips. Terrific. To make matters worse I couldn't immediately remember how to get up from the ground in skis, something I'd been taught decades ago and had slipped my mind. I failed twice, slipping and sliding in the snow before I realised Jade was offering me her hand to help me up. Flushed and irritated, I let her, though she nearly fell down in the process.

Burning with embarrassment I attempted to finish the descent with dignity. We reached the wood-panelled gear room and I hung up my things before shuffling into the spa entryway. I was surprised to see Silvie there – the woman from the first aerial tram station and second half of the pair of china-doll blonds – she'd apparently made her way up to the main building, maybe because she and Renard were considered a set. She was waiting for us with a beaten copper tray bearing two mugs, a steaming pot of herbal tea and another of that mushroom hot chocolate. There was also a plate of very healthy-looking cookies – and I meant that in the pejorative sense.

No one had seen me go outside, I was fairly certain of that. Which meant that there had to be cameras all over the place, monitoring the guests so the staff knew where to provide assistance. Again I wasn't sure if this was good service or deeply invasive. Possibly both. After all, the best service was often both intimate and discreet. I knew that better than anyone.

I accepted a cup of chocolate, because it seemed like the closest I'd get to coffee for a while, and gave Silvie a nod of thanks. Jade patted my arm as if to say, 'You're back on firm ground now', and gave Silvie a nod of acknowledgement, but didn't take anything from the tray. I assumed because she was still on a strict diet which even the seed-filled cookies would break.

Sipping my chocolate, I leaned on the reception desk and nodded towards the doors we'd just come in through. 'Are there really wolves out there? I saw a sign.'

Silvie smiled reassuringly with her perfect teeth. (She really could have got a job at Disney as a real life Cinderella.) 'There are, yes. For a time the population was very low and steps were taken to protect the wolves of Switzerland. However their numbers have increased recently – a problem for farmers, I'm sure, but up here we don't have to worry. The entire complex is surrounded by the fence you saw.'

'It's not very strong looking, even if it is electrified,' I said. 'Don't you get worried? I mean, they could tunnel under it or something.'

She laughed musically and shook her head, sending her blonde hair tumbling over her shoulders. I caught a waft of something rich and boozy, like fruitcake. An odd choice of perfume for a sober retreat. 'The fence extends underground quite a way and it's too high for a wolf to jump. If they did try to bring it down, it would not end well for them – it has more voltage than the usual farm fences. Besides, we have security on-site to keep watch for any intruders. Nothing gets in, or out, of the perimeter without someone knowing about it.'

That went some way to unknot the little ball of tension

in my stomach. I was not a dog lover at the best of times – not since I'd got chased down by a neighbour's German shepherd as a kid. I had a line of scarring around the top of my left arm from where it had bitten me and dragged me down. I didn't think I'd be taking anymore impromptu ski outings, just in case.

I thanked Silvie for the reassurance and headed back to my room. My bruised tailbone required a long, lazy bath, I decided. On my way through I found Patrick and his wife in reception, demanding the return of his luggage.

I sipped my chocolate and quickly entered a waiting lift – it was going to be a long day for the concierge. I was just grateful that for once I wasn't the one having to field questions, demands and shitty attitudes. Maybe this would end up being exactly the break I needed. Laptop or no laptop.

Chapter 5

When I reached my room I discovered that it was already occupied. There was a uniformed staff member by the bed – a redhead I'd not seen before – transferring the contents of my suitcase to the wardrobe. I frowned, as I'd turned down this service only a short while ago.

'Can I help you?' I asked, still with my hand on the door.

The housekeeper, or whoever she was, jumped slightly. A very visible flush sprang up on her pale skin, and she dropped the jumper she'd been folding.

'I'm sorry for any inconvenience, I was just unpacking for you,' she said – her accent clean, sharp and Germanic. Her strawberry-blonde hair was cut into a remarkably unattractive bob, a shame really, as she was otherwise very pretty. Like the rest of the staff I'd seen so far. I wondered if there was some sort of screening process that only let the hot ones through.

'I can manage, thank you,' I said, just icily enough to leave her no choice but to stop what she was doing. She made a hasty exist only pausing at the door to ask if there was anything I needed.

‘I’m fine, thank you. I’ll call if I need anything,’ I said, and she left, closing the door behind her.

I did a quick check of my things. I’d noticed before that my expensive heels were gone – confiscated by the staff. But as I sifted through my clothes and hung the rest of them up I realised that I was missing more than I’d originally thought. A black evening dress with teardrop glass beads, an ecru suit jacket from The Kooples that I’d planned to wear over jeans and a silk camisole and my new suede trench coat. Basically, anything that was clearly designer or in the least bit flashy had been removed. Given that the intruder hadn’t taken anything with her, I assumed these clothes had been removed before and I hadn’t noticed. Perhaps she was just innocently unpacking my things.

With no laptop or phone, that eliminated the idea that she might be trying to access my work files. Which would normally have been my concern. The assistant I’d had before Brie had tried to email himself some confidential client documents with the intent to sell them to a gossip site. Now he worked at a cheese counter in Waitrose. Betrayal was something I couldn’t ever forgive. Especially from one of the few people I’d put my trust in.

I briefly wondered about cameras or something in the room – this place would be a goldmine in blackmail material – but after checking the usual spots I’d hide them if, say, I was trying to find out whether someone was banging the nanny, I found nothing. Again, my work was making me see the worst in people and situations. I sighed and sat down to remove my shoes. I needed to relax.

A bath was just what I needed after the flight and my fall outside. I changed into a comfortable bathrobe and ran the copper tub as full as possible. After sniffing a few jars I tossed in a handful of orange and vanilla bath salts which smelled a bit like I imagined a French bakery would, and added a good tot of tonka bean bath oil. The concoction was vanilla-y bliss and my one regret was not having a glass or two of iced Baileys to go with it.

Wreathed in steam I settled into the bathtub and breathed in the scent of the luxuriant bath salts. There were candles on glass shelves around the walls and a cloche of black-tipped matches by the sink. I'd lit every candle and their flickering lights added to the magical look of the swirling steam. A far cry from my usual hasty shower while listening to voicemails.

The bath was nice and deep too. I'd grown up with fibreglass ones so shallow that I had to choose between my torso or legs being warm. In this one the water came up to my neck, saturating the curls that escaped from my hair claw. Bliss.

I relaxed for a while and then buffed myself smooth with a selection of natural-wood brushes and sponges. I kept letting water out and adding more hot to prolong the experience, but in the end I figured it was getting close to dinner time, judging purely from the rumbling of my stomach.

I wrapped myself in the robe again and padded through to the bedroom, limbs loosened by a hot, decadent soak. I wasn't in any particular hurry to select an outfit for the welcome dinner. Without the bulk of my good clothes, I was left with some nice but plain loungewear, jeans, T-shirts and underwear. There were also some plain black wide-leg trousers, I assumed as an attempt to leave me with something nice but not too ostentatious for the welcome dinner. I slipped them on under a black silk camisole and threw a white lace jacket over the top. That was about as fancy as it was going to get. I had to wear flats with it as all my heels were gone and I had no jewellery or make-up to elevate the look. It was taking detoxing a bit far, in my opinion. What was the issue with a bit of lipstick and some concealer for my dark circles?

At the appointed time, I let myself out of my room and headed for the lift. There was a woman already waiting – a girl, actually. She couldn't have been more than sixteen, and she was so skinny she could have passed for half that age if it wasn't for her height. She was dressed all in white, from her (real) fox-fur hat to her knee-high boots. With waist-length bleached blonde hair she looked like après-ski Barbie. I could only assume that these were the clothes she'd arrived in, which hadn't yet been confiscated. Perhaps the hat had been deemed practical enough for the weather that it was allowed to remain. I pictured Renard and Silvie, the china dolls, putting their heads together over a policy document to debate this.

It wasn't until the lift arrived and we stepped in that I saw her face and recognised her. In fairness I was used to seeing her falling out of cabs or flinging herself around on stage to upbeat, energetic music. She was Carri X (pronounced Carri *kiss*) – born Carrie Harris – another pop star churned out by an American reality show. She was, I realised, the first non-English person I'd met. I wondered if this was by design, and my check-in cohort had been specifically tailored to make us all feel welcome among familiar accents.

Carri was the most famous person I'd met so far. Her debut single was being played everywhere, from shops to adverts and in the summer's blockbuster chick-flick, and the scent of vodka wafting off her was just as inescapable. People like to claim you 'can't smell vodka' but at a certain concentration, you really can, and more closet alcoholics needed to be aware of that.

I didn't say anything because my general rule of thumb is, if someone famous wants to chat, they will. If not, keep it zipped. She was fiddling with her nails, probably missing her phone already. My own hands felt weirdly empty without it. I noticed that her collection of diamond rings (several on each finger – sort of part of her brand) were missing, as were the collection of glittering necklaces that usually had her looking like an ice princess on her way to her sweet sixteenth party.

When the lift reached the ground floor Carri was the first to leave, striding out ahead of me on her sky-high heels. I didn't take it personally. Across the foyer the doors to the grand dining room were open and there were uniformed waiters and waitresses showing people to their seats. Even from where I was, by the lifts, I could hear the burble of conversation and the chime of crystal glassware. Clearly more guests had arrived while I was skiing and soaking my troubles away.

'Miss Wallace?' Renard was by the door at a wooden lectern. 'Allow me to show you to your table.'

He showed me into the dining room, which had ten or so round tables, like those at awards shows, but without quite as much humility on the faces of those seated around them. We passed a woman in a white trouser suit who was talking into an earpiece. The same one from the tram station. Up close I could appreciate her clear skin and impeccable red lipstick. Her winged eyeliner was tattooed on – the mark of a busy woman.

'Has anyone seen Lars?' she was asking as she paced away.

The dining room itself was spectacular – an octagon with only one solid wall – the one connecting it to the rest of the retreat. The rest of it was all glass, including the ceiling and the enormous chandelier that hung overhead. At the far end of the room a platform draped in white served as a stage for a string quartet. The guests were, like me, dressed smartly but not overly decorative. It was weirdly comforting, not being confronted by the finery of the rich and fabulous. Maybe this place knew what it was doing after all. Though it did make it harder for me to work out who was who in terms of type – what was a trophy wife without her giant ring, a sporting legend without a custom watch? A WAG without her Prada?

Renard pulled out a chair for me quite far from the windows, which was fine by me. Given how dark it was outside and the brightness of the chandelier, the windows were more like mirrors anyway. The only things I could see outside were the orb-shaped lights that covered whatever lay beyond the windows – probably an outdoor dining area or something, for use in milder temperatures. The last thing I wanted was to see my reflection as I ate quinoa and kale or whatever this place was going to feed me.

My table was populated with the people I already knew from the aerial tram ride up the mountain. Perhaps this was again intentional, keeping us in the same cluster of guests all speaking the same language, so we'd feel like we were more settled. Or maybe it was just to keep us with others on the same level as us socially, so more famous guests wouldn't fear being gawked at over their bone-broth matchas. Though, if that was the case, I was insulted and annoyed with whoever considered me and Patrick Keegan peers.

The only addition to our group was a woman in her late forties, early fifties, who was fiddling with her water glass. She hadn't been on the aerial tram and might have arrived earlier or later than us. I couldn't tell much about her on first glance, the interferences from The Sorgente's policies hampering my abilities somewhat. Was the lack of jewellery and designer clothing a choice, or something she'd been forced into like the rest of us?

I sat down and we all made our official introductions; Olivia apparently went by Livvy and once she heard that I'd gone skiing that was all she wanted to talk about. Possibly because she was worried the subject of her husband might come up. She was in luck, though, as if there was one person who wanted to talk about her lecherous, embezzling MP hubby less than her, it was me. I had enough of that at work.

The new woman was right by me and I took the time to assess her fully and properly. She had very short nails and hands wrinkled from frequent handwashing, which was what I latched on to in the absence of anything else. Her frown lines marked her as a thinker and she had the kind of squint that comes of many hours spent on detail work. But it wasn't until she started speaking that I confirmed my suspicions – she was a doctor. Specifically, a plastic surgeon. My second guess had been seamstress, but her awfully fitted blouse ruled that out. I realised after hearing her speak that I'd heard her on the radio once or twice and her voice had such a plummy Surrey accent that it was unforgettable. She had famous clients was all I really remembered and she'd overused the phrase 'discretion is paramount' so much I'd turned the radio off.

She shook my hand with surprisingly strong fingers. 'Paula Fairside,' she said. 'How are you finding it? Bit like being back at boarding school, isn't it?'

My only exposure to boarding school was a fifth-hand copy of *Malory Towers* I'd latched on to at a foster home, but I just nodded and gave her a rueful smile.

'I'm Chloe,' I said, leaving off my last name because I'd long since stopped being able to keep track of my enemies. 'Is it your first time here?'

'Mmmm,' Paula said, eyes flicking around the table. 'And I can't see myself coming back. Not that it's not very . . . comfortable, but I can't afford to take too much time off. Not when my practice is so busy.'

I made sympathetic noises. I hadn't heard much about her to be honest. Understandably most people who'd had work done didn't want to shout about it, especially not to the likes of me. But she seemed twitchy, like she'd had too much coffee on the flight in. Perhaps she had, or she wasn't used to sharing air with the likes of Patrick Keegan, who was holding court on the other side of the table. Maybe she thought he was still worth getting het up over. She was that generation. Emmitt was laughing at something he'd just said, and Roberta was peering around Livvy, trying to catch her husband's eye. Whether to remind him to behave or just to try and get some attention.

'Have you ever considered an eye lift?' Paula suddenly asked, and I raised an eyebrow at her. Cheeky cow, I was barely thirty.

'Maybe,' I said – though in truth I'd seen too many botch jobs to ever seriously consider it. Accidents happened, even with the best hand in the world holding the scalpel, and I'd noticed that Paula's hand was shaking a bit as she picked up her water glass to take a gulp.

I knew *delirium tremens* when I saw it. Paula Fairside, plastic surgeon to the stars (or at least, the soap stars) was sobering up and drying out. Now that I was looking for the signs I could see the broken veins under the foundation she must have applied liberally that morning. Deprived of her make-up bag now she'd arrived, I couldn't imagine what she'd look like tomorrow. She wouldn't be the only horror – my dark circles were not a pretty sight without my Clinique eye serum and a generous spackle of concealer. Still, with any luck I'd start sleeping more than four hours a night and wouldn't need the camouflage. My skin might also improve just by osmosis from the many, many jugs of lemon water around the place.

The large doors to the dining room were pulled closed by two waiters and the woman in the white suit I'd noticed earlier took to the stage, where the quartet let their music drift to a stop. The woman tucked her straight black hair behind her ear and smiled at us. Like the rest of the staff she was gorgeous, olive skin glowing with health, hair so shiny a Pantene model would scalp her out of jealousy. She didn't even appear to be wearing any base make-up, her skin was just naturally that clear and smooth. I was jealous but also impressed. Especially because her white suit was so perfect it could have been from a laundry detergent advert, and even my dry-cleaner couldn't accomplish that.

'Good evening and welcome, esteemed guests,' she said, her voice amplified by a hidden lapel mic, which projected her subtle German accent around the room.

‘My name is Aloisia and I have the privilege of managing The Sorgente – I would like to thank you all for choosing to entrust your health and your wellness to us. Every member of staff here considers it our personal goal to ensure you are taken care of, body and spirit. And I do hope you have a very pleasant stay with us.’

There was a polite smattering of applause and Aloisia’s smile widened. She seemed to radiate warmth and understanding and it was easy to see why she had been chosen for her role. I didn’t even believe in most of what this place was selling and I still liked her, trusted her even. She seemed genuine in her fervent wish for her guests to see the benefit of The Sorgente’s wellness regime. As the noise died down again she gestured to the wait staff, who had assembled in a line at the rear of the room.

‘I’m sure you’re all excited to begin your transformative experience here with us. Tomorrow your assigned assistant will have your personalised plans ready and will go through them with you. We offer an extensive range of massage, physical and emotional therapy, artistic outlets, outdoor pursuits and, of course, a full menu of spa treatments. You’ll also have plenty of free time to relax, journal, work on personal craft projects, meditate and embrace the glory of the landscape we are so blessed to be situated within.

‘I know many of you have travelled far to join us. From this moment, put all thoughts of your stresses and obligations aside. Enjoy yourselves and the five-course menu our Michelin-star restaurant and on-site nutritionist have put together in order to make sure you start your first full day with us refreshed and energised.

‘Know that we are all just as invested as you are in the

success of your wellbeing journey with us, and that by the time you leave, you will be a better you.' She paused, still smiling around at us all. 'We will make you better.'

The claps resumed, but despite the outwardly welcoming words, I felt a familiar shiver down my spine. *We will make you better.* It was a promise, yes, but it sounded almost like a threat.

Chapter 6

I kept my head down while dinner was served. I've always been more of a natural listener than I am a talker. People-watching was far less stressful than throwing myself headlong into the action as a kid living in houses packed with other fosters. As an adult, I tended to attract the kind of people who loved to hear themselves talk. Perhaps they sensed that I was a sort of natural vacuum into which they could air their thoughts. Either way, it worked well for me professionally, if not privately.

So I sat and passively listened while Patrick bemoaned the first course (grilled endive – which was perfect, by the way) and Livvy talked about a delicious salad she'd had in Tuscany, and I watched while Emmitt forgot where he was and tried to order some wine. I clocked that Jade was the only person who thanked our waiter – though in Roberta's case I think the mere act of speaking up might have caused her physical pain. I myself only smiled, in case speaking caused someone to talk to me.

The second course was fish, poached, with quinoa and microgreens. The sort of food I was used to eating at corporate lunches with 'the girls', most of whom were on at least two fad diets, as I was. Though occasionally I broke and tossed a bag of mini kievs in the air fryer in the middle of the night, or devoured a herd of turkey dinosaurs. The comfort foods of my childhood, slathered in ketchup.

'Bloody rabbit food,' Patrick moaned, scraping the greens to one side. I noticed that Emmitt had tempeh instead of fish. Either he was vegan or vegetarian. You'd be surprised how many celebrity addicts are very choosy about what they will and won't eat. I've always found that very interesting.

'Surprised they've got fresh fish all the way up here,' Livvy said, to no one in particular. She teased at the flakes of white fish with her knife and wrinkled her nose. 'I do hope it wasn't frozen. I cannot abide frozen food.'

'Probably was,' Patrick said, leaping on the opportunity to complain some more. 'Bertie, I told you to make sure they knew I only eat fresh.'

Roberta mumbled something and Patrick rolled his eyes before glancing over at Emmitt's plate. 'What in God's name is that muck?'

'Tempeh,' Emmitt said, cutting a defiant slice, though I could tell he wasn't enjoying it much. Possibly a new convert to the lifestyle. I'd had tempeh quite a few times and it was actually nice when prepared right. 'It's made of soy beans.'

'Soy's terrible for you,' Patrick said. 'Processed and foreign. It's full of oestrogen too.'

Emmitt, who was rail thin – though, in fairness, more likely from drugs than from his diet – raised his eyebrows in what appeared to be genuine concern. 'Really? Jesus, I didn't know that.'

Jade, in the seat beside me, snorted under her breath and went back to her fish, leaving the pair of them to discuss pseudoscience uninterrupted. She was wearing a sleeveless linen tunic and trousers provided by the retreat – I recognised them as the same type that were hanging in my wardrobe upstairs – and her muscular arms were very much on show. It seemed that she was recovering from her cancer treatment well. She certainly had an appetite – she was one of the only people not pushing food around her plate.

Patrick, having found a captive audience in Emmitt ploughed on. 'It's all been studied but obviously the scientific journals are worried about being called racist. You can't say anything these days. But it's true – soy stops you making testosterone because it's full of oestrogen and that's why all you millennial lot are so weak and emasculated.'

Emmitt looked down at his tempeh and then cautiously cut another bite. 'I haven't had any issues,' he said.

Patrick rolled his eyes. 'Used to be that the only people who'd eat that stuff were communists or queers,' he said as a parting shot, and I felt a frisson of disapproval radiate from both Jade and, surprisingly, Livvy. Roberta seemed to shrink into herself; she'd probably heard the upcoming rant before.

'Or people who give a shit about animals,' Emmitt said. 'Look, I'm not talking crap about your dinner so maybe you can save the commentary for someone else, yeah?'

That startled a little laugh out of me. I hadn't bet on Emmitt standing up for himself, but maybe he was feeling a bit exposed now we were all looking at him. He was probably also still fired up from his encounter with the concierge and security. Though apparently he'd managed to calm himself enough to not be immediately kicked out while I was off skiing.

Patrick's gaze swivelled to me at the sound of my suppressed laugh and his mouth pursed tightly, the corners going white under his spray tan. 'And who are you anyway?'

I felt myself become the centre of attention and inwardly cringed. The safest place to be was behind the spotlight, not in it. But I wasn't about to show weakness in front of a bully like him.

'I'm Chloe,' I said, and reached for my water glass, noting the slices of lemon in it. 'They really love their flavoured waters here, don't they?'

Jade started to say something in agreement but Patrick bulldozed her. 'Chloe who?'

I braced myself just in case he recognised me. 'Chloe Wallace, pleased to meet you.'

There was no recognition in his eyes, but then Roberta leaned in and whispered something to him and his expression soured even further. 'Oh, you're a fixer.'

I bristled slightly. There's more to my job than that. I don't just 'fix' situations, I can make them disappear. Handle them before they even arise. Yes, my job might be grubby on occasion – I've certainly paid off my share of call girls and smuggled rent boys out of hotels, cleaned up cocaine residue before the police arrived, that kind of thing. But my job had given me the sort of life I had only dreamed of as a kid. I owned a home, a car, and could have the heating on all day every day. My TV didn't take pound coins to operate and my clothes weren't just new, they were designer. So, even if I was occasionally a bit depressed about how much of my life was eaten up by my work, I wouldn't let this man get to me.

'That's me,' I said with a smile. 'But I'm not working at the moment, so you'll have to make an appointment for next week.'

Jade stifled another laugh and I could see Livvy glancing at me with interest. God, I hoped she wasn't going to try and hire me. Her husband had already royally fucked his career up, there wasn't anything I could do at this late stage. Unless she wanted some free advice on how to escape the oncoming shitstorm without becoming a national laughing stock. There was perhaps a little that could be done in terms of damage control – starting with publicly condemning her thieving rat of a husband.

'What's that, then?' Emmitt asked. 'Fix what?'

'Oh, she's the person you call to fish dead hookers out of your hot tub,' Patrick said with a nasty smile. 'No problem too big or too grotty.'

I laughed. 'That's a new one. Haven't come across that exact problem yet.'

Patrick didn't laugh and no one at the table seemed in the mood to make light of it either. I'd been outed as an interloper – someone who wasn't famous but who was part of the machinery of fame. A reminder of the world they'd come here to get away from, like a paparazzo crouching in the bushes on their private island. Never mind that I had just as much right as the rest of them to be at The Sorgente. I wasn't welcome.

'You should've said.' Jade looked uncomfortable, which hurt. 'Before, when we were outside.'

'I don't recall you telling me about your work,' I said, stung. 'We're here to get away from all that, right?'

'Yeah, but that's different,' she said. Though she didn't say why. She didn't need to. I was in the same category as the newspaper photographers and the scummy bloggers to her. That made my skin feel tight with shame.

I glanced at Emmitt, hoping for a little support from the last person to bear the brunt of Patrick's mockery. But he glanced away, fiddling with a ratty leather bracelet on his wrist. Fair enough, I hadn't exactly leaped to his defence.

Patrick snapped his fingers in the air, trying to attract the attention of one of the waiters. They were mostly at the far end of the room, clearing plates as they slowly moved towards our side, the nearest to the kitchen doors.

'I think you're at the wrong table,' Patrick said to me, while waiting for someone to come over. 'There must be a mistake.'

'Jesus, can you give it a rest?' Jade finally said, with a roll of her eyes. 'I'm trying to relax at this place, not listen to you whine the whole time. Now put your fucking hand down and eat your fish like a grown-up, eh?'

It wasn't exactly a bold defence of me, but I'd take it. At least she wanted to ignore me instead of having me raked over the coals.

Given Patrick's recent racist diatribe, I doubted he was going to take well to the only black woman at the table telling him to eat his dinner like a good boy. I could feel the air start to coagulate with something more akin to hatred than simple snobbery. Livvy tittered uncomfortably and Roberta hid behind her mousy hair, awaiting an explosion.

I stood up.

The sudden movement made everything on the table rattle and I could feel eyes on me from the other tables around us. It was an instinctive reaction, diverting attention from Jade and breaking the tension at the table. Something I did in meetings with aggressive clients. You had to make yourself big when they tried to make you small. Stand up when they expected you to shrink. Crucially, it also left you in a better position to run away if they started throwing things or tried to physically attack you.

'Cheerio.' Patrick toasted me ironically with his water. 'Hope you aren't offended.'

'I tend not to put too much weight on the words of alcoholic C-list actors,' I said, knowing I should shut up and walk away but not wanting to. I wasn't working, I didn't have to take this shit from these people. 'Though, sorry, are you still C-list if you're not working or are you just unemployed?'

Patrick's mean grin looked more like a snarl now. 'Why don't you fuck off back to whatever squalid little room you could afford here?'

'Suite,' I corrected, and watched his neck turn red. Apparently he didn't have one, or hadn't expected to be in the same kind of accommodation as a lowly 'fixer'. 'And I'll go when I'm ready.'

In the tense silence that followed I picked up my water glass and made a show of draining it right down to the bitter lemon wedge. We'd attracted quite a bit of attention now, both from nearby tables and some of the wait staff who were coming towards us unobtrusively. Whether to herd me out or to smooth things over I had no idea.

As I stood there defiantly I heard glass chiming softly

and looked down. All the water glasses and the carafe were shivering slightly. I watched as the silverware on the table vibrated out of formation. A fork fell from the edge of Emmitt's plate and he looked down, confused.

Looking around I saw other people notice the strange vibrations, as if the entire dining room was under a railway line. I glanced at the waiters nearest to me but they also looked confused. Apparently this wasn't a normal occurrence. I wondered if it had something to do with the spring this place ostensibly sat on, providing all the water we were drinking – one of the only facts about The Sorgente I'd been able to find online.

'What the . . . hell?' Jade muttered, clearly as unnerved as I was.

We all jumped as the tables started to vibrate sideways. A glass crashed to the floor, then another and another. A plate, a carafe, a handful of cutlery. I took a step back from the table and couldn't help but look up, where the giant vintage chandelier was swaying on its chain. It felt as if the entire room was being lightly shaken. The string quartet faltered to a stop and the sudden lack of background noise made the rumbling more obvious, as the confused voices of the other guests and staff swelled along with it.

Was the whole retreat about to come loose from the mountain and collapse into a void carved out by the spring? Hadn't I read somewhere that Vegas was slowly sinking as the underground aquifer emptied and the weight of the city was crushing the porous rock as the sediment was removed along with the water, leaving it weak and unstable? A case study thrown out about the M. Shale expansion?

I saw wait staff taking slim radios from their pockets apparently asking for orders or advice from management. But my eyes were drawn to a few of them nearest the window who were peering out, trying to see. What was out there? A crack in the terrace? A sinkhole?

Then they started running towards us, sprinting for their lives and knocking over anything in their way. I was welded to the spot, watching.

'Is it an earthquake?' I heard someone behind me say, but my eyes were fixed to the dark windows on the far side of the dining room. The windows through which I could only see the illuminated globes of the lights on the terrace. The lights that were going out, one after the other, faster and faster as the rumbling turned into a roar I could feel in my very bones.

The chandelier went out, along with every other light, and abruptly I could see through the windows. We could all see as a wall of snow and ice rushed towards us, studded with dark debris. I took a breath, but someone else screamed it first.

'Avalanche!'

Chapter 7

The room exploded into movement and noise. All around me, people were screaming and shouting and rushing for the exit. Chairs clattered to the floor and tables scraped as guests and staff alike shoved their way past, sending yet more place settings crashing to the floor. I heard those around me yelping in pain as they ran into one another, lost shoes, twisted their ankles, slipped on broken glass and crockery. A man in a dinner jacket climbed over our table to escape the crush, nearly knocking Roberta down.

I was frozen, watching in horror as the wall of snow hit the outside of the building and kept coming as if the retreat was made of paper. The windows shattered as a whole side of the dining room was obliterated. The snow rushed in, folding over itself like a wave, crashing down with a sound like the fist of God. It hit the first few tables, crushing people beneath as it roared towards me. It wasn't stopping, or slowing. It thundered towards me, carrying tables and chairs and people with it.

Someone grabbed my wrist and yanked me down. My knees crumpled and hit the floor hard, jarring my bones. It was Emmitt who'd grabbed me and moments later he was under the table as well. He and Paula were pushing it over, the rest of us sheltering behind. Livvy was screaming and Roberta had curled into a tight ball. I shut my eyes and prepared to die.

The noise was deafening, like a rockslide or a train derailing. It sounded as if the very building was shaking apart and coming down on us. I could hardly hear myself scream, only knew that I was doing so because my throat was raw and my mouth wide open, lungs burning as all my air went into a terrified shriek. My head swam with dizziness and I sucked in air so abruptly that I choked on it.

The barrage of snow hit the table and, had it not been solid wood, it probably wouldn't have held. I shrieked again automatically as the table was shunted several feet across the debris-strewn floor, taking us with it at speed. Livvy grabbed at me and I clawed at the table leg, both of us trying to anchor ourselves to our only form of shelter. My eyes flew open and I watched as snow and ice slid past us in frozen chunks, skating over the shiny floor and smashing against the wall we were sliding towards. The wall we were going to smash on impact.

I held my breath and watched the wall rush to meet us. All of us scrabbling our legs on the floor, trying to slow our mad ride towards death. A shard of something sharp scraped along my thigh and I barely had time to react as we hurtled towards the wall.

I had my feet up to meet the wall when we stopped, only a few inches away. Emmitt flung his arm out against the white plaster and for a moment we were all still, caught in a moment of luck and euphoric gratitude, that we hadn't been smeared against the wall like insects on a windshield.

Around us the noise died down and changed, but

became no less horrifying. The roar of the churning snow dropped to cracking and creaking as the bulk of its weight settled, along with the odd brittle pattering as pieces of ice broke off and tumbled down to hit the floor. And with the lack of grinding and roaring, there came a wave of voices – cries, screams, sobs and people calling the names of other guests, which had previously been inaudible. The hairs on my neck and arms rose at the sound of so many cries of human suffering.

I slammed back into my own body. My arms flung out, one hand on the table leg, the other clenched in Livvy's. One foot against the wall. I pried my jaws open and sucked in a lungful of air, letting my leg drop as my limbs went limp. My ears were ringing from the sudden end to the apocalyptic noise and as I shook Livvy off and started to crawl to my feet, I found that my legs were shaking.

Once I was on my feet, heart hammering, I turned to look at the devastation with my back pressed against the wall. The room was unrecognisable. The far wall gaped open into the night, letting in gusts of icy air, the only light out there coming in the form of pinpricks of stars. The chandelier was still swaying sickeningly. I could hear it creaking and jangling as the thousands of crystals on it shivered in the air. My breath came in a cloud and I wrapped my arms around myself, having been plunged into subzero temperatures.

Around me in the dark I could see the shapes of all the tables and chairs and serving carts that had been shoved towards us. The snow was grey and black in places, with churned-up dirt, and the sight of a leg protruding from the icy mass nearby made me quickly look away, hand covering my mouth as my stomach rebelled.

‘Oh . . . Jesus . . .’ I turned to find Roberta on her feet beside me. It was the first time I’d heard her speak. I realised there was no sign of Patrick anywhere. He must have run for it. I didn’t even have it in me to be angry or disgusted. I was too shaken. At least Emmitt and Paula had thought to overturn the table, to save themselves or the rest of us it didn’t really matter – at least they’d done something. I owed them my life.

‘What do we do?’ Emmitt stuttered, as he was struggling to his feet, Roberta with him as they shook off the strange catatonia that had hit us all after the avalanche. The feeling that death had screamed past us like a runaway train, missing its mark by a hair.

Livvy grabbed my leg and used it to hoist herself up, making me wince as her fingers dug into the scrape on my thigh. Before I could say anything she was running for the door – and she wasn’t alone. Most of the other uninjured guests and staff who hadn’t made it out before the avalanche hit were now rushing for the doors back into the foyer.

The woman in the white suit – Aloisia? – had apparently been sheltering under a table too. She stood up, arms raised as if she was being held at gunpoint. She staggered a little, unsteady on her feet. ‘Everyone, stay calm! Please evacuate to a safe area – anyone with medical expertise, please help us with the injured.’

I glanced around and realised Paula was still under the table, though she’d been at the edge and her jumper was pebbledashed with snow and ice. Her face was pale and doughy with shock but the words ‘medical expertise’ seemed to shake her back into herself. She must’ve been used to acting in a crisis, given her career. Like me she was probably practised at shutting out the noise and the stress and just moving forward.

'I'm a surgeon!' Paula shot up, her hand in the air, already stumbling towards the bulk of the avalanche fallout. She slipped and staggered over chunks of ice and debris, but carried on regardless.

I wavered. I wasn't a doctor or anything like that, but I did have a first-aid course or twelve under my belt. You needed them when you couldn't reliably turn up to a client's house without finding them mid-overdose, having tried to kill themselves or having slipped and fallen down the stairs because they were drunk. It paid to be prepared. But as I took a few steps in Paula's wake, uncertainly following the call to action, someone grabbed my arm.

'Are you mental?' Emmitt hissed. 'This place could fall down any minute. It's not our fucking job.'

I pulled my arm away automatically but followed the direction of his aggressive pointing. Even from this distance, without electric light, I could see that the pillars at the edge of the shattered glass wall were bent. The rest of the glass walls could come down easily, I realised. The entire dining room was structurally compromised.

As if to prove his point, the swaying chandelier above us gave a tortured groan. In my mind's eye I imagined the chain that anchored it to the glass ceiling shearing apart. If it fell, it would take out anyone under its massive bulk.

'Aren't there aftershocks?' Roberta said, head on a swivel as if waiting for the rest of the walls to come down. 'Is that this or earthquakes, or—'

Emmitt shoved her towards the door. 'Move!'

'We should help,' I snapped, glaring at him and taking a step back as he reached for me again. Roberta obediently skittered off towards the foyer and presumably her cowardly whippet of a husband. Although most guests had fled already, there were still staff members and even a handful of guests picking their way over to the snowbank and trying to dig with their hands, gouging at the snow with candlesticks and pieces of shattered furniture.

Close by I saw them pull a woman from the snow. Her blood looked black in the moonlight, running across the snow like ink. My stomach contracted around my meal and I bent double, vomiting poached fish over the floor.

Emmitt backed off in disgust and headed for the door, apparently giving up on me. Suddenly I was alone in the small circle of safety by our table, a puddle of vomit at my feet. Jade must have sprinted for safety faster than any of us could have managed. Though I could hardly blame her. At least, unlike Patrick, she didn't leave anyone she knew behind.

I looked once more at the people struggling to dig at the ice, their progress so slow. The woman they'd managed to excavate wasn't moving and her blood pool was spreading over the floor. My chest was tight with rising panic and I just wanted to get out so I could breathe. It was all too much and I could almost feel the walls closing in on me – despite the barrage of bracing air from the broken window.

I reached the door and stumbled into the foyer with the rest of the crowd. It was dark there too; all the lights were out, even the fire in the central fireplace. Without their phones, the other guests bumbled around in the dark, and I heard muffled curses and sharp retorts as feet were stepped on and people were pushed to and fro. People were sobbing and calling out names as if to locate one another in the crowd. I was hemmed in, breathing in sour sweat and absorbing the panic of those around me, like an animal corralled for slaughter. My hysteria only intensified with every second I was trapped there. I tried to turn and go back into the dining room, but there were already people behind me. A wall of bodies pushing forwards.

A sudden burst of light attracted our attention as a group, as if we were now a flock of moths, desperately seeking the promise of safety. It got our attention more than the man holding it.

'Everyone!' I recognised the voice of Renard, though it was now tight with stress. He was holding a large utility torch, pointed up like a candle so as not to blind anyone. It gave his pale skin and blond hair the look of a scary Victorian child in a horror film.

'Everyone, listen!' he called again, over the general clamour. 'I need you to listen to me and cooperate, for your safety at this time.'

The noise level dropped slightly but I could still hear a woman's voice rising and falling, saying things like 'lawsuit' and 'compensation' in a jarring New York accent with others chiming in to agree. Another woman was openly weeping and several Australian men were blaming one another for the decision to come here at all. Renard ploughed on regardless.

'There are no lights because the utility building is outside and appears to have been hit by the avalanche. I do not know yet if the oil and gas supplies are affected, so be aware that we may be without heating, though as the supplies are outside thankfully we shouldn't have to worry about any leaks indoors. I just need everyone to return to their rooms . . .'

Uproar resumed, tenfold. I winced as the guests around me began to shout and remonstrate with the receptionist in several languages, Italian and Japanese among them – closing in on where he was trapped behind the marble desk. The doors behind him showed no sign of security personnel now that they were really needed. I assumed they were helping those trapped by the snow, or else outside, checking on the power situation.

'Ladies and gentlemen, please!' Renard called, voice cracking with the strain. He was younger than I'd first taken him for. Barely into his twenties. 'I am trying to ensure you are all safe . . .'

'Completely unacceptable, who designed this place . . .'

'. . . no backups whatsoever? How is that in any way . . .'

'. . . going to be hearing from my solicitor . . .'

'I want my belongings back now, and I am getting off this fucking mountain!'

That last brought with it a renewed sense of panicky aggression as people voiced their agreement and closed ranks. Demands for entry to the vault took over the room and guests were fighting with one another to get closer to Renard and make their request the first he had to deal with. Several hands flailed, trying to grab his torch.

Someone stumbled into my back and I tripped over my own foot, elbowing the person to my right. They thrust me back with so much force I nearly fell and would have taken the guest to my left down too if I hadn't managed to get a hand on the wall behind them. Anger at being so roughly shoved about was a welcome tonic – it cut through my stupor and gave me the push I needed to start my brain firing. The only way to combat feeling helpless was to seize control. To act.

Having found something solid in the heaving crowd, I felt my way along it and used my elbows to get everyone out of my way. Eventually, although I was bruised and sweaty, I arrived by Renard. He'd backed up against the wall, one hand out as if to placate the growing mob, the other clutching the torch to his chest. I put my hand on his shoulder and he jumped, but I ignored that and stepped in front of him.

'Everyone, shut up!' I yelled. There was a precious second of stunned silence and before the outraged shouting could return I pushed ahead in the gap I'd made for myself. 'We are all going to get out of here soon.'

Rule One: when in doubt, just tell people what they want to hear. It prepares the way for them to keep agreeing with you and gets them listening to you in the first place. When you have to give someone news they aren't going to like, or an instruction they'll want to disobey, you have to wrap it in something they can agree to. Like giving a cat a pill in some cheese.

'Right now we're still trying to work out what happened and make sure we can all leave safely. For that reason, I need you to clear the area near the dining room and go back to your rooms where it's safe – pack your things,' I said, raising my voice over dissenting murmurs, 'and your valuables will be returned to you shortly.'

'It's pitch black!' someone shouted, and that seemed to prod Renard into action.

'We'll be distributing torches while we attempt to get the backup power online. You'll find matches and candles in your bathrooms. Please return to your rooms and allow us to take care of the situation for you.'

Apparently between us we'd managed to lay on enough reassurance and just plain lies to get everyone moving. Dispersing a crowd is mostly about getting the first few people to leave – once that happens the rest'll start to follow, a lot like sheep. No one wanted to be the last man standing of an angry mob.

Once the majority of the other guests had traipsed away, following one another up the sweeping stairs to their rooms, I turned to Renard. 'Is there backup power?' I asked under my breath.

'Yeah . . . in the same building as the main power supply,' Renard muttered back. 'Which is buried under the snow, if it's even still in one piece. The heating's definitely been taken out – it's going to get really cold in here. Fast. Our landline's not working and there's never any signal up here, so I haven't been able to tell anyone what's going on . . . and no one's told me anything either.'

He looked so young and so helpless. He was clearly desperate for someone to take charge and, in the moment, that was going to be me. I was glad he'd had the presence of mind to lie about the heating maybe still working so the guests wouldn't panic. This place was going to become a very capacious walk-in freezer before too long.

I felt wired and focused, as if I'd managed to score a cup of coffee and a pack of cigarettes after all. I knew it was adrenaline kicking in, a much more concentrated version of the feeling I had when my work phone went off at one in the morning. The urge to hit the ground running and not stop until all the work was done. I leaned into that feeling. It was better than the rising panic and paralysing fear. It was at least going to be more productive.

'Does the tram thing get power from up here, or down there?' I asked.

'From the grid. It should still be working,' Renard said, suddenly hopeful.

'Thank fuck for that.' I sighed. 'We just need to . . . to . . . get everyone out of the snowbank and make sure they're taken care of then. Right?'

A weird chirping noise sounded from Renard and he pulled a slim walkie-talkie out of his pocket. The voice on the other end was just a blur of static to me, and Renard frowned. He pushed a button on the side.

'Répète ça, t'es sûr?' he asked, and I realised that as well as being garbled by interference, the person on the other end was speaking French.

Renard listened and then leaned heavily on the desk. The light from the torch cast his shocked features into harsh relief. He said something back to the person on the other end of the walkie-talkie and then it went silent.

'What's happening?' I asked. 'Please tell me they got the phone working and there are ambulances or fire engines coming, mountain rescue, the army – someone.'

Slowly, Renard shook his head. 'That was one of the security guards, down by the tram . . . It was hit, by part of the avalanche.'

'Can it be fixed?' I asked, already feeling dread climbing up my throat like bile.

Numbly, Renard shook his head. 'It's gone – destroyed. The whole station went over the cliff. And without power, we can't have any helicopters fly in during the night – there's no lights on the helipad for them to land safely.'

'The road,' I said, in sudden inspiration. 'You don't send deliveries up in the tram, right? I saw cars come this way. We can use those, drive out of here as soon as it's light and we can get everyone organised.'

'Right, yes,' Renard got back on the radio, and chattered away to the person on the other end. I looked back towards the dining room door and saw people stumbling around in the dark. I couldn't just stand there and do nothing. The shock had worn off. Now I was just full of nervous energy and even if I couldn't do much, I could at least do more than nothing. If I kept moving, I wouldn't have to think, or let any of what I'd just been through settle on me like a weight around my neck.

Leaving Renard to talk to the security guard on the radio, I walked determinedly back to the scene of the disaster. All the way, I was consciously quelling the shaking in my hands. I just had to keep going.

Chapter 8

In the dining room not much progress had been made. Despite the frantic efforts of the staff who were left and the few guests who had bothered to stay, there were only a couple of dark pits in the snow that suggested people had been dug out. The woman from before was gone, her blood a smear to show she'd been dragged to the side and covered with a tablecloth. I felt a pang of guilt for rushing off but at least I was there now. I could help. Somehow.

Thanks to the mostly glass walls and roof, the dining room was semi-lit by moonlight. My eyes had adjusted a little to the greater darkness while I was in the foyer so I could at least make out the shapes of debris on the ground. Ahead there were figures moving on the sloping mound of ice and snow that had piled into the dining room, blocking the broken window and spilling over the floor. A few of the staff must have gone to get torches because several of them lit up the snow in whirling white lines as people moved around.

I grabbed a metal tray from the floor by an overturned trolley and rushed up the icy slope to where a cluster of people were digging someone out. They were all focused on their task and their faces were set and grim. No one reacted as I joined them, but they shifted sideways to make room. We dug together and I saw how reddened their hands were, though some had tried to wrap them in cloth napkins or their sleeves. Chunks of compacted snow fell away, debris mixed into them – broken glass, gravel, wood splinters and pieces of metal. All the things the avalanche had torn through to reach us.

'Keep going, everyone!' Aloisia panted, and I looked up to see her working away in another spot, her suit jacket wrapped around her hands to help her scoop at the snow. She was luminous in the shadows thanks to her white clothes, shining like some sort of guardian angel. At her urging everyone started moving slightly quicker.

Someone beside me cried out and I realised it was because there was hair poking through the icy crust, dark against the snow. A braid. I dropped my tray and started clawing with the rest of them, trying to dig whoever it was out without hurting them. Within seconds my fingers were burning with cold and one of my nails tore to the quick, but I kept going until there was enough space for the others to reach in and break off pieces of ice, wriggling their raw hands into the space to get a grip under their arms and haul a woman out.

It was Nina, the woman who'd shown me to my room. She flopped onto the snowy slope, unmoving, and I found myself beside Paula the surgeon as we flipped Nina over.

Other people's hands flittered over her, patting for broken bones or injuries. A few people broke away to help others or sat back to regain their energy before moving on to the next rescue attempt. I stayed by Nina, who looked so young in the pale moonlight, limp and unresponsive.

'Airway's clear,' Paula muttered to herself, feeling around Nina's neck. 'No pulse though, must've been smothered.'

'I know CPR,' I said, my own heart in my throat. I knew it, yes, but I'd only had to use it twice – once at a post-BAFTA pool party and once behind the scenes at a press briefing when my client passed out on too many downers.

'Do compressions,' Paula said, tilting Nina's head back to open her airway.

The people around us watched as I pumped at her chest, pausing for Paula to give her mouth-to-mouth. We swapped over as my arms tired and tried again for a few rounds. But when it came time to switch again, Paula sat back and shook her head at me, gasping for air.

'No use – take her down there, we need to keep looking.'

A woman to my right – a waitress who probably knew Nina and had heard Paula just pronounce her dead – burst into tears, and my throat closed up as I fought to maintain composure. I'd spoken to Nina only a few short hours ago and now she was gone. But Paula was right, we couldn't keep trying on one person while there were so many still trapped. I knew that, but it was so awful to have to step back and let the others carry Nina – Nina's body – down to the floor. We'd dug her free and for what? She hadn't made it and now we were back at the start.

I was halfway up the slope, climbing after Paula, when I met Aloisia coming down, slithering over the irregular icy surface. She had a walkie-talkie in hand and grabbed at my shoulder to stop herself slipping over as she reached me.

'You're the woman who helped Renard, right?' she asked, squinting at me in the gloom.

'Uh, yeah, I suppose,' I was still looking up the bank, where Paula was now helping to pull a man from the snow. He was bleeding but appeared conscious. Thank God. Maybe most of the other casualties would be all right. I knew even as I thought it that was ridiculously optimistic. That snow wall had crushed the side of a building – most of the people it had fallen on would have been dead on impact. Or would be by now, having not had immediate aid.

Aloisia's grip on me tightened, bringing me back to earth. Her eyes were wide in the darkness, made even starker by the liner tattooed around them. 'OK, listen. I need your help – we're running out of first-aid supplies already – there were only two kits here at the reception and the kitchen. We need more foil blankets, injectable pain killers, oxygen. I need someone I can trust to go to the medical bay and all my staff are busy trying to help or fix things. You helped Renard. I trust you. So you need to help me.'

That made me look at her straight on. 'Me? Don't you guys have a doctor here?'

Aloisia looked grim. 'We do, but . . . he's under there, somewhere.' She gestured to the pitted mound of snow. 'He was dining with a guest he knew personally. They were right by the window.' For a moment her features were shadowed by grief, then she pulled herself together.

'Shit,' I muttered, my heart turning nervy somersaults. No doctor? OK, we had at least one surgeon but she wasn't exactly giving me a lot of confidence. I could still remember the way her hands shook even before the accident. 'OK, fine – I'll go, no problem. Just tell me where and how to get there.'

Aloisia's tense face relaxed a little. I noticed she'd tied her long dark hair up with an elastic band and there were bloody grazes on her bare arms, probably from falling against the ice. But she seemed unfazed by her injury and the rubber band tearing out strands of her perfect hair. She clearly just wanted to be of use.

She took out a bundle of keys and struggled to take one off before swearing under her breath and pressing the whole bundle on me. 'The medical bay is by the spa – go through there and it's the locked door past the treatment rooms with the snake, stick thing on it, the code for the door before that is 7859, and the key is this one with the blue tag. You might run into Jan – I sent him to man the security room, so he might see you on the cameras. Just tell him I sent you and you're not looting.'

'The cameras still work?' I asked, putting the keys in my pocket.

'On battery, for now,' Aloisia sighed. 'You know about the aerial tram?'

I nodded and her shoulders slumped.

'Please, keep that to yourself for now. I don't want to cause a panic.'

'But we have the road, right?'

For a second I watched her debate lying to me. Even with shadows across half her face it was easy to tell something was wrong. Finally she sighed and shook her head, lowering her voice still further.

'The road's blocked, by snow. We've already been

having trouble getting supplies up here because of snowbanks sliding onto the road but the cameras show the road is completely inaccessible now.'

'So there's no way out until daylight?' I asked, keeping my voice quiet. 'We can have helicopters land then, right?'

She nodded. 'I hope so. Not that we've been able to contact anyone yet but . . . eventually. Come morning the staff for the lower station and gate will raise the alarm, even if we can't get any calls through and the internet's down. The avalanche took everything out.'

I wasn't exactly filled with hope but it was clear that for the moment we were on our own. So getting those medical supplies was very important. I just nodded to accept what she'd told me and then turned and ran for the door. I was still laughably unfit, but my body was humming with adrenaline so much that I didn't care if I ached later. For now I would continue to push myself as hard as I needed to.

The foyer and hallways were completely dark save for a few candles on the marble desk, which someone had lit in my absence. Renard had obviously gone elsewhere to do Aloisia's bidding. It was reassuring to know that there were people all over the retreat dealing with the aftermath. It made me feel less helpless. Less alone.

I took one of the candles – a votive in a glass jar – to light my way. With little to no light coming in from the night sky until I reached the spa with its glass doors, my skin was prickling with fear at being somewhere unfamiliar in almost total darkness. I clung to that candle like it was a lifeline. The building already felt colder, uncomfortably so. My breath turned to mist in front of me and made the candle flame flutter.

When I reached the spa I glanced towards the equipment room and froze. The wolves. The fence that Silvie had assured me would keep them out. Had the avalanche destroyed that too?

For a moment I was paralysed with fear, and every reflection of yellow candle flame or gleam in the darkness was the eyes of a predator. I couldn't hear over my desperately pounding pulse but I strained my ears in case I might catch the sound of a growl or sharp claws on the tile floor. My free hand automatically twitched to my dog-bite scar, and I shut my eyes, trying to get hold of myself.

Don't be stupid, I told myself, sternly. *The wolves can't get in here. All the doors are closed, they could only get through the dining room. I'd hear that. They probably got scared off by the avalanche anyway. Stop being such a baby.*

The harsh words worked and I got myself moving again, though the back of my neck still prickled. I couldn't bring myself to look behind me either. Just in case I saw something.

At the back of the spa area there was a 'staff only' door with a metal keypad lock. I guessed this too was working via battery, or it wasn't electrical, as it was still locked and hadn't popped open. I put in the code and cracked the heavy door ajar, but the hallway beyond it was so dark that I couldn't make myself move forward. Even with the candle, it was too dark and the door would close behind me.

After a moment's hesitation I grabbed a towel from a nearby stack and used it to wedge the door open so some light from the windows would make it inside. The hallway was much narrower than the guest areas, and the walls were white-painted plaster with health and safety posters on them in several languages. Wishing I had a torch instead of a tiny candle, or time to find whatever other candles might be in the spa, I squinted into the darkness and spotted a small sign sticking out from the wall with the 'snake stick thing' aka the caduceus on it. The medical bay. Thank God for that.

I took two steps towards the sign and something hit me in the back of the head. Hard.

I stumbled, crying out in surprise and pain. The candle hit the floor and shattered, spattering my legs with hot wax, which burned even through my trousers. Glass shards spun away on the shiny floor. The back of my skull vibrated with the blow and I'd bitten my tongue. Pain radiated through my head. I turned automatically, throwing an arm up to defend myself from further blows.

It was so dark that as I turned I couldn't see anything but a shadow against the lesser darkness of the spa. Before I could blink I'd been hit in the face. I registered it as a hard, cold thing, not a hand or anything like that. It caught my cheek with such force that I staggered back over my own feet and fell.

I hit the floor, my mouth full of blood, and agony shooting through my cheekbone. My hands met broken glass as I scrambled at the tiles and I yelped. But my brain was so shaken up that I couldn't think straight, couldn't get myself together enough to get away from the glass and back on my feet.

'Help . . .' I bleated, nonsensically, as someone stepped over me. I grabbed stupidly at their leg – trying to stop them, or trying to help myself up I had no idea. Whoever it was kicked themselves free of me and I slumped back to the floor, rolling onto my side and pulling my knees up to my chest. I'd been beaten up enough as a kid that I instinctively made myself small.

The blow, when it came, knocked my head against the floor and I passed out almost immediately. The last thing I felt, through the blasting pain, was a hand taking the keys from my pocket.

Chapter 9

I roused myself with a shaky breath that tasted of blood. My lips were stuck together, my teeth gummed with it. I retched and rolled over onto my knees, hacking up bloody spittle. As I raised a hand to wipe my mouth, the raw cuts on my palm flexed open. I remembered the glass, being knocked to the ground, the figure that had stepped over my body and taken the bundle of keys. My face felt like a mask welded to my bones – it hurt so much my eyes immediately filled with tears, blinding me.

Cupping my face as if the bones would splinter apart without support, I rose in a panic and stumbled backwards into the wall, keeping it against my back so I couldn't be attacked again. It took a moment for the silence and stillness around me to register. The hallway was deserted, and nothing seemed to have changed since I'd lost consciousness. Whoever had hit me was gone and had apparently done nothing else to me once they had the keys.

Squinting into the dark I saw that the medical bay door was still closed, as was the one beyond it. The floor was littered with bits of broken glass and shattered wax. Some of the glass was blue, and I realised it had to have come from whatever I was hit with. A vase or something whoever it was had picked up in the spa itself. I remembered the size of the one at reception and winced. That thing could have killed me.

They hadn't delivered a final blow to end me. That was something, unless they'd assumed me dead. But whoever it was had taken those keys for a reason and I had no idea if they were still close by or not. Unsteadily I retreated to the spa as if it could offer safety.

I reached the nearest door and opened it, finding myself in a treatment room with a massage table and a shelf of lotions, oils and candles. I automatically felt for my lighter but found my pocket empty. Of course, I'd surrendered it with everything else. Thankfully I spotted one of those long 'magic wand' shaped lighters and when I pressed the button on it, an electric current zapped across the end. I took down a heavy three-wick candle and lit it. It cast a lot more light than the other one I'd taken and I felt slightly more comfort from its glow. I slipped the lighter into my pocket. I had a feeling lighters were about to become currency around here. I wasn't about to go without.

Back in the hallway I passed the staff door and crept down the narrow corridor. Aside from the medical bay and the other door, which I could now see said 'Sécurité' followed by what had to be a German and Italian translation, there was another door around the corner. This was a push-bar fire exit, and it was closed. My attacker might have used it to escape, or they could still be nearby.

I knocked on the security door in a panic and got no

answer, tried the handle and found it locked. No help was coming from there apparently. Maybe this Jan person had already left before I got there, to attend to some crisis or another resulting from the avalanche or the guests' stupidity. I still needed to get the medical supplies, I realised. Aloisia would be waiting for me to come back. People were counting on me. But I didn't have the keys anymore. Fuck.

The medical bay door at least had a window, albeit of wire-reinforced glass. But it wouldn't be the first time I'd broken through that – I could vividly remember doing so at school on a dare. One that had got me excluded but, still, I'd been successful. I just had to find something heavy enough to break the glass and the wires. The trick was not getting your arm caught.

I took a moment to assess my options, then went back to the spa reception and selected a likely looking stone Buddha. It was so weighty I had trouble carrying it one handed. Back at the door I set the candle down and swung the statue at the glass. Once, twice, three times. Glass pebbles rained down and soon I had a ragged hole I could just about get my hand through to unlatch the door from the inside. Being careful not to cut myself, I let myself in and immediately started opening drawers and cabinets, looking for supplies.

The medical bay was quite small, room enough for two raised beds with a curtain between them, a desk and two chairs. The walls were covered in built-in cabinets in shiny white laminate. Inside were plastic baskets and storage containers neatly labelled in what looked like Italian. I guessed that was the Sorgente doctor's preferred language. Despite the labelling the contents of each cabinet appeared random and a box marked 'Bende' held two packs of bandages, a bottle of eye drops and some syringes – which seemed completely unconnected to one another.

There was a door on the right – heavy and metal but unlabelled. I felt a shudder pass through me as I realised this must be some sort of walk-in fridge, a tiny morgue for a tiny medical room. I quickly turned away.

Under the desk I found a duffle bag, navy blue and with a teal caduceus beside the Sorgente logo on it. Presumably for if the doctor was called out to the ski route or a guest's room. It had some first-aid stuff inside but I added some small canisters of oxygen, a cool bag full of vials from a little fridge between the beds, and more dressings. Once the bag was packed I threw it over my shoulder and, candle in hand, peered back into the hallway.

It was still deserted, my attacker apparently long gone. Still, I felt uneasy as I left and retraced my steps to the foyer. The shadows had an extra air of malice about them now that I could no longer tell myself there was nothing to fear. I knew now that there was someone out there who was willing to attack me, just for a set of keys. To do what with I had no idea. We were all trapped here until morning anyway.

I felt a wave of relief as I reached the dining room where everyone downstairs seemed to have gathered. Lights and other people made me feel more secure. Then I realised that anyone inside might have followed me in order to steal the keys. There were maybe ten staff members there and Paula, the only guest helping. I scanned the room as I set my candle down on a table that had been righted and covered in first-aid supplies and stuff from the kitchens –

water bottles, scissors, and rolls of foil in the absence of more blankets. No one was looking at me specifically. All seemed busy with their tasks. The light was better, because candles now studded the snow heap and I saw that people were digging with catering-sized spoons and saucepans in lieu of shovels.

'There you are!' Aloisia arrived at my side and instantly took the bag from me, going through the contents and calling to other people. As they came and took things I saw that there were more bodies covered by tablecloths and fire blankets on the ground. But there were also survivors, bundled in foil and clustered together for warmth. Not many, but some.

As the bag emptied and the helpers scattered back to their work, Aloisia looked at me properly for the first time. She held her candle closer to my face, which was still throbbing painfully, my eye in the process of swelling shut.

'What happened?' She reached out and touched my cheek, her fingers probing the growing bruise, and I winced.

'I was attacked,' I whispered, shocked at how fragile I sounded. I turned my head slightly to show her where I'd been hit from behind. 'In the corridor by the medical bay – they knocked me out and took the keys.'

Aloisia looked alarmed, her soft brown eyes widening in shock. 'Why? Who would do such a thing, now? How did you get into the medical bay? Had you already opened the door?'

'No, I had to break the window. You might want to send someone to guard it, just in case anyone goes sniffing around for painkillers or rubbing alcohol.' My eyes strayed to the room behind her as I said this, but I found Paula at the far side of the room, busy putting a sling on someone.

'Yes, that's . . . I'll find someone to do that. But you should lie down – you look terrible.'

Her frankness startled a laugh out of me. It came out a little hysterical. 'I probably do, yeah. Any chance of getting my coffee back?'

Aloisia gave me a rueful smile. 'The vault's on a timer – can't be opened until midnight. We can deposit, but can't get stuff out until midnight security check when a guard takes the belongings of anyone leaving the next day and places them in a small safe.'

'Shame.' I sighed. 'Know anyone on the staff I could get a cigarette from?'

'I'll ask around,' she said. 'But don't hold your breath – go get some rest and hopefully by the time you wake up . . . we'll have a way out of here.'

'Wouldn't that be nice,' I murmured, eyes straying to the covered bodies that had been retrieved from the snow. 'Wish they had the same option.'

The moment of off-kilter humour was over. We were both brought back to reality with a sharpness that nearly took my breath away. Aloisia squeezed my arm sadly and went back to her work. I turned away, wondering if she'd ever imagined that this would be something she'd have to take responsibility for. To manage, as if there was any way to manage a tragedy of this scale. I felt for her, I really did. Never in my life had I been tasked with something so important, or that seemed so impossible.

Tired to my bones, I picked up a smaller candle – leaving the larger one behind for them – and made my way towards the stairs. On my way back up to my room I kept my ears pricked for the sound of footsteps behind me, alert in case I was about to be attacked again. But there was nothing. Apparently whoever it was had what they wanted and they either weren't in the building anymore, or were lying low. I wished that brought me any sense of safety but it didn't. My head still throbbed and my cheekbone sent shocks of pain through my entire face. They could have killed me and probably didn't even care.

The door to my room wasn't locked – as with all the other room doors up here, the key card locks had disengaged without power. Once inside I did a quick check of the dark suite and then returned to the door to put the chain on. It was better than nothing, even if any sufficiently motivated person could kick it open if they wanted.

The air in the room was distinctly chilly and the temperature only seemed to be dropping further. I set my candle by the bed and retrieved some more from the bathroom. The bath was still wet from my luxurious soak earlier. How had all of this happened in such a short time? When I went to rinse my hands clean of my own blood, the water was cold.

At least I wouldn't run out of candles anytime soon. I got a thick wool jumper out of the wardrobe and put it on over my dinner outfit, then shed my wax-spattered trousers in favour of some of the fleece-lined leggings The Sorgente had provided, and a pair of shearling slippers. I was so desperate for some relief from the pain in my face that I opened the balcony doors and put handfuls of snow from the railing into a flannel to place on my cheek. Outside the darkness stretched on forever. Not a single light anywhere. Either the power grid was down or the barn and the security lodge were closed for the day. It was eerie, like we'd been transported to the surface of the moon. Lifeless and silent.

I shut the doors and, bundled up under a duvet and weighted blanket, I faced the door and lay my aching head down for a rest.

It only occurred to me that going straight to sleep with a head injury and possible concussion was a bad idea, when I woke suddenly in the dark. So at least I hadn't died in my sleep or fallen into a coma or something.

My candle was still burning and the windows were still dark. Night without electricity seemed endless. I'd taken it for granted my entire life that my world didn't stop when the sun went down. Especially not in London, where there was always something open and the streets were never empty of cars and buses, the streetlights and shopfronts chasing away the night. It was hard to get used to this perpetual helplessness against the dark. I sat up with a wince, my hair pulling at the dried blood on my scalp.

That was when I heard it again. The sound that must have woken me – running footsteps in the corridor outside.

I held my breath and listened, waiting. The footsteps receded into the distance. Was it someone rushing back to their room after going down to ask a question of the staff or demand answers? Or was it someone else – someone up to no good? Whoever it was, they were fast and not stumbling at all even in the dark. Perhaps they had a torch, or they knew the way well.

I didn't want to find out, to be honest. My skull was already aching enough from trying to 'do something helpful'. The swelling around my eye had gone down but

I was out of adrenaline and emotionally wrung out from the night that would not end. I didn't want to involve myself in anything else.

Yet still I forced myself to get up and went to my door, peering through the peephole. All I could see was the mezzanine rail and the pale wall of the opposite side of the building across the foyer, mostly lost in shadow. No sign of movement or anyone standing out there. Mind you, in dark clothing whoever it was would have been invisible even right in front of me. I couldn't see very far to the left or right and like hell was I opening the door and sticking my head out.

I listened a moment longer, alert for the sound of doors slamming, a scream, anything. But it was silent.

Still uneasy, I shuffled back to bed and sat with my back propped against the headboard. The blankets were warm and I tried to tell myself that it was only the chill in the air that had me shivering.

It took me a long time to get back to sleep.

Chapter 10

When I woke up, pale daylight streamed in through the gauzy curtains. I was glad that I'd neglected to drop the 'relaxing' blackout blinds down. Never in my entire life had I been more grateful to see sunlight. I could see why cavemen had got so excited about the solstices and sunrises. The sunlight signalled safety and the return of normalcy after the chaos of the dark. The nightmare was over; I was going home.

As I shrugged off my mound of blankets I heard movement outside. Lots of it. Voices and footfalls, the trundling of many expensive pieces of luggage and the thud of doors being yanked shut in a temper. The other guests were clearly as ready as I was to get the hell off this mountain and back to the safety of an airport lounge, with complimentary champagne and hot coffee. My mouth watered just thinking about it. Who cared if I had to leave my tech and my lighter in the vault for a week? They could ship it to me at their expense.

The room was even colder than it had been last night and I shivered convulsively as I crossed the room. It was almost as cold inside as it had been out on the ski route.

I thought of the outdoor coat and wondered if I should go and get it or if I'd be leaving too soon for it to matter that much.

In the bathroom I winced to see the size of the bruise that had formed across my cheekbone. It was a hefty one, moody purple and alarmingly dark around a cut that must have been left when the glass thing I was hit with shattered. My eye was a little bloodshot but didn't show any signs of damage, thankfully. My vision was fine but my face hurt when I frowned at myself in the mirror, and I winced.

The back of my head was even more tender to the touch and my hair was crusted with blood, though it didn't seem to be bleeding now. I'd made a real mess of the pillow I'd slept on, smudges and smears of brownish-red all over the pristine high-thread-count linens. They could whistle for any cash from me for that, though.

I sluiced my head wound as best I could with cold water from the shower, bending over the moss-filled tray so as to not get my body wet. The water was like ice melt – apparently Renard hadn't been exaggerating about the heating going off. I wondered how long it would take the pipes to freeze up completely. I carefully towelled my hair off and left it down, because trying to pull it into a ponytail hurt like hell.

My stomach growled, reminding me that I hadn't finished dinner last night, and had thrown most of it up anyway. I was desperate for a cup of coffee, though a tea would have sufficed – a room temperature Red Bull even. Just a few micrograms of caffeine to get me through the day. Maybe I really did need to detox from it, but not today, that was for sure.

I didn't bother putting on fresh clothes, the leggings and jumper I'd slept in would do for the airport. If anyone emailed me wanting that stuff back they'd get one hell of a reply. Instead of packing properly I just scooped everything out of the wardrobe and into my suitcase, jammed the lid down and zipped it up. All ready to go. Then I took a deep breath and let myself out of my room, ready to face whatever was happening downstairs.

There weren't many people about on the second floor anymore. Most had probably already gone down to the foyer. There went my chance of being in the first helicopter out of this place. I didn't want to rush and risk falling, though, as it was still a little gloomy away from the windows. I descended carefully with my eyes on the stairs themselves instead of the wider foyer.

I heard them before I saw them, the same mob they had been last night. Raised voices and mutinous muttering filled the high-ceilinged space. I reached the bottom of the stairs and looked around. It appeared to be the exact situation I'd defused last night, only without the benefit of darkness to hide how pissed off everyone looked.

I hadn't really noticed how many people had made it out of the dining room last night. They'd all been scattered around. But from the looks of things our numbers had been hit hard by last night's catastrophe. The dining room had maybe held a hundred people, including twenty staff. There were between twenty and thirty guests in the foyer. That was it. Fewer than half had survived. For the first time the full scale of the casualties hit me and for a moment I couldn't breathe for the pressure in my chest.

Yet with all the suitcases and yelling, the room felt cramped. More like the gate at a busy airport than the foyer of an exclusive retreat. As if the remaining guests were trying to make up for the drastic loss by being twice as loud and taking up double the space.

Half the guests were wearing outerwear – coats, hats and handbags – as if ready to depart imminently. The rest were in casual clothes and leisurewear as if they'd just come down for breakfast. Which appeared to be the case as I started to make out individual voices in the noise. It sounded like some were ready to leave immediately and some wanted to be fed first. None of them appeared to be getting what they wanted. None seemed to have really registered the impact of last night's horror.

The desk was unmanned and I could imagine no one wanted to come and face this mob. That or they were all still busy elsewhere, trying to save lives instead of scheduling breakfast for us lot.

One voice suddenly rose above the rest of the crowd. It was Jade. I'd lost track of her last night when she must have made a run for it when we saw the avalanche coming. I couldn't judge – if I'd been a competitive sprinter I too would have got out of there at speed. It was survival instinct.

'Shut. UP!!' Jade yelled, and when the volume only dropped slightly, I watched as she kicked over a huge Samsonite suitcase and climbed onto it, prompting a noise of complaint from its owner. 'I said shut up! I can barely hear myself think in here with you moaning!'

That had the desired effect and the general volume softened to sulking murmurs. It was the first time I'd seen Jade lose her cool. Maybe all the stress and noise was triggering to her. There was a slightly wild look about her, as if she might just run away again. Or punch someone.

Jade hopped down and stalked towards the staff door, which, for all their bustle and complaining, the rest of the guests were still respecting as a boundary. I noticed that Jade had changed her clothes since yesterday – she was all in black, leggings, long-sleeved skintight jacket and black trainers. Like a cat burglar. Her hair was still in tiny, meticulous curls and she looked well rested despite her obvious annoyance. Maybe she was used to the early morning starts and late nights due to her training schedule, which had to be intense.

She opened the door and turned right without pause. Did she know her way around from being here before or was it the only choice? I had no idea, but she vanished and a few moments later returned, bringing Silvie with her. I couldn't really tell if she was frogmarching her out to face us, or if she'd offered Silvie enough reassurance that she felt able to finally come out from the staff corridors. Silvie certainly looked like a rabbit cowering from dogs, her doll-blue eyes huge and startled. Yesterday I'd been transfixed by how perfect she was, from her pearly teeth to her creaseless sheath dress. Today she looked more human – her clothes were the same as yesterday, crumpled and limp, and her long blonde hair was scraped up into a bun to keep it out of her face. There were dark circles under her eyes and I imagined that she, like most of the staff, hadn't got much sleep. If any.

I felt a pang of remorse that I hadn't been able to do more before going to bed – the attack had really taken it out of me. But it was clear that in my absence the remaining staff of The Sorgente had soldiered on. I wondered if they'd dug everyone out of the snowbank by now, and how many of those people were still alive but weren't in the foyer. My guess was not many could have survived being crushed and then buried in the freezing cold for hours. That tiny medical bay wasn't going to be enough, I thought with a shudder, and neither was that morgue.

With Jade beside her like a bodyguard, Silvie took a deep breath and tried to arrange her face into a customer service smile. It didn't quite work but it was at least a reminder of the normal order of things.

'Good morning. I apologise for the delay – I was called away . . . I'm sorry but, unfortunately, due to damage from last night's disaster, the helipad is currently out of commission and sadly thc aerial tram is also non-operational . . .'

'So get some cars round here!' Patrick called, stepping forward in the crowd and elbowing his wife aside in the process. 'And where are all the housekeepers? I need my bags packed up so I can get out of this death-trap!'

Silvie's eyes shuttered slightly and I recognised the look of someone who was reaching the limits of their training. If this went on much longer, she'd snap. I'd seen it before when a PA crashed out behind the scenes of a morning show. They'd thrown six coffees, mugs, tray, custard creams and all, at the host and then torn a hairpiece off an assistant producer. It had turned very ugly, though she had her reasons – which was why I was on the scene, making sure said host stayed in line. Which, regrettably, he hadn't, despite my threats and cajoling.

I took a step forward, trying to get closer to the desk before Silvie snapped. But Jade was already there. She shot Patrick a dick-withering look and pointedly turned her attention back to Silvie. 'Carry on,' she said, loudly enough that her voice carried across the entire foyer.

'The road is, at this time . . . blocked by the avalanche,' Silvie said. 'Although we have every faith that our situation has been reported to the authorities by ground staff at our dairy and the lower tram station, it will take them a while to send the machinery needed to clear the road as it's on private property and will be considered less vital than public and more well-trafficked routes.'

No one interrupted now. Everyone in the foyer was hanging on her every word, waiting for the 'but', for the solution, their way out. None was forthcoming. Although I'd already known most of this, the news about the helipad was a new blow. We really were stuck up here for the foreseeable.

'For the moment we have no internet and no phones due to the utility building being destroyed – likewise, no power. I've just been informed that there's an issue with the septic tank pipes freezing, so for now I must ask everyone to refrain from flushing the toilets.' Silvie gave us another brave attempt at a bright smile. 'But food will be distributed via reception shortly and we aim to make sure everyone is comfortable until we are able to leave. Anyone with any injuries should report to the spa, where we have set up triage rooms. In the meantime all treatments and activities are suspended and we would ask that you remain in your rooms as much as possible to keep warm and to limit the possibility of accidents or further distress.'

Silvie ended her little speech and waited, as I was waiting, for the first dissenting voice to pop off. How she handled that would give a good indication of how today was going to go. It didn't take long.

Patrick cleared his throat loudly and puffed up

in preparation for a fresh assault, but Silvie headed him off. She gestured to her left like a flight attendant demonstrating where the exits were on a flight already delayed by four hours.

'Line up this way to collect your breakfast – a further update will be provided here in two hours. Thank you.' That last she directed mostly at Jade, before stepping backwards and vanishing through the staff door. I could only imagine that she was leaning against the wall on the other side, desperate for a cup of coffee or stiff drink.

'This is ridiculous,' Patrick bugled, as if trying to get her to come back. But the bulk of the crowd was being led by their stomachs and began lining up from reception along the corridor towards the spa. I assumed that the kitchen was connected to the front desk for room service delivery purposes. It was good we had a back way in, as the dining room was off limits now for obvious reasons.

It looked like the queue for food was going to be a long one and I wandered in the opposite direction to avoid the crush. The doors to the grand dining room were closed and someone had put what looked like a bike lock through the handles to prevent access. I peered through the windows and saw the shapes of people laid out under makeshift coverings – a double row across the dining room like they'd come out of some sort of grim factory. I'd been right about the lack of survivors. There had to be at least fifty bodies in there, probably more still buried in the ice.

'We had to secure the doors, there's no way to barricade the broken windows.'

I turned and found Renard behind me. He looked rumpled and exhausted. His hands were chapped raw where they were clasped around his elbows. Likely from digging in the snow. His uniform was just as wrinkled and there were sweat patches under his arms. He'd had a long night, just like Silvie had. I noticed that his formerly pierced earlobe was bleeding – he'd probably been picking at it nervously.

'Secure?' I echoed. 'From what?'

He checked over his shoulder but we were more or less completely alone now. Those few people left in the foyer were too busy talking to one another to notice us. Only Jade seemed the least bit curious about what we were doing. I caught her glancing at us and then away as if embarrassed that she'd been caught eavesdropping.

Renard sighed but seemed to decide he could trust me after yesterday's events. 'The avalanche took out more than just the utility building . . . the perimeter fence isn't just without power – it's come down, a whole stretch of it.'

A cold fist took hold of my heart and suddenly I found it hard to breathe. The wolves. The wolves could get in? Renard must have seen the horror on my face, because he touched my shoulder in an attempt to reassure me, having no idea how close his fingers were to the scar left by a dog's jaws.

'Even if there are wolves nearby and they get into the grounds, they can't get inside the building. The doors from in there to the kitchen are locked too. Our security team also have a rifle for the rare chance that one might appear outside. We're perfectly safe as long as we stay inside,' he said.

I nodded, forcing myself to take steady breaths. He was right. With the doors to the dining room secured, nothing could get in from outside unless someone let it in. Given that the guests seemed to need their bags packed for them, it seemed unlikely that they'd willingly face the elements outside without the promise of hot chocolate afterwards.

'Do you know where Aloisia is?' I asked. 'I wanted to ask her if there was anything I could do now we're stuck here . . . I can't just sit around waiting in my room.' Neither could I see myself eating anything, not after seeing those rows of shrouded bodies.

Renard's brow creased. 'No . . . no, I haven't actually seen her since late last night. Or, I suppose, early this morning. She was helping to take the casualties to the spa rooms with that doctor. She didn't come back that I saw.'

'Paula? The surgeon?' I asked and he nodded.

'Maybe she decided to sleep there. The staff quarters are a separate building and even though it's not been damaged, she said it wasn't smart to have us all go over there. What with the fence being down and the guests possibly getting . . . difficult,' he said, rather diplomatically, in my opinion.

'They do seem like they're ready to start ripping copper wire from the walls in lieu of a refund,' I sighed. 'OK, I'll look for her at the spa. Maybe she told Paula where she was going.'

'I'll come with you. She only gave us instructions up to making sure there was cold food for everyone. I need her to let us know what we're meant to be doing now.' Renard looked fretfully at the marble reception desk, now deserted. 'We lost a lot of staff last night, I don't think she's taking it well.'

For the first time I wondered how it might feel to be one of the remaining staff at The Sorgente in the cold light of day. To hear guests demand refunds and talk about how inconvenient this all was, expecting service while staff grieved their friends and tried to mentally recover from their own near-death experiences. How long until they all snapped, one after the other, and left the clients to fend for themselves? How long until the guests realised that, despite all the deaths, they still outnumbered the staff?

I didn't like the idea of either option. The sooner we got off the mountain the better.

Chapter 11

Renard accompanied me on my way to the spa. We passed clusters of other guests who'd already got their food and were scoffing at the cold options on offer – which appeared to consist of ham, cheese, bread and yoghurts. I suppose we had to at least be thankful that it was so cold everywhere, and we had snow or cold air to keep things fresh. Even if it meant no hot water and no way to cook anything, plus the delight of frozen toilets. I made a mental note to take the cheeses out of my room's snack drawer and stash them somewhere no one could find them, so at least I'd have a small private supply of food to fall back on.

A horrible thought occurred to me as my mind went down the supplies route and I made sure we were far enough from the other guests before I voiced it to Renard. I didn't want to spark additional panic.

'Aloisia said you've had trouble getting supplies up here because of snow blocking the road, right?' I said. 'She said the weather's been bad or something.'

'Yes, but nothing like the avalanche. Usually it melts, or worst case we can clear it ourselves with shovels eventually, but it's been difficult the past few weeks. The weather's been bad – that's what's caused all this. The avalanche.'

'Does "supplies" mean . . . food?' I asked hesitantly, hoping I was wrong.

Renard stopped in his tracks and shut his eyes for a moment as realisation hit. He swore in French and then looked helplessly at me. 'Yes. Damn it, it does. I need to talk to Aloisia about that now as well. We were expecting another delivery to cover the shortfall from having missed a delivery a few days ago, but now . . .'

'How long do you think we can last on what we have?' I asked, because I didn't want to be one of the people not in the know. This was pretty critical and at least knowing what was going on put me in a slightly better position than the rest of the clueless guests.

'I'd have to ask the kitchen staff but . . . I know we were getting very low and Chef wasn't happy it would take until Monday to get a delivery up here. He was having an argument about it with Lars – the deputy manager. I've never seen him that angry.'

I swallowed hard. It was Saturday now, so hopefully we'd be out of here in a day or so. Otherwise things might start to get a bit desperate. Although we wouldn't need fancy dinners, we also wouldn't be able to cook most of the food, so we'd be quite limited. Starting a fire outside would mean braving the possibility of wolf attacks. I could only hope there was some extra snack food hidden in the vault if we really needed it.

'I never said thank you, by the way – for yesterday,' Renard said as we carried on up the corridor. 'Thanks for helping get everyone under control.'

‘Don’t mention it – honestly you guys deserve a fucking medal for still trying to keep it together after everything that happened last night,’ I said, eyes fixed on the hallway ahead. ‘Can’t imagine you were trained for this.’

‘Still . . . thank you. And I’m sorry you were hurt afterwards. Silvie told me you were hit in the head?’

‘Oh that wasn’t to do with that,’ I said, then frowned. I didn’t actually know that, did I? I’d assumed the keys had made me a target, but really they might have been besides the point. It was possible one of the other guests got annoyed at me for throwing my weight around and saw their chance to put me in my place. I could see Patrick wielding a vase and then snatching the keys – as keen to have an advantage as I was. Whoever had them possibly fancied a little look around the vault, or an opportunistic visit to the pantry after hours. I hoped Aloisia had security watching out for anyone going where they weren’t meant to be. Though how long the battery power for the CCTV system would last was anyone’s guess.

As we reached the spa the doors opened and Carri X stumbled out. She was still wearing her Barbie winter wonderland outfit, apart from the fox-fur hat, which she’d either left in her room or lost in the intervening time. Her blindingly blonde hair was mussed and she’d thrown a crochet duster on over the top of her skimpy skirt and top, though her hands still looked almost blue with cold.

‘Hey, d’you know where the food is here?’ she asked as she got closer, tripping over her own feet. The smell of vodka that had clung to her last night had only grown stronger. Had she bathed in it? Some misjudged attempt at a ‘cleaning hack’? Even Renard recoiled slightly as the aura of pure alcohol stung our eyes.

‘Kitchen’s back there,’ I said, and gestured. ‘There’s a queue at the moment though.’

‘D’they have, like . . . bone broth?’ Carri asked, squinting at me as if I was the one dressed head to toe in white and it hurt her eyes to look at me. She was slurring slightly so she’d definitely drunk the vodka and not spritzed it on. Where the fuck had she managed to get alcohol from? I wondered if she’d been the only person smart enough to smuggle some in undetected. Or, if she was using that old model trick – soaking a tampon before inserting it. But then she wouldn’t smell like she’d just rolled around on the floor of a student union and that wouldn’t have got her this blotto.

‘I don’t think so – only cold stuff I think,’ I said, looking to Renard for confirmation. But he was still looking askance at Carri, like his staff training was at war with the unique situation we’d all found ourselves in. I supposed in ordinary circumstances a drunk guest would warrant intervention and a full-scale search of their belongings for previously undetected contraband.

‘Fuck,’ Carri sighed, succinctly, and went trotting unsteadily in the direction I’d indicated. I wondered, watching her go, if she even knew about the avalanche or if she’d left the dining room before it happened. I couldn’t remember seeing her in the aftermath.

‘Should we . . . help her?’ Renard asked.

I considered for a moment, then shook my head. ‘She’ll be with everyone else, so, she’ll be OK. No idea how she’s managed to get even drunker since I saw her yesterday. Does anyone on your staff have a sideline in dealing vodka miniatures?’

‘No, absolutely not.’ Renard looked scandalised at the

very thought, eyes darting around as if he was worried someone would hear me.

'OK, I was just joking,' I said, raising my eyebrows.

'Sorry, it's just we all take our work here very seriously, and anything like that would mean an instant dismissal,' Renard muttered and began to walk. He shoved open the doors to the spa before I could comment again and we stepped into the spa.

Where yesterday it had been empty and quiet, today there was a sense of occupation and activity. Paula was at the reception desk scribbling away on blank printer paper and I could hear the telltale beep of a heart monitor coming from one of the treatment rooms. The candles had been moved around to light the place and most were extinguished now that the night was over.

Paula looked up as we arrived and pushed her brown bob out of her face. She looked exhausted and as if she'd aged five years over night, at least. I guessed she'd been working hard and, unlike me and the rest of the guests, hadn't had a chance to sleep. The concealer and heavy foundation had worn off and her broken veins were as red as her eyes.

'Is there news?' she asked briskly, and I realised she hadn't heard the morning meeting in the foyer.

'Looks like we're stuck here for a while – road's blocked, helipad and the aerial tram are damaged,' I said, when Renard didn't jump in to explain. He was probably exhausted. Paula's shoulders slumped. 'How are things looking in here?'

'Pretty awful,' she said, not mincing her words. 'I've been writing up notes to keep track of treatment but we're already running out of painkillers and antibiotics. There's one heart monitor with a battery, no idea how long that's going to last and . . . we've already lost two more people,' she said, lowering her voice. 'So the morgue is full . . . and why am I telling you this? Where is the manager?' She rubbed at her face again, chasing off exhaustion and causing more make-up to pill and crumble away.

'We're looking for Aloisia – was she not here with you?' Renard asked.

'She was but she said she was going to sit down for a minute and then she never came back,' Paula huffed. 'Is there any danger of someone bringing me a cup of coffee or some food? I've been on my feet all night trying to keep these people alive and it seems everyone else has just forgotten about that. And none of the taps are working now, so I can't even get a drink.'

'I'll go and get you something, though we don't have coffee here,' Renard said.

'Not even in the staff building Aloisia was talking about?' Paula challenged.

'Not unless you fancy racing the wolves to get to it,' I said, putting a stop to the argument before it could fully begin. I was too tired to keep breaking up spats.

Renard left to go get some food for the good doctor and I glanced down to find that her hands were no longer trembling. I got the sense that the stash of rubbing alcohol in the medical bay had taken a significant hit. I only hoped she could keep it together until rescue came.

'How many people are being treated?' I asked, glancing towards the treatment rooms.

'Last count was five – two serious concussions, one with a broken finger. Broken leg and ribs, one impaled on a piece of metal from the window frame . . . if we don't get that one to a proper hospital they aren't going to make it.'

I winced. Five survivors was not a lot and it looked like we might lose more. 'I don't know that there's anything we can do. I would say let's try and clear the road but . . . the fence is down and we'd probably end up getting attacked by wolves, with our luck.'

Paula inhaled through her nose and let out a long breath. I wondered if she'd learned that technique while studying for her medical degree. She nodded and squared her shoulders. Despite her apparent drinking problem, I liked her. She seemed like the kind to get stuff done.

'All right then, I suppose we just have to cope,' she said, and bustled off back towards the treatment rooms. I was left by the reception desk, wondering where Aloisia could have gone to. If she wasn't able to get to the staff building and hadn't wanted to find an available guest room in case she was accosted, there were limited places she could be.

I guessed Paula would have mentioned if she was in the treatment rooms and so did a check of the reception in case she was in a nook somewhere. There was the security office, but that door was probably still locked. I opened the door to the outdoor clothing and equipment room last and found her there, sitting on the bench, asleep among the coats.

I shook her gently by the shoulder, wincing because she looked so done in. There were dark circles carved into her olive skin and she'd bitten her lips to pieces. She woke with a groan and looked at me through bleary eyes. 'Oh no . . . I only meant to sit for a moment, in the quiet . . .' She rubbed at her face and stretched with a grimace. 'What time is it? What's happening?'

‘I’m not sure, actually. You don’t really go big in for clocks up here, do you? It’s morning, I’d guess maybe nine, ten-ish? Not much going on except the potential for a guest riot. It’s freezing cold, we’re stuck here and the toilets aren’t working.’

She groaned again and stood up, easing her back after spending a good few hours sleeping upright on a bench. I heard footsteps behind me and Renard returned with a tray of fruit, yoghurts and stale-looking bread rolls, probably leftovers from last night’s dinner.

‘This was all that was left,’ he said, setting the tray down at reception. ‘Everything the kitchen staff served up has been cleaned out.’ He spotted Aloisia and looked relieved. ‘We’ve updated everyone on the situation – told them about the helipad being compromised. What should we do . . . now?’

Aloisia shook off her obvious exhaustion and steadied herself. ‘I want to speak to Jan – he was manning security last night. I meant to check on him before, but I just sat down and . . . I need to relieve him and we need to check the CCTV to find Lars and whoever attacked . . .’

‘Chloe,’ I filled in. ‘What’s with this Lars guy? I think I heard you trying to find him last night at dinner.’

‘He’s my deputy.’ Aloisia sighed. ‘He wasn’t at yesterday’s pre-dinner briefing. Someone said he was back at the staff lodge but he never appeared and then I didn’t see him in the dining room but . . . now I’m starting to think he *was* there and now he’s . . .’

Buried in the snow with the other people we can’t dig out, I thought but didn’t say. Still, that knowledge seemed to weigh Aloisia down. She was, after all, just the manager of a wellness retreat, not someone who’d been prepared to be the voice of authority in what felt like a warzone.

'If we check the cameras I can at least find out if he was or wasn't in the dining room and if there's any use in looking for him,' Aloisia said. 'And we need to get my keys back and make sure whoever's attacking my guests doesn't do it again. Renard, can you radio for someone to relieve Jan? See if Nils or Lionel can come over from the kitchen now they're done distributing the food.'

I followed Aloisia as she strode to the staff door and onwards to the security office. Renard followed us, chattering on the radio as he tried to locate another guard to take over from this Jan guy. I was thinking about the video footage we were about to see, proof of who'd hit me over the head. What would we do with whoever it was? Lock them in a side room and hand them over to the police when the road was cleared? What if they fought back? What if it wasn't Patrick or one of the guests but someone else? Someone on staff? Could there be an intruder given all the steps it took to get here? I doubted it, but so far my stay at The Sorgente had been nothing but surprises.

Aloisia knocked on the security door and called for Jan, but there came no answer. She sighed, reaching for her pocket before remembering that her keys were lost.

'Probably asleep,' she muttered, automatically trying the handle anyway.

The handle clicked down, and the door opened under her weight.

I still don't know why, but the moment that door opened, unexpectedly unlocked, I knew something was really, really wrong. People like to say that when they look back on awful events. Make out like they felt or saw it coming. But in this case I knew that door had been locked tight last time I was in that hallway. I'd tried it myself.

'Jan?' Aloisia said, stepping through the door. 'Are you—'

I never heard the end of that sentence. She just stopped talking, stopped moving. Just stood there in the doorway, looking at the lake of red illuminated by a handful of almost dead candles. And after a second, a single heartbeat, she began to scream.

Chapter 12

The candlelight made the whole thing appear much more sacrificial. The unsteady flames gave the room a Gothic, ritualistic look – reflected many times over in the monitors and framed certificates on the wall. Without those few guttering candles, the room would have looked almost ordinary: a bank of screens, a large desk with three keyboards, a door marked 'WC' and a pair of swivel chairs. Only one of which was occupied.

I could see him over Aloisia's shoulder, the figure in the chair. He was slumped, arms over the sides the only thing holding him up, his legs vanishing into the shadows under the desk. If his head hadn't been bludgeoned to bits he might have been sleeping. Perhaps he had been, when someone caved his skull in like ice on a puddle. Or perhaps he had just fallen into the chair when his body went limp in death.

Aloisia abruptly stopped screaming, the sound drying in her throat until she closed her mouth with a clack of teeth. She took a few dazed steps into the room, heedless of the blood spattered over the grey carpet tiles, the painted walls and the rows of monitors. I could hear her ragged breathing, the only sound other than the relentless chattering on Renard's walkie-talkie behind me.

I looked away from the horrific sight of the body and saw a hole punch sitting on top of a short filing cabinet. One of those massive office hole punches that could do a hundred sheets of paper at once, or crush bone. It was covered in blood and a sticky pool had formed around it, dripping down the side of the gunmetal grey cabinet.

'Jesus . . .' Renard murmured, and I sensed a flurry of movement like he was crossing himself. Aloisia sagged to the side and leaned against the wall, eyes still fixed on the man in the chair.

'Jan . . .' she finally murmured, peeling her dry lips apart. 'Oh God.'

Behind me, Renard was being sick in the hallway. He hadn't even entered the room. My empty stomach roiled but there was nothing to throw up. Instead my throat felt tight, coated in acid. I edged into the room and circled the body in the chair to push open the WC door. Inside there was nothing, just a stainless steel toilet and sink combo in the tight space. No one hiding. I wasn't sure if I was disappointed or not. The idea that whoever had done this might be in the room with us was terrifying, but so was the thought that they were roaming The Sorgente unchallenged, master key in hand.

'Why would he . . . ?' Aloisia asked no one in particular, her voice shaking. She tried and failed to get a hand into her pocket twice before taking the walkie-talkie out and pressed the button to bring it to life. 'Security staff, come in. Report, security team . . .' She let the button go and listened to the dead air for a moment before speaking again. 'Nils? Lionel? Max? Report immediately.'

This time a voice crackled over the walkie-talkie, followed by another. Aloisia sagged with relief. 'Nils? Please respond.'

Dead air again. Aloisia looked at me and I shrugged helplessly. Renard was still on his knees heaving in the corridor.

'Come to the security room, at once. Code White.' She put the walkie-talkie back in her pocket and straightened up, still looking at Jan's body but apparently steeling herself for action.

'What does that mean? Code White?' I asked.

'Security code for a sudden death . . . I'd say this qualifies,' she said. 'I don't want other staff hearing about this on the radio and panicking. How did this happen?'

'I don't know, but the door was locked when I was here – I tried it after I was hit and it didn't open. I suppose if I'd been thinking more clearly I'd have tried yelling for help but the medical supplies seemed more important in the moment.'

'So he might have been alive when . . .' She couldn't finish the sentence, just shook her head at the insanity of it all and turned to Renard, now leaning in the doorway. 'Do not tell anyone about this – not even Silvie.'

I wondered why she'd specified, but it didn't seem like the time to ask. Renard nodded, wiping his mouth. He was as pale as a Victorian orphan, eyes bloodshot from the vomiting.

'Can I . . . May I please go?' he asked faintly.

'I might need you to help search for Nils, for whoever did this, since you already know what's happened,' Aloisia said, after a pause. 'Go sit in the spa reception, direct Max and Lionel up here and . . . prepare them, as quietly as possible.'

Renard didn't need telling twice. He left on unsteady feet, one hand on the corridor wall. Aloisia turned to me. 'You too, I'm afraid. You're involved now and I could use the help since Lars is still missing, Nils won't respond and now Jan . . .' She swallowed. 'Do I need to tell you to keep this quiet?'

'I'm used to it,' I said, looking at her rather than the bloody mess to try and regain some sense of normalcy. 'Never anything quite like this, but I understand discretion being the best policy.'

'I don't know how this happened. I'd never have thought anyone here could do something like this.' Aloisia looked truly unsettled, as well she might in the presence of a murdered colleague. The savagery of the attack, as evidenced by the whip-cracks of blood on the walls, was horrific. It was shocking even to me. 'We check the background of every member of staff before hiring them – criminal records, social media, even a credit check to make sure they're not going to succumb to bribes from our more . . . insistent clientele. I can't believe that a . . . murderer slipped through that process.'

'So you think it was a guest?' I asked.

'I don't know what to think.' She gnawed at her thumb for a second, then looked to the security system. 'I'm hoping we have it on camera, so we'll know for sure who's responsible. My God, my bosses are going to lose their minds. This whole situation is . . . it could be the end of this place.'

I felt sickly responsible for Jan's death, at least partially. The keys had been in my hands when they were taken and it seemed to follow that whoever had killed Jan had used those keys to gain access to the security room. Had they come in while he was facing away and surprised him? The hole punch had been left close to the door – maybe that was where it had always been kept. Or else someone had let themselves in while Jan was in the tiny toilet and then hidden just out of his view as he retook his seat. As to why they'd done it I hadn't the faintest idea. It seemed so random and brutal. With everything else going on, who would want to add to the death toll?

Footfalls thudded up the hallway and we both turned to see two men arriving. I recognised them as the pair who'd backed Renard up yesterday – the tall, hefty blond who'd climbed from the pages of Hansel and Gretel, and his shorter, dark friend, looking like even more of a starving French poetry student with his fresh dark circles. They spotted the body and stopped in their tracks. Renard must have warned them as Aloisia instructed, because they seemed less shocked and more disgusted. The blond turned away and the dark-haired man didn't seem to be able to tear his eyes from Jan's body. Like he was rubbernecking at a car crash.

'Have either of you seen Nils?' Aloisia asked, wasting no time.

'Not since last night,' the blond guy said.

'Max?' she asked of the shorter guy. Which made his taller, blond companion Lionel, I supposed.

He closed his eyes for a moment as if trying to get his thoughts in order. Or erase the sight of Jan's smashed skull from his mind. 'No . . . last I heard from him he'd confirmed the road was blocked and he was going to the staff lodge. We were trying to get a full list of survivors and had to check to see if anyone had snuck out early to go to bed once dinner was being served.'

'He went outside?' I asked disbelievingly, though I supposed someone had to for the news about the helipad and aerial tram to be discovered.

Both Lionel and Max looked at me in obvious confusion. They clearly had no idea who I was. They had no reason to, after all.

'This is Chloe, a guest – she was with me when I found Jan. And last night she was attacked just outside and had my master keys stolen from her,' Aloisia filled them in.

'Have you checked the CCTV to see who it was, to see if they came in and . . . did that?' Max asked.

'No, I have no idea how this system works. We were going to ask Jan to . . . Can you please log in and see if you can bring up yesterday's videos?' Aloisia asked, sounding overwhelmed.

Max looked like he'd rather do anything else but approach the body, but he went around to the PC towers and started pushing buttons, gingerly avoiding the blood. I guessed that the security computer was running off whatever backup battery the rest of the system used. Yet nothing happened as he tried to turn it on. He stepped back, frowning.

'Max? You're better with it – why isn't it working?'

The dark-haired man reluctantly approached to help, kneeling down and checking under the desk. I heard wires rattling together and then bits of plastic hit the floor as he checked connections. Moments later he emerged, looking shaken.

'It's been fucked with,' he said, and held up a cut wire as evidence. 'By someone who had no idea how to work it – instead of deleting stuff they've just cut wires, pulled out anything they could and it looks like they hit the computers with something heavy – trying to batter the hard drive.'

'Shit.' I'd been hoping for easy answers from the security system but apparently the killer had known enough to screw with that. 'Can't we plug something else in and view it from the cloud or whatever?'

'It wouldn't have been able to back anything up since the power went down and we lost Wi-Fi,' Max, apparently the resident tech expert, said. 'The hard drive copy was all we had and I don't know if it's salvageable even if we had a working PC to plug it into. It looks pretty badly damaged.'

'OK.' Aloisia rubbed at her temples, apparently fending off a monster headache. I sympathised – my own head was throbbing, a line of pain bisecting my skull between the wound on my cheek and the one on the back of my head.

'OK . . . No CCTV, then. We'll have to see if the hard drive can be fixed after we get out of here. For now we need to find Nils and Lars. I want to know what happened and where they are. We need as much help as possible if there's a . . . killer, up here with us,' Aloisia concluded.

'We should arm ourselves as well,' Max said and he went to a tall cabinet that had been hidden from me by the bank of monitors. 'Nils took the pistol in case of any wolf incursions. Said he didn't want the guests to panic if they saw him with the long gun. Pistol's easy to hide. What the—'

He'd opened the cabinet, which was either unlocked already or had an electronic lock that had failed since the power cut. He now stepped back, ash white, frowning first at Lionel and then us. Lionel cursed under his breath.

'The rifle's gone,' Max said, confirming what I'd been fearing since he looked into the cabinet and went pale. 'Whoever killed Jan must have taken it.'

We stood in tense silence as we all absorbed this new development. We weren't just trapped on a wolf-infested mountain with almost no food – now we were at the mercy of an armed killer.

Chapter 13

We were all still silently trying to process the theft of the gun when there came a commotion in the corridor. I could hear Renard babbling something about 'authorised staff only' and lots of footsteps coming our way.

'. . . Someone needs to tell us what the fuck is going on,' Emmitt's voice carried to us.

'It's not acceptable. You can't just keep us here and ask us to survive on yoghurts. There's no hot water and we can't use the loo, for God's sake.' That was Livvy; I recognised the plummy accent of the MP's wife. 'No heating either, we'll all get pneumonia – my fingers are already turning blue!'

'Can you shut up about hot water – there's a literal life or death emergency? Someone needs to point me to the coats, because we can't just leave her out there,' Jade was saying, suddenly very close.

Aloisia and I went for the door at the same time, but didn't get it closed fast enough. The three of them, with Renard in the rear, arrived at the half-closed door and Emmitt shoved it open with a surprisingly strong hand. He gawped at the body and his face drained slowly of colour, his mouth working as if trying to dredge up a word from somewhere deep inside his brain.

'Oh, dear Jesus . . .' Livvy's hand flew to her mouth and she turned away, going the same yellowish off-white as her bob.

Jade, still in her all-black outfit from earlier, just stood and stared. Her eyes flickered over everything, taking in the details. I watched her muscles tense under the tight outfit, like she was preparing herself for a fight, or to flee.

At Aloisia's nod, Renard corralled them into the room. At the back of my mind there was a tiny voice squeaking about 'preserving evidence' for the police. But we were operating in what felt like a new and separate reality to the one we'd been in before the avalanche. The real world was far away and, as of right now, unreachable. Besides, I'd done my share of wiping fingerprints and hiding bloodied clothes before. I wasn't exactly the poster child for correct crime scene procedures. It'd be hypocritical to start getting precious now.

Renard pulled the door closed and Livvy was the first to break out of her shocked stupor. She grabbed at her throat, fingers twitching as if searching for a string of pearls to clutch.

'What is the meaning of this?' She looked between all of us as if afraid we were about to produce knives from behind our backs and lunge for her. 'What – who – did this?'

Aloisia was apparently at the end of her rope. I could see it in her slumped shoulders. It was my turn to step up and take command of the situation.

'There's been a murder,' I said, as calmly as possible, because if you start treating something as gossip-worthy, that's what it becomes. 'We only just discovered this and no one else can know – or there'll be a panic and more people could get hurt.'

Jade looked away from the body and at me. 'You mean whoever did this might start offing people if they get spooked?'

Damn it, she was unfortunately perceptive. I weighed the benefits of trying to swerve that question and decided against it. 'Yeah . . . that's exactly what we're worried might happen. So, like I said, it's important to keep this quiet.'

Jade nodded slowly, absorbing this.

'And you haven't called the police yet?' Emmitt said.

'We can't call anyone.' Max was looking at him with the dawning realisation that he was addressing an idiot. 'None of the phones are working. We can't get any sort of signal either and the internet's down.' He muttered something to Lionel in French and the blond-haired man snorted.

'We need to find Nils and Lars – they work here,' I said, interrupting before Emmitt could notice he was being mocked. 'And, no offence, but we can't have you lot running off unsupervised now you know about this. Maybe you ought to just stay here.'

'No, I say we split into two groups,' Aloisia said, to my utter bewilderment. She must have noticed the look on my face because she elaborated. 'The fewer people wandering around unchecked, the less likely we are to have another death, right? One group can go to the staff lodge to find Nils and the other can muster the rest of the guests together in the foyer so we have eyes on everyone.'

'Go outside?' Emmitt asked. 'What if something's happened to the fence? There could be wolves?'

'Wolves?!' Livvy's voice climbed three octaves, fingers digging into her throat with new vigour. 'Absolutely not, I am not going out there.'

'I'll go.'

We all looked at Jade and I was honestly a little impressed. Also doubting her sanity more by the minute, but even so. I hadn't expected anyone, especially not another guest, to go outside without a weapon when there were wolves prowling about. Why she'd offered was what had me confused.

She crossed her arms. 'Look, I saw that American pop star girl go out the front door – no coat or anything. We need to get her back inside, so I might as well go with you and hopefully we find her on the way.'

So that was why Jade was stepping up. Carri was outside in just the outfit I'd just seen her in. She had to be really drunk to not come running back in right away due to the cold. Forget the wolves – she'd have frostbite if we didn't get her back inside ASAP.

'OK – Renard, you and Max go with these two back to the foyer and start rounding everyone up,' Aloisia said, easily slipping back into control as if the past few minutes were just a blip. 'I will go with Lionel, Chloe and . . . ?'

'Jade,' she said. 'Do you have guns, by the way – in case there are wolves? Or in case a murderer sneaks up on us?'

'. . . No,' Aloisia said, and her eyes briefly flicked to mine. Interesting. She didn't want to tell them that the killer had taken the rifle and that Nils had a handgun on him when he went out. I wondered if this was just to try and stop the spread of scary information or if she had another reason for keeping it between her staff and me.

At least I now understood where the whole 'split into groups' thing was coming from. She wanted one security guard to stay behind in the main building, to keep order. It made a kind of sense, for now she only had two trained guards, and taking both away from the bulk of the guests would mean chaos.

I was also panicking because she'd put me in the 'going outside where the wolves are' group. My heart felt like it was being strangled inside me. I couldn't. I wouldn't. It was probably my imagination but the bite scar on my arm felt like it was throbbing – fresh and angry. The memory of that terror crawled over my skin.

'All security are trained to deal with wolf encounters, gun or no gun,' Lionel put in drily, answering Jade's question. 'You don't run or they chase you, you don't look away, and you scare them off by being big and loud.'

'So literally like trying to get home from the club, got it,' Jade said. 'All right, can we get moving? There's a drunk woman out there in the snow and she's only getting further away while we stand here chatting.'

I clenched my hands at my sides, trying to keep myself calm. Yes, there were possibly wolves outside but what were the odds of us seeing one? I told myself harshly that I lived in London – a city with a very high dog population. I saw dogs all day every day – on the Tube, in coffee shops and even the gym once – and kept myself calm even when trapped in a lift with one, or when one shot out from under a Starbucks table, barking like a hellhound.

A dog is not a wolf, a tiny part of my mind reminded

me. *Just like how you're only good for dealing with miscreant MPs, not murderers.*

I silenced that part of myself. I could do this. I was not going to stay behind and be left out of the loop. I was not going to abandon Aloisia. At this point I wasn't sure if she would tell me about anything I didn't directly witness either. I had to stay informed. It was the only power I had in this situation.

I would be fine. Security knew how to handle the wolves if they showed up. The staff lodge couldn't be far and soon we'd find Nils and his gun and we'd be even safer.

We left the security room and Max locked it up with his keys. No one else was going to stumble upon Jan's body while we were gone. That was something, at least. Paula was still bustling around in between treatment rooms and I hoped she hadn't overheard us while the door was open and we were talking to the others. If she had, she gave no sign.

Livvy and Emmitt seemed relieved to be away from the body – as were we all – and even more so to be part of the 'staying indoors' contingent. Lucky bastards. Renard and Max walked on either side of them as they left for the foyer and I hoped they'd be able to keep them in check.

Myself, Jade, Lionel and Aloisia stopped at the equipment room to get coats and boots and then Aloisia decided we'd be best off leaving by the side door as it was closest to the lodge. She pulled a hat on one handed while holding the outer-equipment room door open for the rest of us.

'We'll focus on finding Nils first – he can help keep us safe while we look for Carri,' Aloisia said, once again deciding not to mention the gun in so many words. I couldn't deny that her logic was sound, but I was starting to wonder if she wasn't more concerned with having as much backup for herself as possible, instead of being worried about the safety of a missing guest.

Outside I sucked in a breath as the bracing cold rushed at me. No matter how chilly it was getting inside, it was still leagues better than braving the unforgiving icy air. I saw Jade huff out a few puffs of fog, adjusting to the cold. It didn't seem to bother Lionel at all. I supposed he was used to it. That or he was putting on a front for our benefit.

We crossed the start of the ski route I'd taken only the day before and went through the gate I'd noticed then. The path beyond was clear of snow like those out the front of the retreat had been yesterday. No new flurries had fallen. My heart sank a little – if Carri had stuck to the paths we'd have trouble locating her. The same went for Nils. I could only hope that one or both of them had taken a shortcut across one of the flowerbeds or verges that still had snow on them.

The staff lodge was down a path that was really more of a graduated staircase, each 'step' being about two metres long and only a few centimetres high, and all of them paved in a sort of cement mixed with gravel to provide grip. Our hard-soled boots rumbled over the rough surface and I found it hard to pick up on any other sounds besides that. I kept my head up and looked from side to side, worried I'd catch a glimpse of grey fur through the surrounding trees. My pulse was thundering in my ears and I couldn't stop my eyes roving the area in fear that I might see a pack of wolves rushing at us, teeth bared.

When the lodge came into view I could feel everyone's relief alongside my own. It wasn't as impressive as the main building but had the same sort of square, modern style. Most of it was screened off from the guest's view by a line of evergreen trees that had to have been planted for that specific purpose. We passed them and I got a good view of the front door – glass and metal, with a key card lock. Which I realised wasn't working as soon as Lionel pulled it open. Fantastic. Anyone could be in there.

We trooped in, glad to at least have a door between us and any potential wildlife. A staircase with vinyl flooring branched off to the left and a corridor led towards the staff canteen and gym.

Silence reigned inside the lodge, not a single squeak of a shoe on the floor, nor the clunk of a door. The place felt unoccupied, but that didn't necessarily mean anything.

'Should we split up?' Jade asked. 'Two up, two down – search the place faster?'

The rest of us exchanged looks. We knew that the killer had a rifle. Splitting up was probably not a good move. Jade seemed to pick up that something was wrong but she didn't ask outright. She probably assumed, correctly, that we would lie to her.

'We should stick together,' Lionel said eventually. 'Downstairs first, then we go up.'

Still looking down the long corridor to the cafeteria with my back to Lionel, I nodded. It sounded as good a plan as any. I only hoped that Nils had decided to skive off for whatever reason and we'd find him napping in his room. We could really use that pistol, especially as we had to walk back up to the main building out in the open.

I turned to Lionel to ask where we should start and immediately froze, a strangled cry caught in my throat.

One by one the others glanced back and saw what I'd seen. Standing dead centre of the path we'd just walked down was a wolf, looking right at us through the glass door.

Chapter 14

I couldn't speak, couldn't blink. My eyes were fixed on the wolf and it felt as if it was staring right back at me specifically. Into my eyes. Watching and waiting for me to so much as twitch before it came at me, teeth bared and throat snarling. I had the inexplicable feeling that it knew I was the most terrified of everyone there. It knew and it was going to get me for it. As my eyes blurred I saw the German shepherd that had sunk its teeth into my arm. I already knew how much a bite from that thing would hurt. Only this time it wouldn't be just one bite.

'What do we do?' Jade asked, barely audible, like she was worried the wolf would understand her. Or maybe it was just my thundering pulse drowning her out.

'Nothing,' Lionel said, a lot calmer than I felt. 'It can't get in here.'

'The door isn't locked,' Jade pointed out, as I tried to swallow my own spit without moving a muscle. I was trembling.

'It's a pull door.' Lionel's voice was level and even, like he was convincing himself and not just us to remain calm. 'It can't open it . . . Aloisia? Can you pass me that plant?'

It was such a weird request that it partially shocked me out of the hypnotic state of horror the wolf had sent me into. Aloisia moved, stiltedly, to the side and dragged a planter over. It had a sort of mini palm tree in it – a crown of spiky leaves and thick trunk marked with horizontal lines. I watched and held my breath as Lionel pulled it from the pot and stuffed it through the door handles, barring them.

Relief coursed through me like a drug. I sagged a little and nearly stumbled over my own feet as my knees weakened.

The wolf still hadn't moved. It watched us curiously and sniffed at the air, then it was gone, loping across the path and circling around to the right. Was it looking for another way in, or on the trail of something, or someone else? I thought of Carri and shivered, hoping she was elsewhere and not being actively pursued by a predator – animal or otherwise.

'What happens when we have to go back out there?' Jade asked.

'We either make it or we don't,' Lionel said, still looking at the door. 'Hopefully by then we'll have Nils and his gun.'

'Gun?' Jade echoed. 'You have *guns* – why don't we have a gun?'

Aloisia shot Lionel a look that said *Why would you tell her that?* and then reluctantly addressed Jade. 'We have – had – two guns. A rifle and a sidearm. We think the person who killed Jan may have taken the rifle. Nils had the handgun when he came over here.'

Jade scoffed. 'You were just going to keep it to yourself that there's a murderer on the loose with a rifle? Fuck you.

I suppose you knew this too?' she said to me. 'Jesus, you look awful.'

'I'm fine. I just . . . don't like dogs. And I didn't want anyone to start panicking,' I said. 'Which they would if they knew they could get shot at any time.'

'Better to panic and know what we're up against than to get shot in blissful ignorance.' Jade folded her arms. 'Whatever, can we search this place and get this gun before someone comes to kill us?'

Her words were spiky but there was a tenseness to her voice. She was afraid, like we all were, and I couldn't exactly blame her for that. There were a lot of reasons to be scared at the moment and Jade knew all of them now. She was one of the few 'in the know' and while that conveyed a little power and control, it also brought with it anxiety and dread. The price of knowledge.

'Follow me, and keep quiet,' Lionel advised. 'We'll need the element of surprise if there's an armed person in here.'

We went slowly up the corridor, checking the side rooms. No one was there and nothing looked out of place in the little TV room or the recreation room with its abandoned game of pool and stack of board game boxes. It reminded me slightly of some of the foster placements I'd had. The only things missing were the ratty-haired dolls and balding teddy bears. Were it not for the tension in my spine I'd have felt right at home. The gym was as silent and empty as the rest of the ground floor, though as we turned to leave Aloisia knocked a forgotten water bottle over and we all jumped out of our skins as it hit the floor and rolled.

'Be. Careful,' Lionel said through gritted teeth and Aloisia flushed pink.

In the cafeteria Aloisia paused by the kitchen door. 'We should take anything useful back with us – we might not be able to risk coming back here with the wolves around.'

'It'll slow us down,' Lionel said flatly. 'And we might need any advantage if we get attacked out there. Can't risk being weighed down with bags of food.'

Was it just my imagination or was there a sort of quiet power struggle going on between those two? Since we'd left the main building, Lionel had taken control. He was giving the orders. Was that why Aloisia hadn't wanted Max to come along with us? Divide and conquer? She was after all just a manager and the old command structure wasn't exactly built for this situation. Was she worried about losing control?

To be fair, I could understand both sides of the current debate and not just because I'd just laid eyes on a catering-sized drum of Kenco. In the short term, Lionel was right and we couldn't overburden ourselves. But in the long term the food stored here could mean the difference between rioting guests and maintaining order until rescue came. I supposed if we became desperate we could risk another trip out to the lodge, but that meant two extra attempts at crossing the open area between. Tempting fate. I knew from professional experience that doing a stupid, risky thing more than once was like begging to be caught.

'If we find the gun, we can revisit this,' I said, while Aloisia and Lionel looked at each other, waiting for the other to back down. I didn't like being the referee but they'd left me no choice. 'Let's just take a look upstairs.'

We retraced our steps to the barred door, finding it still

secure. No one had left that way – they'd have had to remove the plant and wouldn't have been able to put it back once outside. Lionel was a clever man.

As soon as we reached the second floor it was clear something had happened there. There was a duffle bag in the hallway that appeared to have been ripped open. Clothes, cash and pre-packaged food littered the floor, some of it stepped on and crushed. Multiple doors were open and Lionel went around and cleared each one.

'Looks like someone's been ransacking the rooms – turned them over looking for . . . something,' he said, returning to us. 'Probably money.'

'Who though?' I asked. 'And why? It's not like anyone can get out of here, money or not.'

Lionel looked to Aloisia, but she just shrugged and looked away. I knelt down by the bag and started to go through it. I was looking for anything with a name – passport, credit card, even a nametape sewn school-uniform style into the duffle. But there was nothing. Whoever had been packing in such a hurry had apparently had their ID and stuff on their person.

'Only thing I can say is most of these clothes look like men's – but they could be unisex.' I sighed. 'And, if all this stuff is stolen, it could be anyone's.'

'Damn it.' Aloisia shook her head. 'Is it too much to ask for a straight answer?'

'Apparently,' I muttered, turning over a few bits of gold jewellery but finding no engravings. It was good stuff, though, and call me a snob but it wasn't the kind of thing I thought the hotel employees could afford. One item was a Dior ring that I knew for a fact cost around £300 – probably nothing Livvy would notice losing down the back of the sofa but easily a week's wages for someone working in hospitality. Though maybe The Sorgente paid really, really well, much better than any such job I'd ever had.

Aloisia cursed in German and leaned against the door behind me. It swung open with no warning and she stumbled, cursing again. All the doors were keyed locks instead of swipe cards. I guessed because they were cheaper and employee security wasn't as important as guest security. Even more reason why I'd never have a Dior ring if I lived here. Aloisia's keys presumably had a master key for the staff quarters. Clearly whoever had taken them from me had made good use of them.

'Might as well check every room – they might not have left the doors open but can't rule out they've been in,' Lionel said. 'Maybe we'll get lucky and find where most of this stuff came from – find the empty hangers and drawers, figure out who was packing in a hurry.'

It was the only plan we had. We went from room to room opening doors and checking inside. Most rooms had a drawer or two open, whether from someone rushing to get ready for their shift or someone looking for cash. But nothing too suspicious and no empty drawers or hooks where a duffle might have hung. If someone had packed only their clothing, they had enough still hanging that it wasn't obvious some was missing.

Lionel pushed at the last door in the row on the left, and it opened an inch before hitting something. He frowned, pushed the door again, but with the same result. It sounded like it was hitting a mattress or something – soft and dull.

'Maybe they dropped something while packing?' Jade said. 'Could be this is the room where they started off, made the most mess.'

'I don't think so,' Aloisia said. 'This is Lars's room – he's my deputy manager. He'd never steal. He does our background checks, for God's sake.'

Jade snorted. 'Because no one's ever been a hypocrite before.'

Aloisia shot Jade an annoyed look. 'I don't think there's any point searching in there, is what I mean. We should be getting back.'

'I thought finding this Nils guy was important?' Jade retorted. 'You're giving up?'

'No one's giving up,' Lionel said, and shouldered the door firmly. It shunted inwards, dislodging whatever was blocking it with a heavy thump. The door opened and as it did so a lake of blood spread across the linoleum floor. Jade gasped and I felt my heart lurch.

'Lars!?' Aloisia hesitated but then leaped over the blood to peer behind the door. 'Oh my God . . .'

Lionel followed her and I stepped over the blood pool to get into the room. Jade backed off, shaking her head. She wasn't in a hurry to see her second dead body of the day. I could understand her reluctance but I needed to see this for myself. After all, I'd already been attacked once – I wasn't about to let whoever did it get away.

The room was a more deluxe version of the others, owing I supposed to Lars's position on staff. It had a double bed rather than a single and the room had space for a desk, sofa and smart TV. It was clean and well kept, almost military – everything on the small dressing table arranged in lines. The kind of room I'd expect a no-nonsense manager to keep.

Lionel eased the door shut. Aloisia was in the few feet of space between the end of the bed and the wall behind the door. She was bent over the crumpled body of a man at the foot of the bed, whose shirt was soaked in blood. There was so much of it – on him, on the floor. But I asked anyway.

'Is he—' I broke off when Aloisia let her hand fall from his throat and nodded.

'He's . . . cold,' she said in a small voice. 'He must have . . . He's been here a while.'

Lionel knelt to check him over and stood up again, looking a little grey, but angry too. For all his efficient calm I wondered if he'd ever seen anything like this before. He was a security guard at an exclusive retreat, not an active duty police officer in a big city.

'He's been shot,' he said. 'Looks like it was with the rifle because of the . . . damage.'

By 'damage' I assumed he meant the spray of blood and bits up the wall, as if the man's back had exploded. I looked away from it and tried not to breathe in the coppery smell of all that blood slowly congealing on the floor.

I heard a choking sound coming from outside. 'Jade? Are you OK out there?'

'I'm fine . . . just don't like blood, that's all,' she said, her voice faint.

Aloisia hiccoughed a sob and touched the face of the dead man as if to convince herself that he was real. There was a roaring growing in my ears like that which had proceeded the avalanche. I could feel my knees going a bit shaky and I sat down hard on the carefully made bed, bile on my tongue.

'You think Nils shot him?' I asked, my own voice sounding far away.

'*This* is Nils,' Aloisia said, words coming out in a harsh rush. 'I don't know why he's in here but . . . this is Nils.'

'Does he have his gun?' I asked, drowning in unreality.

Lionel came over and wordlessly forced my head down between my knees. The rushing, roaring feeling started to fade away, for which I was grateful.

'At a guess, Nils caught someone packing in a hurry, being suspicious and they shot him with the stolen rifle,' came Lionel's voice, slightly muffled by my position. 'But the handgun isn't here, so . . . whoever shot him, they took it with them.'

'They have both guns now?' Jade's voice filtered through the door, louder than before. I supposed she'd recovered a little from the shock of the blood. 'Fantastic.'

I sat up slowly and took several deep breaths before looking to Aloisia, who was still crouched by Nils. I think maybe she was taking this one harder because he still looked like himself. Jan's face had been . . . unrecognisable, really. But Nils still looked like the person she must have known. It was strange, the things the brain was capable of in situations like this. The ways it rallied or fell apart weren't always one size fits all.

'Do you think it was Lars?' I asked, after giving her a moment's grace. 'This is his room and you said he was missing before the avalanche . . . maybe Nils interrupted him packing, trying to make a run for it on foot?'

'No, Lars isn't capable of this. He'd have no reason to.

Besides, it would be stupid to try and get off the mountain like that,' Aloisia said, finally standing up and sniffing, getting herself back under control. 'And Lars isn't stupid.'

'But he might have been desperate,' I said, looking at Nils's sightless eyes. 'Desperate enough to try.'

Chapter 15

We didn't want to hang around long after the discovery of Nils's body, but we had to search Lars's room. Aloisia still stubbornly insisted Lars couldn't be responsible for any of the violence we'd seen. But I was determined to find anything left lying around that might help us work out why he'd missed the pre-dinner briefing and gone AWOL. We'd found a dead man in his room; that warranted an explanation.

Aloisia reluctantly opened his wardrobe and started going through his pockets, while I checked the desk and Lionel dug around under the bed. Jade waited outside and I wondered as I searched what she was thinking about or how this latest shock had affected her. She seemed to keep her feelings close, something I supposed she'd learned to do while getting used to competing professionally. That was a lot of rejection and criticism to absorb from a young age.

'His dinner jacket isn't here,' Aloisia said, flicking through hangers. 'That's weird.'

'Why?' I asked, poking through a desk drawer, which contained only pens, paperclips and a few DVDs of American sitcoms from the nineties.

'He'd only wear that for the formal dinners, which means he must have got ready for the welcome dinner on the night of the avalanche. But . . . if he'd come back here he'd have taken it off, surely? If he was going to run off he'd want something more suited to the outdoors – right?'

I thought about this for a moment. 'It might have had blood on it if he was wearing it when he attacked Jan. So, maybe he did change but he took it with him so no one would find it and realise what he'd done?'

Aloisia looked crestfallen. She clearly wanted to believe in Lars's innocence. It had to be difficult, knowing both the victims and the suspect so closely.

'Nothing down here.' Lionel got to his feet and dusted himself off. 'Not that we really know what we're looking for. But it's just his suitcases and extra blankets.'

'Chloe?' Aloisia asked. 'Did you find anything?'

'I can't find anything that looks out of place,' I said, pushing the drawer closed – or I tried to. It stopped about an inch short of closing flush and I frowned. The drawer had been closed just fine when I found it. I jiggled the handle a bit and heard something drop.

'What the . . .' I pulled the drawer out and found a small notebook in a plastic document wallet, taped to the underside of the drawer. It had come loose and got stuck, then pulled mostly off. I retrieved it and took it out of the wallet, flipping through the pages.

'What is it?' Aloisia asked immediately. 'A diary?'

'I don't know,' I said thoughtfully, scanning the handwritten columns inside. 'It looks like accounts or something?'

'That doesn't help us,' Lionel sighed. 'Can we get out of here?'

'Seconded,' Jade said, through the door.

I ignored them and showed Aloisia the pages, which had been neatly divided into columns, each unheaded but full of initials, dates and amounts of money. Aloisia frowned as she read over them, then shook her head.

'I have no idea what this means. Could it be . . . betting? The dates could be games or matches these initials bet on and the amount they owe? Entertainment is at a premium for the staff after all . . . though that doesn't seem like something Lars would involve himself in. And not for so much.'

'Hmm . . . and there's no minuses. So, if he was running a book, no one ever won anything. Seems unlikely, unless he was blackmailing people, or . . .' I had a sudden brainwave. 'Maybe he was taking note of what was going into the vault and how much it was worth? Could he have been planning a robbery?'

Aloisia glanced at Lionel. 'I don't want to think so but . . . with the CCTV system sabotaged there'd be an opportunity. The avalanche happening might have forced him to move early. But, if he was planning to steal from the vault, he hasn't yet. I checked at midnight last night and it was secure. It won't open again until tonight.'

'In which case we need to be at the vault when that happens,' Lionel said. 'To catch him. The bastard isn't going to get away with this.'

'It might not be that,' Aloisia said. 'Even if he was trying to steal . . . Lars wouldn't kill people . . .'

'Aside from you, he's the only one with the code to open the vault,' Lionel pointed out. 'He helps himself to food and stuff all the time – he's not as clean as you think.'

Aloisia glared at him, her eyes hard. 'Stealing from the kitchen is a long way from murder.'

'I thought you said the vault's on a timer?' I said, interrupting their stand-off once again. 'How is he the only other person that can get in?'

Aloisia looked reluctant to answer, but she did nonetheless. 'It is timed – but you need the code to open it once the locking mechanism disengages at midnight. Two-step security – either myself or Lars checks the vault contents against an inventory every night,' she sighed. 'Lionel's right – only the two of us have access.'

'So he'd know exactly what was in there too,' I said. 'What if there's an emergency like, I don't know, someone accidentally gives you their insulin and you lock it up. Can you override the vault and get it open earlier?'

Aloisia thought for a moment. 'He wouldn't be able to right now. If that did happen we'd have to call in to the security firm that fitted it and they can remotely reset the timer if we give them a code phrase but, we don't have signal or any working phone lines, and the Wi-Fi is down so . . . there's no way to remotely access the vault. If he wants in, he has to wait until midnight.'

I relaxed a little. That was something at least. If it was Lars behind this and, from what Lionel was saying it seemed pretty likely, we could lay a trap for him by the vault. By midnight this could all be over. Then we'd just be stuck in a hotel without heating or working plumbing or much food until rescue came. But I'd take that over an active murderer any day.

I pocketed the book, which neither Aloisia nor Lionel seemed happy about but they didn't argue. Jade wasn't right outside the door as I'd thought – she was at the other end of the corridor by the stairs, pacing. We went downstairs, where the door remained secure. No sign of the wolf outside. Yet. I wondered if it was near the building because it could smell the body and all that blood inside, and whether that meant it could now smell it on all of us. I checked my shoes and found no blood, thankfully, but that didn't mean the scent of it wasn't clinging to me, calling out to the nearby animals.

When Lionel removed the tree from the door handles he didn't open the door right away, but turned to look at us. His expression was set and he looked even tenser than he had before. I suppose because we now knew that there were wolves in the near vicinity and we'd failed to secure a gun for ourselves.

'Everybody ready?' he said.

We all nodded, but I don't think any of us were, actually. Had I not known about the body upstairs I might have insisted on staying in the lodge until rescue came, but I didn't want to be alone in there with a corpse, waiting for a killer to come back for his bag.

'Remember: don't run. Look big. Maintain eye contact. I'll bring up the rear, keep an eye behind us. Make sure you're checking to the sides as well and call out the second you see something move,' Lionel said.

Then he opened the door, with the air of someone sliding open the side of a helicopter and bidding us to jump. Jade went first when it became clear I wasn't going to move and Aloisia was still frozen in fear. She followed reluctantly and Lionel had to push me along to get me moving after her.

I heard the door shut behind me and kept walking, eyes flicking from side to side so fast that I started to make myself dizzy. I stumbled over the first step and glanced down, then whipped my head back up. *Eyes on the trees*, I told myself. *Keep watching*.

Halfway up the staggered walkway, I started to panic. We were now too far from the staff lodge to bolt back in and yet still not close enough to make it to the hotel at a sprint. I knew we weren't meant to run either way, but we were too exposed out there between the two buildings and I started to spiral.

I nearly screamed when Jade stopped moving entirely in front of me, nearly causing a pile-up, and yelled, 'Over there!'

I turned. As I did so she started to run and I felt a rush of panic.

It was Carri. She was wandering in the snow just off the path, by the trees, bent over and doing something on the ground, pressing snow together. A snowman, I realised through a haze of residual fear and adrenaline. She was rolling a ball to make a snowman.

My laugh came out hysterically and I clutched at my chest, where my heart still felt like it was about to erupt through my ribs. We were scuttling back to the hotel afraid for our lives from an imminent wolf attack . . . and Carri was building a snowman. In a minidress, knee-high boots and no coat. Just that crochet cardigan. Even from this distance I could see how raw her hands were from rolling the snow into balls. The snowman's body was already standing by the trees I noticed. She must have started work on it right after we passed by.

Jade reached her, a figure all in black to Carri's white ensemble. Without preamble she grabbed her around the shoulders like a bouncer and steered her forcefully back towards the path, at speed.

'But I'm almost done!' Carri whined, kicking her legs in the snow and sending white puffs of powder into the air. 'Lemme go!'

'Get her other arm,' Jade said, as she got close to Aloisia. Between them they got her under control and started marching her up the path. I looked around and followed, glancing back at Lionel, who was sidestepping, watching our backs.

We got through the gate by the ski route and closed it behind us. We were nearly there, nearly free. Aloisia let go of Carri in order to open the outer door to the equipment room and I sucked in a breath of freezing air in relief.

Relief that turned out to be premature, as Aloisia hauled on the door and it didn't budge. She yanked again and looked back at us with huge, frightened eyes. 'It won't open.'

'It's probably iced up,' Lionel said, without turning round. 'Chloe, give her a hand.'

'It's not ice, it's . . . stuck,' Aloisia protested, jiggling the door, which banged against the frame as it opened an inch but no further. She jammed her hand into the gap as I reached her. 'There's something through the handle . . .'

Just like Lionel had done with the lodge doors, I realised with a jolt of irony. We were barricaded out. Someone didn't want us getting back into the main building, it seemed. They'd effectively condemned us to death – by freezing or by wolf.

'Hurry up,' Lionel murmured, as if barely opening his mouth.

I turned to snap at him that maybe he should help, and saw what had him so stressed. There was a wolf – the same one? I had no idea – on the path we'd just climbed.

And it was padding towards us. Not running exactly but not wandering aimlessly. It was coming after us.

'Shit.' I shoved Aloisia out of the way and got my hand into the gap. It felt like a ski had been stuck through the door handle and angled to hit the wall on either side. I tried to force it down at one end or up at the other, but the gap was too small for me to get a proper grip. I screamed through my teeth in frustration and fear.

'We're gonna fucking die,' Jade said, disbelief seeping into her voice. 'Oh my God, we're gonna die here.'

'Everyone look big, start yelling,' Lionel said, still staring down the wolf. 'We can maybe scare it off.'

'Lemme go . . .' Carri mumbled. 'I wanna pet him.'

I pressed my mouth to the gap. 'Help! Help us!!' I shrieked, hardly recognising my own voice it was so strangled by panic.

Aloisia turned and started waving her arms at the wolf, yelling 'Help!' as loud as she could as well. All I could think of was teeth sinking into my skin, clamping down on bone and tearing off a chunk of steaming flesh. I was going to die, horribly. We were all going to die. Could we run around to the spa terrace? Break a window? Would there be time to get away – for some of us at least?

'Help!' I screamed through the narrow slit of space. My voice broke into a sob, tears freezing on my cheeks as soon as they escaped my eyes. 'Help us!'

Someone pushed the door abruptly closed and I yelped, pulling back just in time to not lose the tip of my nose. There was a scratching, clunking noise and then the door was opening fully and Paula was standing there, holding a ski and looking utterly bemused.

'What the hell is going on? Where did you— Hey!'

she snapped, as we all shoved our way through the door, thrusting her backwards. Lionel was the last one through and he pulled it shut and locked it with his keys. I collapsed onto a bench, my legs like jelly, and Aloisia followed suit.

Carri staggered away into the spa itself and I heard her being loudly sick, while Jade leaned in the doorway, panting as if she'd just run a hundred-metre race.

'What's going on?' Paula asked, clearly peeved.

'There was . . . a wolf . . .' Jade managed. 'Get her . . . a blanket . . . hypothermia.'

Paula's face went grey and she continued to ignore Carri in favour of bleating. 'A wolf? Why the hell were you outside with a wolf?'

'Did you see who barred this door?' Lionel asked, sharply.

'No. I've been busy with my patients.' Paula put her hands on her hips and glared at him. 'Are you going to tell me what the hell is going on?'

'We went to the staff lodge to check for anyone not accounted for,' I said, because I didn't have the energy to explain it all to her and although it was probably inevitable that the other guests would have to be told that there was a killer on-site, it would be best to do it all at once. 'You sure you didn't see anyone come in here? Did anyone visit the spa at all?'

Paula looked unimpressed by my explanation but appeared to consider before replying, 'A few people came by to check on their friends . . . someone brought me some of that herbal tea? Apparently they got a fire going in the foyer and made some. Wasn't half bad.'

'Who came here?' Lionel asked sharply. 'Describe

them. We told Renard and Max to keep everyone in the foyer.'

'I don't know. I was quite busy tending to my patients, alone,' Paula snapped. 'Maybe four people visited? Guests and staff. It was a woman who brought the tea. Blonde. Very blonde.' Paula shrugged. 'All wrapped up in a coat like yours, but I assume she works here.'

I fought not to roll my eyes as the panic receded and frustration took its place, my brain returning to normal as the adrenaline wore off. A blonde woman could be anyone, especially if they'd been wearing a coat and were not visibly in uniform. Would a guest be making tea and taking it round though? I doubted it, but Renard or Max might have ordered it to be brought down here.

'We should ask around after her,' I said. 'And find out who else was here. And we should update everyone . . . I don't think we can keep this to ourselves anymore.'

'Keep what?' Paula said, and finally turned to grab a large bath towel with which to swaddle Carri's shivering form as she staggered back towards us, her bleached hair looking ready to snap off in the cold.

'Let's go to the foyer and tell everyone together,' Aloisia said, defeated. 'This is going to be painful.'

Chapter 16

As soon as we got within earshot of the foyer, it became obvious that a situation had been developing in our absence. The guests stuck inside were a churning mass of annoyance and outrage. Raised voices echoed around the high-ceilinged space and it was clear no one was happy with being kept in one room.

It appeared that everyone was now collected together, including the remaining staff. Of the hundred or so people who had been in the dining room that night, plus whoever had been working in the kitchen, there were maybe forty people left. Most of those were guests, who outnumbered the staff at least three to one. Maybe more. It was hard to tell as everyone was wearing blankets or coats over layers of clothes. Coming in from outside it felt warmer within the retreat, but it was still freezing. The red noses and clouds of breath around me told me so.

I spotted Max the security guard posted by the staircase – effectively barring the way back up to the guest rooms. Renard was standing on the marble desk with Livvy on one side and Emmitt on the other, preventing anyone from circling the desk to get at the staff doors.

Silvie was behind the desk and looked close to tears. I wondered if she knew about Jan now, despite Aloisia's orders.

The fireplace, a sort of modern chrome bowl on a stalk with a similarly shaped fume hood and chimney, had been relit. Though we'd doubtless run out of fuel for it at some point, it was at least warming the centre of the room – as was the press of bodies – though it did little to take the chill off the wider foyer. A catering-sized saucepan was wedged over the logs and a table had been dragged up next to it, covered in cups and boxes of teabags. I spotted a carving fork by a pile of bread and realised someone had been making toast. My stomach grumbled – reminding me that I hadn't eaten since last night and apparently I was past the point where horror would suppress my appetite.

'Calm down! Please, calm down!' Renard called as we pushed through the throng and the volume of their complaints grew.

'I saw a wolf!' Patrick shouted over the din. 'A wolf, through the window – walking around the grounds. Are we even safe in here?'

Beside me, Aloisia heaved a sigh and then headed for the stairs to the second-floor landing. Max let her pass and I watched as people registered her reappearance and turned to watch her as she climbed the stairs. At the top, she leaned on the banister and looked down at us, waiting for silence to fall. I respected the move – she was taking back control from the mob.

Slowly everyone fell silent, except Patrick, who was still hissing insults at Livvy and Silvie as his wife pawed at his arm ineffectually, trying to get him to calm down. Livvy looked ready to slap him or cry, perhaps both. But eventually the pressure of expectant silence quietened him as well.

'I'm afraid I have disturbing news,' Aloisia began and I felt tension swirl around the room. She was good – I hadn't given her enough credit. Clearly we both knew our way around a crowd.

'Last night, in the aftermath of the terrible catastrophe that befell all of us here . . . one of my staff members was murdered.'

The whispers rolled through the crowd like hissing waves and I watched people look at one another in shock, in fear and, yes, in suspicion. Silvie started to cry harder, confirming my suspicions that Renard had already told her about Jan's death. After a beat of silence, Aloisia continued.

'Today, while looking for another member of my security team, we discovered he had also been killed, apparently around the same time. We now believe the killer to still be on the premises . . . and that they are armed with at least one firearm.'

Hearing a quiet sob I turned and spotted Silvie covering her mouth, her red eyes fixed on Aloisia. Another death would not calm her down. I wished she'd at least try to hide how badly she was taking the news. We needed everyone to keep it together.

Patrick's nasal voice broke the spell Aloisia had woven over the crowd. 'What the hell are you doing about it then? Keeping us here when this murderer could open fire and kill us all?'

Panic blossomed and the crowd shifted as people looked towards the exits, the only viable ones of which were the spa hallway and the staircase that Max was blocking. People shuffled towards them slightly, and I could sense that they were gaining momentum – soon we'd have a stampede on our hands.

'At the moment, we are our own best weapons against this person,' Aloisia said, though I heard the silent 'or persons' that she'd left off the end of her speech. After all, if it was Lars, he'd been very active in the time since the avalanche, killing two men in separate buildings with wolves in between them. Maybe he'd had help. Despite Aloisia protesting his innocence I was fairly certain he had at least something to do with what had happened to Nils and Jan.

'That is why I want all of you to stay together and keep watch over one another,' Aloisia continued. 'The two deaths we've been investigating happened when we were all scattered around the retreat and, hopefully, by staying together we will have strength in numbers.'

The rumbling around me suggested that some of the crowd believed her and some didn't. It was a reasonable suggestion on her part but fear and self-interest are powerful motivators. I've never been one to believe in the selflessness of mankind, even before falling into my line of work. From my experience, at the first sign of rising water it was every rat for themselves. And I was no exception.

'Food will be distributed shortly, and I will assemble small parties to go and fetch bedding and essentials from the rooms up here – but in the meantime I will ask that all of you make yourselves at home in the foyer, and hopefully we can avoid further incidents until rescue arrives.'

'Which will be when, exactly?' Patrick heckled.

He had a point. We still had no idea when help would arrive, or if anyone even knew we were stuck up here.

Aloisia seemed sure that the staff for the security building or the aerial tram's lower station or at the dairy would raise the alarm, but what if they didn't? What if they couldn't even get to work because of snow elsewhere? Or what if, as on the day we arrived, the person at the lower station was someone who lived and worked up here, like Silvie?

'. . . Soon,' Aloisia said, losing a little of her assertive calm. 'It will be very soon. As I said, all we can do is wait. Wait and . . . take care of one another.'

Patrick scoffed but, looking around me, I got the impression that most of the other guests had taken Aloisia's words to heart. Or at least for the moment were clinging to them as a lifeline in all the madness. Looking to the side I spotted Paula leaning against the wall in the corridor frowning as if trying to work something out. I made my way over to her through the crowd.

'How's Carri?'

'Who?' she looked genuinely confused.

'The girl we brought in with us – skinny, young . . . basically an icicle?'

'Oh . . . She should be OK. I don't think that woman was out there all that long. I wrapped her up in some more towels and gave her some of the tea. She shouldn't be at risk for any complications.'

'That woman' – why was my one witness to who had locked us out so self-involved as to be basically face-blind? Bloody surgeons and their god complexes.

'Right . . . she is wasted though,' I pointed out. 'Isn't that something that makes the cold hit you harder? Messes with your circulation, or . . .' I trailed off as Paula suddenly focused on me, and I remembered I'd had her pegged as an alcoholic. Shit.

'She's drunk? How did she manage that, here?' she asked.

'I don't know,' I admitted, though honestly I wouldn't have told her if I knew. We needed our one and only medical professional to be somewhat fit for work. 'She actually seemed a bit tipsy when I met her last night, before dinner. But she's got worse since.'

'She probably has a stash then – that or someone else here does and she bought it from them or stole it.' Paula looked thoughtful. 'Anyway . . . I'll go check on her. Can't be too careful when mixing hypothermia with a vasoconstrictor.'

I watched her go. She was obviously off to pump Carri for information about her alcohol supply, but to get any straight answers she'd first have to get her sober and warmed up, so that was something. I made my way towards the front desk and found Renard now behind it, comforting Silvie. Emmitt had left his post and I spotted him by the fire, making toast. Livvy had collapsed into the chair behind the desk, rubbing at the pouches of loose skin under her eyes as if to erase her exhaustion.

'Make sure you all get some food before it's gone,' I advised. 'Have either of you seen Lars since yesterday, by the way?' I asked Silvie and Renard.

Silvie's eyes welled up with fresh tears and she shook her head, clinging tighter to Renard. He shrugged.

'He didn't show up to the pre-dinner briefing. He could have been at dinner – there were so many people and we were all so busy . . . I haven't seen him since, anyway, do you think he's . . . still in there?' He jerked a head towards the dining room.

'I don't know. He wasn't in the staff lodge, I can tell

you that much. But we did find Nils – the security guard – in his room. Shot dead.'

I heard Livvy, clearly earwigging, draw in a ragged gasp, but ignored her.

'We still don't really know why,' I said, keeping my voice low. 'If it was Lars that did it, we're not sure what he's trying to accomplish. But it looked like he was maybe trying to pack up and leave when he got interrupted. He just left stuff behind.'

Renard looked troubled. 'Do you think he was the one who took the keys? He had his own set.'

'Maybe he lost them?' I shrugged. 'Or left them somewhere he couldn't get to them after the avalanche, with all the confusion. Lionel thinks he might be planning to make an attempt on the vault tonight, so the plan is to lie in wait and trap him before he can do any more damage. We'll need your help.'

'Sure, I don't want to have to worry about him on top of everything else,' Renard said.

'You mean to say someone is trying to rob us?' Livvy interjected, slightly louder than I was comfortable with, given the crowd still shuffling around into ever reconfiguring knots of gossip.

'Shhh,' I hissed. 'And . . . maybe. I mean, the vault is full right now and that's a lot of expensive jewellery he could smuggle out of here easily. Must be pretty tempting, especially if he'd already been planning it. Plus he's killed now, so he'll be desperate, and it takes cash to disappear.'

Aloisia parted the crowd and came towards us, giving Silvie a sharp look as she came to a halt at my elbow. Apparently I wasn't the only one who wanted her to keep herself together.

‘I want to search the whole building – top to bottom. There’s a chance we can find Lars and get to the heart of what’s been going on. I think finding him sooner rather than later would be best for everyone. And, Silvie, for God’s sake, calm down. I need help, not hysterics.’

Silvie sniffed wetly. ‘Sorry . . . I’ll try.’

‘Thank you – I know it’s hard but we all need to work together.’ I sighed. ‘It feels like this is going to be a long day.’

Chapter 17

I wolfed down a sandwich of one piece of bread wrapped around some smoked ham and Emmental cheese, washing it down with a cup of slightly smoky green tea. Not the best or worst meal of my life, to be fair. While I did so I contemplated asking Aloisia if there was any chance of getting my coffee out of the vault once we'd caught Lars. It didn't seem like a big ask to be honest – stop a crazed killer, get a hit of caffeine. I wouldn't even ask for a vape.

Scratch that, I was absolutely gasping for a cigarette as well. If she let me in there I was leaving with my hands full of lung-rotting goodness and as many coffee beans as I could carry. As God was my witness, I would never go smokeless or caffeine free again. Or however that quote goes.

I was starting to worry that I was cracking up a bit. My brain was all over the place and by the time Aloisia began to assemble search parties to try and find Lars, I felt cold and jittery with nerves. How much more could I go through before I snapped? Before this all found a home in me and I was different, forever? How much of this could I really recover from? I didn't want to think about it. Getting out alive was my priority, getting out sane a close second.

To maintain order in the foyer, Aloisia decided to leave Renard and Lionel in charge. Max would come with the two of us to search for Lars. Now that everyone knew what was going on there was no real need to keep Emmitt, Livvy and Jade occupied and none of them volunteered to join the search. I think, like me, they had all seen quite enough horror for one lifetime.

But Aloisia needed all the help she could get and, probably for the first time in my life, I actually cared about the person I was trying to help. She wasn't some disgraced CEO or pop-princess caught driving with a suspended licence. She was just a normal person, trying to do her best in an insane situation. I respected that and I felt as if she respected me.

I convened with Aloisia and Max by the stairs. Both of them looked tired but determined to power through, just like me. Max knocked back the last of his tea and set the cup on the end of the banister.

'Shall we go?' he asked, his dry French accent sounding bored even in the midst of this chaotic mess.

'Yes, I think everything's stable down here, for now,' Aloisia said. 'Lionel can keep things that way.'

'You really think Lars might be up here?' I asked as we began to climb the stairs, ignoring the curious looks and downright resentful stares of the assembled guests. They might have simmered down for now but it wouldn't take much for them to kick off again. Once the fire went out I expected chaos close behind. I remembered my primal joy at seeing the sun rise – we were all cavemen now.

'I don't know. He's not on the ground floor and he wasn't at the staff lodge, so . . . there's only so many places he could be,' Aloisia said. 'Though if he has both guns he can move around outside a lot more freely than we can. That's *if* – I still can't imagine him doing anything like this.'

'Are there many places he – or anyone else – could hide out there, comfortably? Considering there's no electrics?' I asked. We'd reached the landing and she gestured left towards the main bulk of the guest suites. The other way was my room and the dead end at the other side of the mezzanine where it met the lifts.

I was tense the moment we set foot on the second floor. As far as I knew, Lars could be behind any of those doors. Hiding away and waiting for a chance to kill again. After all, the suites had been empty since early that morning. Plenty of time for him to sneak by the limited capabilities of Max, Renard, Emmitt and Livvy to get up here. They could only notice so much and I had no idea where the fire exits and other ways in and out were located or if they were being guarded.

'I don't think there are many places, no,' Max said, lowering his voice as we approached the first room to check. 'Utility building's gone, aerial tram's down, there's an equipment shed and the garages, I suppose. He could use the cars to keep warm but there's nothing to eat out there.'

He nudged the door open and we did a quick sweep of the room beyond. Aside from clothes scattered over the sofa and the unmade bed there weren't any signs of habitation.

'One down,' Max muttered. 'Only about fifty to go.'

'Can we get to the garage to check it?' I asked as we let ourselves out.

'It's further than the staff lodge,' Aloisia said, giving me a look that said she'd rather jump from the mezzanine than try and make it over there. 'All the way on the other side of the property, near the exit road. I did hear something about them originally intending to put a tunnel in underground so deliveries could be made more discreetly, but I think those plans were shelved due to costs. It would've come out right into the main building.'

'Great.' I opened the next door and Max passed me, doing a professional-looking sweep that he'd probably picked up more from action films than his real life job. Another empty room. We moved on.

By our fourteenth empty room, the tension in my body was seeping away. It was seeming less and less likely that we'd randomly stumble across Lars just chilling in someone's bed or patching up a wound in their pristine bathroom. It was also very cold up there and I wished we were back by the fire, for all the good it would do. The sheepskin boots I'd put on yesterday were wet from the path outside and my toes were numb. Even with my coat still on I was cold to the bone. It seemed such a stupidly small thing to care about just then but as my fear subsided those little concerns were seeping in.

We completed the left-hand side of the second floor with no incidents and returned to the top of the stairs to go right. So far the only thing we'd discovered was how many people had ignored the 'don't use the toilet' rule.

Looking down into the foyer I saw several faces turned upwards, watching us. Their expressions weren't exactly friendly. In their shoes I had to admit that I too would have been annoyed to be separated from my possessions and the warmth of my own bed, the privacy of a bathroom. Perhaps they were thinking they'd be better off barricading themselves into their rooms and waiting this out alone. I couldn't disagree.

'That's my room,' I said, as we reached it.

'We still need to check,' Max pointed out.

'I know, I was just saying as, you know, a point of interest,' I sighed. And, sure enough, like all the others it was empty.

'I've barely spent any time in here,' I mused, out loud. 'If it weren't for that housekeeper letting herself in while I was out I wouldn't even be unpacked. But she started so I figured I'd finish.'

'Hmm?' That seemed to get Aloisia's attention. 'Sorry, what happened?'

'Oh, I just told uh . . . Nina? My welcome guide, that I didn't need my stuff unpacking but when I got back to my room after skiing, there was this other woman going through my case. Some kind of mix-up.' I felt bad, actually – I'd been so cold to her and anything might have happened to her now. I hadn't seen her, so perhaps she was dead. Just like Nina.

'What did she look like?' Aloisia asked.

I turned and saw her frowning at me. 'It's not a big deal. I'm not looking to get her fired or anything. I mean, God, we have bigger issues and she's probably . . .' I cut myself off, feeling a bit ill the more I considered that possibility. 'I . . . haven't seen her, since then,' I finished, not wanting to think about what that might mean.

'Please – just, humour me,' Aloisia sighed. 'This isn't

about getting anyone in trouble but it might be important if she was acting weird. Did she say anything to you when you caught her in here?'

'No, nothing. She just made an excuse and left. She was . . . youngish? Pretty. Had strawberry-blonde hair – you know that kind of not-quite-ginger thing? Awful bob.' I shrugged. 'She left quick enough.'

'Lilli,' Aloisia said, and shook her head with a disbelieving smirk. 'Oh, I should have guessed. She's a recent hire, splits her time between housekeeping and waitressing. At least she did until I fired her yesterday.'

'Why?' I asked, curious now as we moved on to the next room. 'I didn't report her.'

'I don't know when she was in your room but about . . . half an hour before the dinner she was caught going through a wardrobe in that young singer's room?'

'Carri?' I said and she nodded.

'It was her third warning and this time she didn't have any reason to be in there. So I fired her on the spot – we don't tolerate thieves, or liars. Sent her down on the aerial tram myself and said her things would be forwarded on to her home address.' She laughed bitterly. 'She was the last person to leave before the avalanche. Probably halfway home by the time it hit.'

The irony of that was not lost on me. 'What was she even trying to steal? I mean . . . all the valuables get taken to the vault, right?'

'All the major ones, yes,' Aloisia confirmed as Max went into the next room to begin his sweep. 'But almost everything our guests bring is expensive – the more ostentatious clothes and shoes are confiscated, but that leaves plenty of more discreet designer clothing to go through. Little bits of jewellery or make-up get missed because our focus is anything that might disrupt the guest's wellness experience. And guests are so preoccupied with what's been taken to the vault they probably don't notice the odd pair of leggings or cashmere scarf going missing. It's not worth much to them – but for someone like Lilli it's an extra few hundred in her pocket.'

'What a little weasel,' I muttered, only half-annoyed. Everyone had to get their little 'bonuses' after all. When I'd worked temporarily in a B&B I'd taken the half-used White Company products and married them together like a waitress with bottles of sauce. Then sold them as new. Perk of the job, just a little extra cash. Everyone did it. Yet Aloisia had been so passionate in her defence of Lars before, of all their staff. Hearing her being so quick to call Lilli out was jarring. Maybe it was because she was new, whereas Aloisia had known Lars for a while. Maybe it was management sticking together.

'A lucky one, though,' Aloisia huffed. 'Oh, this is Miss Harris's room.'

Carri's suite was almost exactly like mine and, if anything, appeared even less disturbed than all the other rooms. As if she hadn't so much as slept in the bed, which I supposed she hadn't. Her set of pristine off-white Michael Kors suitcases were arrayed in size order in front of the wardrobe and that was about the only sign that she'd ever been in.

'I wonder if she's got her booze stashed in here,' I said idly, as I checked the bathroom and found it completely unused.

'I have no idea how she's managed to get it in,' Max muttered irritably. 'We check everything that comes in to

The Sorgente – luggage, personal bags – and it's not as if she has a lot of pockets in that outfit.'

I had to agree. 'She could have got it from someone here, though, right? I mean, you already told me you had a thief on staff . . . and maybe also a murderer. It's not really a stretch of the imagination to think someone else might be passing out party favours at a heavy mark-up.'

'I'm starting to believe anything could be possible. I certainly see now that I had no idea who some of my colleagues were.' Aloisia sighed. Perhaps she was letting go of the immediate instinct to protect the reputation of her staff. After all, if Lilli could be a lying thief, why couldn't Lars be more than he seemed as well?

We finished checking the rooms with no more of an idea on Lars's whereabouts than when we had started. Though at least we now knew he wasn't hiding anywhere in the bedrooms. Max checked the only other way in or out – a fire escape down the back of the building – and determined that the door hadn't been opened, as it could only be done from inside. He checked the green zip-tie attached to it and nodded, satisfied. 'This would be broken if the door was used. No one's been out this way.'

That was something at least. I realised that the night I'd been attacked, if I'd known about the tag I could have checked to see if my attacker had left by the fire exit or backtracked into the foyer. Now the knowledge wouldn't really help me much; everyone had moved around in the intervening hours.

On our return to the foyer, it was clear people were chomping at the bit to reclaim their things. A crush of guests had formed at the bottom of the stairs with Patrick at the fore, facing Lionel down as he barred the way, despite Lionel being broader and taller than him.

'Can we get into our rooms now?' Patrick demanded archly. 'Or do you seriously want us to sleep down here without so much as a pillow between us?'

I could almost hear Aloisia counting to ten before she responded. 'The upper floor has been cleared and you'll now be allowed up to your rooms in groups of ten.'

Patrick scoffed. 'Treating us like children – really?'

'Well you are acting like one,' someone – who sounded a lot like Jade – heckled from the crowd.

I bit the inside of my cheek to keep from smirking as Patrick's head whipped round in a futile attempt to identify the person who'd spoken. He nearly knocked his wife over in the process.

'Lionel will allow you upstairs in stages,' Aloisia said, cutting across whatever Patrick was about to say next. 'You'll have five minutes to grab anything you might need – bedding, a change of clothes, medication and any food – and then you need to be back here. Apart from anything else we can at least try and keep this room warm for you and provide hot drinks.'

She was playing up the comfort angle and I approved. Although the foyer was too open to really keep properly warm, it would be easier to keep tabs on everyone. Especially if someone was stationed up on the mezzanine to keep watch.

There was a lot of grumping as Lionel separated out ten people to go upstairs like he was filling cars on a Disney ride. I noticed that Patrick was not in the first group. Apparently Lionel had decided not to reward his constant complaining with preferential treatment. Possibly the first time that had ever happened to Patrick.

I spotted Emmitt sitting beside a pot of bamboo, either sleeping upright or trying some sort of meditation he'd learned in rehab. Whatever helped in a situation like this, I guessed. We were all stressed and exhausted and probably traumatised by the events in the grand dining room – maybe I'd ask him for some tips.

'We'll settle everyone down for the night and then go to my office – it's back there,' Aloisia said, indicating the doors behind the marble desk with a tilt of her head. 'The vault's in a side room just off it, also accessed from the hallway. I think that's the way Lars would come in, considering there's an outer door there to make it easy for him.'

'Do we have a plan yet for what to do if and when he does show up?' I asked, noticing that for the first time she seemed sure that it was Lars we were waiting for.

'. . . Hopefully we can catch him unawares and separate him from the guns. I just . . . I want to know why. Why he would do this. We take the guns, and then make him explain himself.'

It didn't exactly sound easy, simple or like Aloisia had much confidence in what she was saying. Then again, I supposed that like the rest of us she'd never been in this kind of situation before. 'Can we shut him in the vault once he goes in there?' I asked.

'There's a release inside, overrides the timer. In case someone gets stuck in there,' she said drily. 'Unfortunately it wasn't designed to hold a prisoner.'

'Might be something you want to upgrade, once all this is over.' I offered her a brittle smile. 'All right . . .

not long left to go. Let's set a trap and just . . . hope it works.'

Neither of us said it but I saw in her eyes that she was thinking the same thing I was. That the consequences of failure would be sudden and, likely, violent.

Chapter 18

It took a long time for the guests to go up in tens and troop back down with duvets, pillows and other essential comforts. Most of them took longer than their allotted five minutes and arguments broke out between those waiting and those finally returning from upstairs. Many had layered on clothes to keep warm and brought candles, matches and other useful things down with them. Including food, which they were carefully guarding. The spirit of sharing was pretty much dead, if it had ever been alive in these people.

'Someone's taken my cashmere leggings,' Livvy pronounced from the top of the stairs, like she was Miss Marple announcing the death of a countess. 'And my merino tights.'

Unsurprisingly no one owned up to the theft and most of the assembled guests and few staff members seemed intent on ignoring her. Livvy puffed up and pursed her lips, but there wasn't much she could do. I doubted these would be the only thefts reported. No one could be trusted right now.

In the end, after another round of teas made on the

fire and the distribution of the last of the cheese, some fruit and yoghurt with cereal, most of the people in the foyer settled down. Despite being told that the 'toilets' they'd be using were catering pans stashed in one of the spa rooms, and they'd have to ask to be escorted there. Every pipe in The Sorgente was iced up now. We were on bottled water for the foreseeable. Then snow, I guessed.

The best sleeping spots – those near the fire and away from the windows, filled up quickly. I noticed Max and Lionel discreetly moving through the crowd, securing excess bedding to give to the kitchen staff and the few housekeepers and waiters still with us.

I wasn't really thinking about where I'd sleep. After all, I'd be busy until midnight and probably a while after. My bedding was still up in my room. If I did get it, I figured it would be stolen before I came to use it. Sleep was pretty much the furthest thing from my mind anyway when I reconvened with Aloisia and she took me through to her office.

The hallway behind the staff doors was similar to the one off the spa area and turned left at the end, presumably towards the kitchen. Only this one was painted an inoffensive oatmeal colour and bore framed photographs of The Sorgente, the assembled staff and some certificates of excellence. In one photo Aloisia and a colleague in a pristine suit accepted goodie baskets from a tanned and toned man I took to be the owner of the retreat, or his representative. Squinting I made out the name tag on the other gift recipient. *Lars Haldorson.*

He looked so . . . ordinary. The kind of man you'd see about thirty of in any given supermarket on a Sunday. Short grey hair, neat metal-framed glasses, large even teeth arranged in a polite smile. He wasn't young or old and he was medium build, medium height compared to Aloisia. The most ordinary, boring man you could imagine. He looked like he ate muesli and enjoyed 'brisk walks'. Yet this man had apparently murdered two people – violently and bloodily.

Aloisia had gone into her office but I was transfixed by the photograph. Lars beaming as he clutched a cellophane-wreathed hamper of biscuits, chocolate, amber liquor and champagne, the silver bow ridiculously Christmassy against his corporate attire. If that picture had been presented to me by my assistant, Brie, as one of a potential client, I'd have had a hard time categorising him. He didn't have the 'butter wouldn't melt' look that signalled a real deviant, or the crinkly-eyed charm of a serial adulterer. Given that we thought he was a thief I was expecting a tightness around the mouth – oddly like drawn purse strings – the tell of every embezzler I'd ever come across. There was something about him that unsettled me, but then again I was looking at him with the knowledge of what he'd done, so I was probably reading in to things.

'Are you . . . Oh,' Renard had followed us in, trailing Silvie like a lost puppy. Max and Lionel were dealing with someone just outside the door. It sounded like Patrick was once again demanding answers, with support from a handful of other vocal guests. 'That's Lars.'

'I see that,' I said. 'What was he like, to work with, I mean? Before. I can't really tell. He looks like . . . if sparkling water was a person.'

Silvie slipped past me and scurried into the office. Renard watched her go with a frown before answering me. 'He was . . . normal. Just a normal boss, you know? Boring. But we were all still so new, so I can't say I've talked to him more than a handful of times since he hired me.'

I hummed in thought. It was just like I'd picked up on from his photograph – Lars was nothing noteworthy. As Renard moved past me I turned towards him. 'Silvie seems really upset, is she OK? I mean, I know none of this is OK, but she seems more on edge than everyone else.'

He looked suddenly defeated, shoulders slumping. 'It's just hitting her very hard, all this. She's a really bubbly person normally . . . got on so well with everyone. Everyone's best friend since we got here . . . and now a lot of those people are dead.'

I nodded in understanding, though truly I had no idea how that must feel. I mean, I found it disturbing enough that the dining room was full of the bodies of strangers. I couldn't imagine what it would be like for those to be people I knew. That I'd spoken with, befriended, complained to about work. I briefly thought of Brie and shivered. We weren't close or anything, but I saw her every day. I worked so much that she was probably the person I saw most, spoke to daily. I knew her expressions and the sound of her voice and the songs she hummed in the break room. The thought of her lying cold and still, suddenly made alien to me by death, was deeply disturbing. Almost as disturbing as the realisation that I had no one else in my life other than my assistant. I hadn't gone on so much as a coffee date in three years.

I followed Renard into Aloisia's office, still trying to shake off the image of Brie's lifeless eyes. Max and Lionel came in behind me and shut the door. The office was decorated in the same sleek modern style as the guest suites. A door on the right seemed to be accessed via another button keypad. The only sign of Aloisia in the place was the desk's surface, where she'd left a lipsticked coffee cup. Judging by the neatness of the rest of the room, that used mug was a sign of just how much strain she'd been under since the night of the avalanche.

I noticed a spare tie hanging ready to slip on from a brass coat rack. The tie – a boring plain blue one, neither cheap nor expensive, seemed to match with what I now knew of Lars. Perhaps she shared this office with her deputy.

Aloisia was sitting behind the desk and on the wall above her was a large frame displaying blueprints, or at least some sort of architectural sketch of The Sorgente, signed and dated. I made myself comfy in one of the two brown leather chairs opposite the desk. Silvie was already seated in the other one. Renard, Max and Lionel squeezed onto a love seat.

'Not long now,' Aloisia said, looking distinctly anxious. 'What do you think is the best way to handle this? Obviously we need to surprise him – not give him any time to use the guns.'

She was directing the question at the two remaining security guards and it was Max who answered. 'I think we need to have at least two people in here – the door from this room into the vault area puts you behind anyone coming in from the side door, so that's a good position. We also need someone back at the reception desk to cut him off if he tries to make an escape through the foyer instead of going outside. Which just leaves the rear kitchen door and the outer door at the end of the corridor to cover once he's in – and he could get in either one . . . Whoever does that can wait in the custodian's cupboard – there's a grille to look through and I doubt Lars would go in there before reaching the vault.'

'What about hiding someone in the vault room, is there any chance of that?' I asked.

Aloisia was the one to answer me. 'There's nothing in there aside from the vault door and a spare cart for moving its contents. There's nothing to hide behind.'

Lionel shifted on the sofa. 'I'd feel most confident if one of us – meaning me or Max – was in here, waiting to surprise Lars, with the other one of us covering the outer door. Those seem the most likely positions to encounter him directly and . . . well, it's sort of our job to keep the rest of you safe, so . . .' He looked to Max, who nodded.

Aloisia seemed to think for a moment, not automatically agreeing. I'd thought her reluctance to have Max and Lionel together in a group was about controlling the other survivors. Perhaps that was part of it but she seemed uneasy at the prospect of them working together even now. Did she suspect them of something? Or was she worried that if they caught the man who'd killed two of their colleagues, they might kill him before she got her answers.

'That sounds . . . reasonable,' she said, eventually.

'What about the rest of us?' Renard asked. 'I can man the door to the foyer?'

'I'll wait in here as well,' Aloisia said firmly. 'Lars is my responsibility.'

'And me?' I asked, wondering if she wanted to stay here to monitor the security guards.

'You could go and get some sleep?' Renard offered in

the ensuing silence. 'There are four of us – that's more than enough, right?'

It was tempting and I almost accepted. But the thought of starting tomorrow off with another surprise death made me rethink. No matter what happened tonight, I wanted to be part of it. I wanted to know why Lars, the human communion wafer, had killed two people. At least if I was here and something happened it would be because of my failure and not my inaction.

'I'll wait up with you,' I told Renard. 'Two sets of eyes are better than one, aren't they?'

'I'm not sure we can let you do that. I mean . . . Lars might shoot someone tonight,' Aloisia said. 'That's a very real possibility.'

'So was getting attacked by wolves, but I still went out there,' I pointed out.

'Well, had I been thinking more clearly I wouldn't have allowed that either,' Aloisia sighed. 'But I suppose you're entitled to make your own decisions.'

'Plus, I'll take the slim chance of getting some coffee even with the possibility of being shot,' I said, as a stupid attempt at a joke.

Only Max let out a small snort of laughter; everyone else seemed too on edge. Lionel especially looked tense. Something was off with him and Aloisia, I could feel it.

'. . . What about me?' Silvie asked softly. Her eyes were red-raw from crying and her once sleek blonde hair was limp and greasy from running her fingers through it and anxiously redoing her bun. She reminded me of a pet-shop mouse, pink-eyed and cowering under a pile of wood shavings.

Aloisia and I exchanged sideways glances. I don't think

anyone wanted Silvie anywhere near the vault or our half-cocked attempt at a trap.

Renard cleared his throat and mustered a kindly expression. 'Why don't you switch with Chloe and stay with me by the foyer doors? You can get some rest and, that way, I'm right there if you need anything.'

I wondered if there was something going on with those two, romantically. They seemed very close, and Aloisia had specifically instructed him not to confide in Silvie. But Renard had said Silvie was 'everyone's best friend' so maybe it was only close on his side and he was taking this opportunity to play white knight to her damsel in distress.

'So I'll be in here with Aloisia and whichever one of you two ends up staying here while the other goes in the cupboard,' I said to Max and Lionel, because no way was I being edged out of the in-the-know crowd at this late stage. Neither of them looked happy about it but there wasn't much they could do aside from dragging me out of the room and tying me up somewhere.

After a lengthy debate, Max and Lionel resorted to the very professional method of rock, paper, scissors to decide who would wait in the office and who would hide in the cleaning cupboard waiting to cut off Lars's escape route. Max won the right to be in the office. Lionel, being a lot taller and broader than him, didn't seem too thrilled to be consigned to the cupboard. Still, as we took our positions and started to wait for midnight he went to his post to keep an eye on both the rear kitchen and the outer door.

Renard and Silvie retreated to the foyer. They had instructions to keep everyone quiet, calm and to extinguish any candles in case Lars was waiting for the lights to go out before he snuck in.

'Stay quiet,' Max advised us, as he waved Aloisia and myself behind the desk. 'And stay out of sight in case he looks in here.'

Max took up a position where he'd be hidden by the door once it opened and could listen for movement in the vault room. Both he and Lionel had helped themselves to knives from the kitchen and he held a cleaver in his hand, a wicked-looking filleting knife in his belt.

And so we waited.

I sat behind the desk with my knees tucked under my chin, trying to breathe quietly. My neck started to ache from keeping my head down out of sight but I didn't want to adjust myself in case it somehow gave us away.

Aloisia had brought her desk clock – gold and etched with mountains – under the desk with us so we could keep an eye on the time. I watched its tiny gold hands tick closer to midnight and chewed my lip raw.

Aside from Aloisia I was sharing the space behind the desk with the two gift hampers that had been given to her and Lars – one with gold ribbons and one with silver. They were piled in a corner to the left of her chair and had obviously been raided as the cellophane was screwed into a ball and the boxes of biscuits and chocolate were open or missing. It was such an ordinary workplace thing – the half-eaten packet of biscuits back in my desk drawer in London could attest to that. It made me feel suddenly and violently homesick for my day-to-day life.

Aloisia shifted a little and her foot hit a bottle of cognac with a gold bow on it, sitting beside the rest of the hamper contents. She winced and slowed her movements as she finished rearranging herself into a slightly more comfortable position on the hard-wearing carpet. I caught her eye and we shared a look of mutual anxiety. Midnight was close now. Only minutes left.

I strained my ears, listening for any sound from the room next door. I couldn't see Max from where I was crouching but I would probably hear if he opened the door. Or so I assumed. The paper-thin plan we'd managed to cobble together didn't feel that comforting now that it was about to come into action. I only hoped that, between him and Lionel, they could subdue Lars before he attacked us.

The hands ticked to midnight and seemed to pause there longer than a second. As if, like us, the clock was bracing itself for what might happen next.

Chapter 19

We waited, holding our breath as midnight passed and time ticked on.

Where is he? I mouthed at Aloisia, but she just shook her head, confused and tense as I was. It was gone midnight, the vault was open, and yet Lars was nowhere to be seen or heard. By ten past the hour I gained enough courage to poke my head up and look at Max, still stationed by the door.

His eyes met mine and I saw that he had no more idea of what was going on than I did. Which wasn't at all comforting. He held up a hand and spread his fingers. A clear sign for 'five more minutes'. I nodded and ducked down, mouthing his instruction to Aloisia.

'What if we're wrong?' Aloisia whispered.

Meaning, I supposed, what if she was right and it wasn't Lars we were waiting on at all? I had no idea. If not him, who?

Five more minutes passed in strained silence and then I carefully unfurled my body and eased myself up onto my feet. Aloisia did the same with my help and we picked our way over to Max in silence. He shrugged and indicated the door, then gestured at his ears. Nothing to hear in there apparently.

I pointed to his walkie-talkie, still clipped to his shoulder, but he shook his head and leaned forwards, showing me that it was switched off. Probably because the chattering and beeping of it might give him or Lionel away. So we had no way of knowing if Lars, or anyone else, was in the corridor or the vault room right now, waiting and listening.

I'd picked up the clock and now showed it to Max. Almost twenty minutes past midnight. He frowned and then leaned in to whisper. 'The vault resets half an hour after opening. Security measure in case no one's there when it deactivates.'

Any prospective burglars were almost out of time. So where the hell was Lars?

'I'm going to look,' Max whispered. 'Stay here.'

Aloisia grabbed his arm to try and stop him, but he shrugged her off and eased open the door, sliding through. I caught a glimpse of the vault room – white walls, grey carpet, a black metal door that had to be for the vault itself. Then the connecting door closed and it was just me and Aloisia looking helplessly at each other. It hadn't looked like Lars was in there but what if he'd taken a leaf out of Max's book and hidden behind the door?

'I need to make sure everyone else is OK,' Aloisia whispered, waving at me to stay put. She headed for the other door out of the office, back towards the foyer.

I waited alone and listened, alert for any sounds of a struggle. There was nothing, just the vague shushing sound of Max's boots on the nylon carpet. I was listening so hard for any tiny noise that I wasn't even breathing.

The gunshot was so sudden, so loud, that I couldn't keep myself from screaming. My heart jolted in shock and I clapped a hand over my mouth almost as soon as I broke my silence. Terror, both at the source of the sound and the fact that I'd given myself away, jabbed like a shard of glass under my ribs, hurting with every breath.

After a few seconds, I realised the shot had come from the foyer. I rushed towards it. I'd love to say this was bravery, some instinct towards saving my fellow man. In reality, I think I was just doing what I always did – chasing after catastrophe, hoping to find something out before anyone else did.

I ran along the hallway, glancing behind me at the sound of heavy footfalls, my heart in my throat. But it was Max and he was sprinting, gesturing impatiently at me to move aside. He must have used the other door out of the vault room, into the corridor.

'Where's Lionel?' I panted as I hugged the wall and he shot past me.

'I don't know – the cupboard was open, he's not there,' he called back, barging through the doors and into the foyer. I could hear the screaming and thunder of many people moving around, the crash of breaking glass and metal clattering to the hard floor as things were knocked over or thrown. It was like the avalanche all over again and I was seized with panic.

I threw myself through the door and cried out when someone grabbed my arm and tugged me down. It was Renard, cowering behind the reception desk with his other arm around Silvie. I dropped down beside him and peered at them both in the dark.

'What's happening?' I had to almost shout to be heard

over the din as guests ran every which way. I could hear them above, disregarding the order to stay downstairs and fleeing to their rooms, tripping on the stairs and barging into one another in the near total darkness. Even the moonlight coming through the windows was dimmed by cloud.

'I don't know – someone came through the doors, we just heard a shot and . . . How did he get past you?' Renard stuttered.

'I didn't see . . . Did you see Lionel come out?' I demanded. 'Where's Aloisia?'

But Renard's response was drowned in a shriek and a tumbling thump as someone fell down the stairs. I automatically stood up, turning towards the sound and Renard tried to hold me back. I avoided him and stepped into the darkened foyer.

My heart was beating harder than it did after no sleep and a triple espresso with a Red Bull chaser. There was a man with a gun in there and I knew it. The darkness was all I had. I hoped he wouldn't hit what he couldn't see. Though I supposed there was always the chance of an accident.

The foyer had mostly cleared out – the guests had stampeded upstairs and only a few people remained, cowering in the corners behind potted bamboo. I spotted the shape of the fallen person. With the foyer almost deserted, even though it was very dark, there was enough clear space to make the body on the floor obvious to me, the light-coloured wood practically white in the faint moon glow against the black of his clothes and the inky darkness of his blood.

Overhead I heard Max shouting for calm, trying to

get information from the hysterical people still rushing around in an attempt to put a door between them and a killer. I dropped to a crouch and peered at the face of the man on the floor. It was Lionel, no doubt about it. But he wasn't dead.

He gasped and gaped at me like a landed fish, and I caught one of his flailing hands in mine. The blood pooled around his legs and as I patted him over with my free hand I found his trousers already soaked. He'd been shot somewhere low down, the thigh or something. He was bleeding fast, the puddle visibly spreading across the floor. I looked around helplessly for something I could use as a tourniquet, half-remembered first-aid courses flying through my mind.

'Max!' My shriek carried around the expansive foyer, cutting across the muted sobs and whimpers of people sheltering there. 'Renard! Someone . . . Lionel's hit!'

His hand went slack in mine and I looked down to find his pale face tipped back. Eyes open and sightless. He was dead. Just like that, in seconds. I hadn't been able to help him, or even to comfort him. His killer was possibly still in the room with us and there was nothing I could do about that either. I felt useless, helpless.

Aloisia appeared opposite me, making me jump as she threw herself down and grabbed at his shirt. It took her a few moments to realise what I knew already and then she collapsed, silently weeping, her shoulders heaving as she sawed air in and out. Another life lost on her watch. Another person she knew killed outright.

I went to pat her shoulder, realising just in time that my hand was covered in Lionel's blood. I let it hover awkwardly for a moment, trembling in mid-air, then lowered it and rose unsteadily to my feet. One thought was rattling around my head – the vault.

We'd all left the vault.

I ran back towards the desk, stumbling over my own feet in the process, sliding on shards of something that had smashed on the floor. Renard asked me what was happening but I ignored him and flung myself through the door. My skin was sticky with cold sweat and I felt like I might throw up from the combined shock and exertion, but I made it back to Aloisia's office and the door to the vault room. I tore it open, heedless of my bloody hand and went inside.

The vault door was closed, just as tightly as it had been when I'd glanced in before. I walked over and tugged on it, but it wouldn't open. Had it reset itself undisturbed, or had someone been in and out in the time it had taken us to scatter to the foyer and for me to return?

Why had Lionel gone out there without telling anyone? Why would he leave the door unguarded? What had he been thinking?

Still reeling, I turned to the hallway door and saw that it was open. Slowly I crossed over to it and peered out. On the other side I found the outer door closed – though that wasn't proof no one had entered from outside. Lars could have been in and out and there was even a mat on the floor, so he wouldn't have left any wet footprints.

A clatter to my left made me jump and I realised the door through to the kitchen was open. I froze and heard someone moving around, the soft unsticking sounds of plastic-soled shoes on linoleum and harsh breathing. Had Lionel let someone in from outside, then been betrayed?

Was he heading for the foyer to attack someone specific, or to prevent interruptions?

What could I do now? If I moved the intruder would hear me, if he hadn't already. I was out of shape and breath, but if it was Lars, he was older, so it was anyone's guess who'd win that struggle. I reminded myself that he didn't need to do that either. He could easily shoot me in the back.

Then I heard footsteps moving rapidly up the corridor – the others were returning. I heard them talking in hushed voices but not the individual words. The movements in the kitchen ceased suddenly and I waited to hear a door or something. A sign that he'd left the way he'd come in. But there was nothing.

Suddenly a dark shape shot out of the kitchen and came straight for me. I threw my arms up and screamed as it collided with me – also screaming. We fell over, hitting the hard floor with our combined weight. The air was driven from my lungs.

I fought against the flailing figure tooth and nail. It attacked me back and I wasn't sure if the smears of blood I saw were fresh, or from Lionel's blood on my hand. My eyes were barely open, screwed up in fear.

'Chloe!'

There were other hands now, grabbing at me and the person on top of me, dragging us apart. I crawled into a corner and looked on as Paula was hauled to her feet. She was smeared with bloody handprints and white as paper aside from a flush high on her cheeks. Her hair was in disarray and, now that I wasn't drowning in terror and adrenaline, I could smell the alcohol on her.

My heart rate lowered to a speed just below sickening.

It was Paula – sneaking around looking for alcohol. Wherever Lars was, it wasn't here. He'd got away, and taken with him our one and only chance at ending this before it could get worse.

'Get off me!' Paula snarled, blindly trying to free herself from Max and Aloisia's grip. She finally tore herself away and staggered sideways, attempting to straighten her clothes.

'She's drunk,' said Max, disbelievingly and also slightly redundantly.

'I am not,' Paula snapped.

'Where's Carri? Is she OK?' I asked, managing to keep a tremor from my voice as I got to my feet.

'She's fine – completely fine,' Paula muttered, now smoothing her hair back into order.

'And, let me guess, she told you where she'd managed to get booze from?' I said, anger asserting itself over fear.

Paula rolled her eyes. 'I confiscated it, for her own good.'

I sighed. 'Where was she hiding it? Do you know how she got it in?'

Paula mimed locking her lips and throwing away the key, then giggled and stumbled sideways into Max. He steadied her, pale and exhausted-looking. I realised he'd just lost another colleague, maybe even a friend. Both he and Aloisia had. Carri and Paula's drinking was inconsequential in the grand scheme of things. My desire to know wasn't important right now.

'I'll take her back to the spa to sleep it off,' I said. 'We should . . . uh . . . we should move him, before the other guests come back. It might cause more of a panic if they realise he was killed.' Though there were still people in the foyer who might spill that secret, at least they wouldn't have to see the grisly evidence of the murder.

The reality of the situation felt heavy and thick in the air after the heady adrenaline of rushing here and there on a desperate mission. My legs felt like they were hauling concrete blocks instead of my feet as I took Paula by the elbow and guided her away from the kitchen. I paused at the desk to light a candle and herded her onwards towards the spa. I was very aware as we walked of the watchful eyes of the few guests who dared to look down from the mezzanine at Lionel's body.

As we drew closer to the spa I wondered if Lars had come this way, if he was lurking there. The fear made me slow my steps but in the end I carried on – it was more likely he'd taken the nearest exit. What could he possibly want in the spa? More importantly, had he ever been here, or had I already looked into the eyes of Lionel's killer? Max could have shot him and run back down the corridor, pretending to have never left. He was fast enough. Aloisia had been out there, all the guests and other staff. While we chased the shadow of Lars, had someone else been picking us off?

Paula seemed to have run out of steam, entering the sleepy stage of drunkenness. She was easy to lead now we were underway. I found an empty treatment room and got her into it. Judging by the smell that still hung in the air, this was where she'd done her drinking earlier in the day.

'Get changed into this, OK?' I said, shoving a clean white robe at her with my unbloodied hand.

She took it from me and started to undress, dropping her bloody clothes every which way, heedless of whether

I saw her naked. My arm was drying, tacky with blood. I looked around for something to clean it with and spotted some hand sanitiser. Fortunately for me it was alcohol free, otherwise the bottle might have already been emptied. I poured some out onto a spa towel and scrubbed my hand and arm clean.

Paula had finished changing into the robe and collapsed onto the massage couch. I gathered her stained clothes up with the towel and hunted for a bin I could take the bag from. I found one tucked beside the wooden cabinet of oils and spa knick-knacks. I scoffed when I saw that it was full of paper tampon wrappers and clear plastic tubes. I picked one up and sniffed it, confirming my suspicion. They were fake tampons for smuggling booze into festivals and onto cruises. Carri must have made herself a stash and it hadn't been found during the bag search. Underneath those was a hairbrush missing its end. I clocked the markings of a screw cap and sniffed it. It too was hollow and smelled of vodka – probably a fake brush. No wonder they were both plastered. I didn't want to imagine how many other stashes Carri had – more bottles of sun cream or shampoo that were actually vodka in disguise. There were an alarming number of products on the market for smuggling booze. I couldn't quite believe that, out of everyone, Carri had managed to bypass The Sorgente's bag searches so cleverly.

With Paula snoring softly I crammed the clothes and towel into the binbag and tied it up, then left the room to check on Carri. I found her in the second treatment room I checked. Like the rest of the patients she seemed to be fast asleep, chest rising and falling under the towels she was tucked in with.

I heard a low rattling and left the room to see the vault trolley being steered into the hallway. Max was pushing it and Lionel had been laid on top, his face covered by Max's jacket. Renard followed after him, looking just as drawn as I felt.

Without a word I stepped aside as they wheeled the trolley to the security room. Max unlocked it and Renard held the door and pushed the trolley inside. Then the door was closed and locked again. Out of sight but not out of mind.

'What do we do now?' Renard asked softly, as the three of us stood there like loitering mourners waiting for the buffet to be laid out.

'Aloisia's told all the guests to stay where they are until morning. She's cleaning up the blood so . . .' Max swallowed hard and then shrugged. 'I suppose we wait for first light. Try and get some rest.'

I noted that he didn't say 'sleep' because I doubted any of us would be able to get any of that for quite some time.

Chapter 20

We passed the hours until dawn in the foyer. Aloisia had been busy while we were in the spa and there were candles to light the space and a lit fireplace. The air smelled of disinfectant and there was a wet, gleaming patch on the wooden floor. The only sign that anything had taken place there. Even the broken glass and cups had been swept up. Despite that, only a handful of people were left in the room among the abandoned duvets and pillows. No one, it seemed, had returned from upstairs. I couldn't blame them. I was actually surprised the people left downstairs hadn't bolted but maybe they were too afraid to move.

Renard sat up beside Silvie while she sobbed quietly on a makeshift bed. Aloisia and Max were silent and still – he looked straight ahead, lost in his own thoughts, and she chewed her nails, looking at the wet oval on the floor. Aside from us the only other people were a pair of kitchen staff, still in their uniforms under some blankets and crammed into an alcove by a plant, Emmitt who was passed out so completely that I wondered if he'd found some booze too, and Roberta, once again left behind by her husband.

Looking at Aloisia and given how late it was, I thought we could all use a moment's rest. I certainly could. I'd seen three dead bodies since I woke up – one of them had died in my arms. I could feel something breaking apart inside me, part of my head or my heart that would never be the same again. It was excruciating and draining all at once. I just wanted to be still for a moment. To reorientate myself around what I could not change.

When I sat down in the shadows by the dining room door – not my first choice due to the bodies inside, but it at least offered a good view of all the exits and everyone else – Roberta picked herself up and crept over to sit with me. I didn't look at her but neither did I tell her to go away. Like a stray cat she settled at my side in silence, as if waiting to see what my response would be. She pulled her knees up, sensible shoes squeaking on the floor.

'Do you know what happened?' she whispered, after apparently satisfying herself that I wasn't about to tell her to get lost.

'No . . . Do you?' I asked, my voice coming out weirdly flat.

She shook her mousy head. 'I didn't see anything – too dark, too many people. I wondered if you knew . . . who shot him?'

I shook my head, increasingly sure that I knew nothing. Nothing at all.

'I tried going up . . . Patrick won't open the door to our room. I said it was me, but . . .' She trailed off.

I wished I'd found just one remaining shot of vodka in that bin. Something to dull the ache between my temples. After a full day of rushing around my head wound was making its presence known again. 'That's because he's a fucking arsehole,' I muttered.

Roberta let out a surprised huff, like a kid frightened but thrilled at the use of 'bad words'. Then she giggled. 'He is, isn't he?'

'Yep,' I said, still staring straight ahead.

She hummed in agreement. 'Can you keep a secret?'

I shut my eyes and rested my head against the wall. I was starting to feel distinctly unreal. Between the pain and the trauma, this all seemed like a nightmare. 'Sure. What's one more?'

Roberta took in a long, slow breath. 'I'm leaving him.'

Despite myself I cracked an eye open and looked sideways at her. She'd done the thing I'd least expected – made me like her. 'No shit?'

She nodded, an expression of secret glee transforming her face. The dowdy clothes and hunched posture, I realised, were hiding quite a pretty woman. Not beautiful – few people are truly beautiful, and I'm certainly not one of them – but she was pretty. Especially when she smiled. Prettier than Patrick deserved, to be honest. He wouldn't pull another one like her now his career was in the toilet.

'That's why I booked us a place here. He thinks we're waiting out the storm, having a break and fixing his image . . . Right now I have a team of hired movers taking all my things out of his house and driving them up north, to my parents' old place. Still in my name . . . It's got a lovely herb garden, space for hens and this perfect apple orchard which just bakes in summer.' She sucked in a breath and let out a long, shaky sigh. 'I want to see it again . . . I want to make it back.'

Roberta's smile wobbled and crumpled. She started

to sob quietly – like everything about her, her tears were minimised for the convenience of others – and I awkwardly put an arm around her and let her cry into my shoulder until she tired herself out and fell asleep. I had no reassurances left to offer her, and honestly I doubt she'd have believed them. But at least she wasn't alone. Neither of us were.

The sun rose slowly, a pale golden line crawling across the floor until it found the spot where Lionel had bled to death. It had reached the reception desk by the time Aloisia stirred and got to her feet, wincing after hours spent sitting on the hard floor. Her shoes were muffled by the duvets and throws that still littered the ground as she picked her way to the desk and leaned on it as if gathering strength from the impressive marble structure. Then she turned back and cleared her throat. A summons to the rest of us – her rapidly diminishing team, of which I was now an honorary member.

Max rose and so did Renard. Silvie was finally asleep. I slid my shoulder out from under Roberta's cheek and left her leaning against the wall. The four of us converged on the desk and Aloisia's face twitched as she tried to offer us a smile and then thought better of it, or else realised she couldn't quite make it happen. But her words were all business.

'I don't think we'll be able to get most of the guests out of their rooms. Not now. So might be a case of distributing food door-to-door and reassuring them by turn.'

'Fuck that,' Max said with surprising venom. 'I'm not going around waiting on a bunch of spoiled idiots after everything that's happened. They want to eat, they can come and get food.' He glanced my way. 'No offence.'

'None taken – trust me I am very aware of the kind of

idiots that pay to stay here – I'm one of them.' I turned to Aloisia. 'Why don't we use the time we're not being flocked by said idiots to take stock of what we've got supply-wise and plan from there?'

'What about Lars?' Renard lowered his voice, glancing at Silvie where she lay sleeping. 'He's killed three people and we have no idea what he might do next. What if he sets the building on fire with us in it or something even worse . . . We need to focus on finding him.'

'Finding him where?' Max demanded. 'The only place we haven't checked in here is the fucking roof. He might not even be here to find!'

'I . . . I don't know – he has to be somewhere!' Renard hissed. 'The garage maybe?'

'You offering to go outside where the wolves are and wander over there – in plain view of about a hundred different places he could shoot you from with that rifle?' Max crossed his arms, his expression thunderous. 'If he is here, he's killed three of my friends. Your colleagues. You think you can take him, be my guest. But we both know you don't have it in you.'

There was a sharp silence and Aloisia held up her arms in limp appeasement. 'Please can we not do this? I think Chloe is right. There's not much we can do about Lars – assuming it is him – at the moment, because we don't know what he wants. If not the vault, what? What could possibly be worth all this death?'

That was a good question. Though we still couldn't be sure he hadn't been in the vault. Maybe, best-case scenario, he'd grabbed whatever he wanted and run off. Maybe we were in the clear so long as we managed our food supplies and waited for rescue.

Then again if Lars had taken what he wanted, why not leave through the kitchen or the outer door? Why make a break for the foyer? But if so Max ought to have seen him before the gunshot and we hadn't heard him yell. He'd been the only one in the vault room. Max had only left once I was already on my way to the foyer. Either he hadn't seen Lars . . . or he was working with him.

I thought of raising this to Aloisia but couldn't bring myself to with Max right there. Something weird was going on with this sudden attitude and I wasn't really sure if I wanted to start questioning his actions right in front of him like that. It might have just been his way of coping with last night's incident, but he seemed riled up about something more than that. Better to keep everyone on side as much as possible. Aloisia, it seemed, already had some sort of unease about Lionel, but did she trust Max? More than me? It would be a gamble.

'How about Aloisia and I go take an inventory of the kitchen and you and Renard stay out here and work on a plan for Lars?' I said, framing it as a compromise. What I really wanted was to get Aloisia alone so I could talk to her frankly.

'I can help.'

I turned along with everyone else and saw that Roberta had apparently woken and caught the tail end of what I was saying. She produced a pen and notebook from a modest little cross-body bag and held them up sheepishly. The notebook had Winnie the Pooh on it, I noticed. I'd had her pegged more as a Piglet.

'I'd like to keep busy, if that's OK?' she said.

Aloisia nodded, apparently resigning herself to the fact that she was losing control of the situation and waved her over to the reception doors. I followed the pair of them and hung back a little in the hallway, then took Aloisia's shoulder and gently pulled her to a stop, putting my finger on my lips. She frowned at me, but halted and waited for me to speak.

'Why do you think Lars is only killing security guards?' I whispered. 'If it's not about the vault is it . . . personal?'

She cast a wary eye towards the doors back into the foyer – apparently I wasn't the only one worried about Max overhearing. Interesting.

'You were also attacked,' she pointed out.

'Yeah, but we don't know who did that. What if it was someone else entirely? We could be overlooking a pattern here. One that says Max is next on the hit list, or that he's involved. So . . . did Lars have anything going on, between him and security?'

She chewed her lip, then shrugged. 'I don't know, he got on well with everyone. All right, not "well" – he was too . . . earnest to be liked. I think the other staff found him a bit uptight. But professionally he was perfectly reasonable. If there was something else to him, I didn't know about it. Do you think he really wasn't after the vault? Then why come here last night?'

I sighed. It was my turn to reluctantly reveal my ignorance. 'I don't know, but why go through the foyer instead of out the other doors, which only had Max in the way? Either he specifically wanted to kill Lionel or . . .' I shrugged helplessly. 'Or it was something else and we just don't know it yet.'

Aloisia's eyes brightened with sudden inspiration. 'Do you think he wants the book?'

I automatically touched the shape of it in my pocket. 'Why?'

'Well, we don't even know what it means, so maybe it's important. Or he doesn't want to leave evidence lying around. Or it might have information about bank accounts he put stolen money into . . . I'm just trying to guess!' She hissed, on seeing my doubtful expression. 'We should burn it – then he has no reason to come after us.'

'But what if that makes him angrier? And why would he think Lionel had it?' I asked. 'The only people who even know we found it are me, you, Lionel and maybe Jade. Right? We were alone in that room and Jade was outside. Unless one of them told someone else and we just don't know . . . but who else? Max?'

That seemed to stump her. To be fair, it had also stumped me. I hated this, not having the full facts of a situation. It made me feel vulnerable and at a disadvantage. But there was also a slight thrill of the chase. It was like a challenge, a puzzle to work out. As grim as it sounded, given all the horrors around me, I was invested in this odd mystery now. I wanted an answer, because searching for it would at least keep me going. Right up until it drove me round the bend.

We'd delayed enough and quickly caught up to Roberta in the kitchen. She'd propped open the door to the storeroom and was going over shelves – giving each one a page in her notebook and carefully writing down the contents. Aside from the storeroom there was a walk-in fridge, which obviously was no longer working. I opened it and found it mostly empty – Renard hadn't exaggerated, they really had been low on supplies. We'd probably eaten the last of the dairy over the past two days.

The storeroom had plenty of food but not all of it was

stuff we could use – huge containers of dried spices and beans, rice and pasta. I supposed we could try and cook it on the fire if we had to, but it would take ages to make enough for all of us, three meals a day. We'd run out in a few days anyway if we did that. I hoped we'd be rescued by then.

'Maybe tonight we can get some stuff out of the vault? People must have tried to smuggle in junk food and treats,' I said, hopping up on a chest freezer at the far end of the storeroom to take a seat. 'We can check the inventory against the contents as well – see if anything's missing. We did run off and leave the vault exposed after . . . well, you know. He could have got in then.'

'Good idea.' Aloisia was turning jars and tins around so Roberta could more easily list them, but clearly thinking hard. 'It looks like someone was really searching in here. Chef usually keeps it very neat.'

'Paula was probably looking for cooking wine or something,' I said. 'Sorry, I probably should have told you before that she had a problem with alcohol.'

'Well, she's out of luck – we don't use any in the food.' Aloisia picked up a bottle of vinegar and set it down again aimlessly. Obviously she was still turning the Lars question over in her mind, as I was.

What could one of the guests have brought to the vault that was worth killing three people over? I couldn't imagine taking that kind of risk for a few handfuls of jewellery – even if it was really good stuff, a hundred thousand pounds or so wasn't worth what was going to become an international manhunt. Something else? A file or something saved on a piece of tech? That was more likely – information, secrets, were worth a lot more than diamonds to certain people. Myself included. But what secret and, more crucially, whose?

I fiddled with the latch by my thigh, turning the padlock on the freezer one way and then the other. *Click-clunk*, like a fidget toy. *Come on brain, think*.

Blackmail material? Corporate espionage? The location of fucking buried treasure? Livvy's recipe for the perfect apple crumble? What?

I tried to put myself in Lars's sensible managerial shoes. What would be worth the lives of three people to me if I was a man like that? Something either very valuable to someone else or very personal to me.

'Chloe?' Aloisia said, gesturing to the freezer. 'We need to inventory that.'

'Sorry . . . I'll help – I was just thinking.' I slid off the freezer as she came over with Roberta, ready to catalogue its contents. Aloisia tried to lift the lid, noticed the padlock and frowned.

'Why is this locked?'

'Uh . . . for the investor dinner?' I said, pointing at a piece of paper taped to the lid, now slightly crumpled from where I'd sat on it and slid off.

'That food hasn't been delivered yet . . .' Aloisia said quietly, as if to herself. She jiggled the padlock and looked around. 'Do you see a key?'

'The chef or whatever probably has it, right?' I said, glancing at Roberta, who immediately perked up.

'I can go find him?' she said, eager as a sheepdog.

'It'll take forever – we have no idea which rooms people ran to yesterday . . . Can you grab me something I can use as a crowbar?' Aloisia seemed to be getting a bit stressed over the freezer and I couldn't really work out why.

As Roberta rushed off to fulfil this request, Aloisia frowned down at the freezer, then turned and caught my eye and the question in my expression.

'I think the kitchen staff might have decided to hoard supplies.' She sighed. 'We don't lock this – ever. Jesus, that's all we need.'

'Sort of smart though – you know that as soon as there's no one watching, the guests'll be down here looking for stuff they can stockpile in their rooms. Just look at Paula. It's every man for himself right now.' I clicked my tongue. 'You think they threw the frozen stuff out and put tins or something in here? That's what I'd do,' I admitted.

'Maybe,' Aloisia shook her head. 'I expected better of them. I don't know why – it's not as if any of us have been through something like this before. I mean, how are you even supposed to act in a situation like this?'

'No idea,' I said. 'But I think most of us are just trying to make sure we get through it.'

Roberta returned with a hefty metal ladle and a marble rolling pin. 'I couldn't decide which was better. I thought this for prying and this for bashing?'

Honestly, Patrick was going to be lost without her. I could already tell. If we made it off the mountain and she fancied working in London, I could really use her. She had that rare thing – initiative.

We tried the ladle, putting it through the lock and twisting, but the metal handle bent after a few seconds of pressure. It was only aluminium. So in the end Aloisia and I took turns battering the padlock with the rolling pin until the housing cracked and we could wrangle the thing off. Luckily it was only a household padlock, nothing too sturdy.

I pushed up the lid to reveal a freezer still packed with peas, ice cream, and other frozen staples. All of it still kind of cold but definitely thawed and squishy. There was certainly nothing in there I could see the point of hoarding. It was all perishable and well on its way to perishing. More disappointment, I was becoming used to it by now.

Roberta's shriek caught me off guard. Aloisia jumped and clasped a hand to her chest. I turned to glare at Roberta and found her pointing at the freezer.

I followed the direction of her trembling finger and saw what had made her scream. A greyish pale finger, pointing back.

Chapter 21

The three of us stared at the finger protruding between a bag of baby carrots and another of raspberries. A pale, bloodless finger, shrunken around the nail. I was breathing hard through my nose, trying to quell the rising shock. Roberta's scream died away and she shrank back against the shelving and slowly dropped to the ground, hugging her knees.

'Jesus Fucking Christ,' Aloisia whispered. 'Who the hell is that?'

Boots pounded the hallway and within moments Max had arrived, panting. He looked between the three of us – Roberta sobbing on the floor, myself and Aloisia standing like statues over the freezer.

'What's happened?'

'There's . . . a man in here,' Aloisia managed.

Despite myself I looked again. I guessed she was right – that was a pretty mannish finger, blunt and unmanicured. Though I had no idea how she'd managed to process that in the shock of finding it. And what if it was *just* the hand in there? The idea of that made me shudder.

Max came over and swallowed hard when he set eyes

on the freezer contents. Then, slowly – as if waiting and hoping for someone to stop him – he started to remove the saggy packages of defrosted food and set them on the floor. He uncovered the person in stages, and I watched as the form buried in the freezer took shape.

The body was, in fact, complete. A man in dark clothes sort of folded up into the freezer on his side, in the foetal position, the food crammed back in around him and layered on top. One arm was angled sideways to get his shoulders into the freezer, the arm underneath him angled up and over his body. The packets must have settled after the body was stuffed in there, or else whoever had put him in there hadn't noticed the finger poking out, thanks to the body's awkward position. Gingerly, Max reached in and tried to turn his head so we could get a better look at him. He withdrew his hand as if stung.

'He's still . . . solid,' he said, through gritted teeth. 'Mostly.'

I shuddered. Though perhaps it was a mercy – God knows how long that body had been in there. If he hadn't been frozen he'd have probably started to . . . go off.

Max tilted his head and bent to get a look at the guy's face. He stood up suddenly, one hand grabbing at Aloisia's arm.

'It's Lars! It's fucking Lars!'

Aloisia gaped at the body. I tried to recall the details of the picture I'd seen. I supposed it was him, though being sideways when he froze had done something to his face and his hair was dark with water from the melting freezer contents. They were right – it was Lars in the freezer, dressed in a black tuxedo, minus the bow-tie.

'What the fuck?!' Max looked between us both, shock evident on his face. I was right there with him. We'd been rushing around trying to find Lars for how long and he'd been right here . . . but since when?

'I don't— When did this happen?' Aloisia said aloud, clearly struggling with the logic of what we were seeing. My mind was moving quickly, sorting through what I'd heard about him from everyone else and coming up with an answer that wasn't exactly comforting.

'You said he wasn't at the pre-dinner briefing,' I said, slowly. 'But he is dressed for dinner – right? That's the suit you said was missing from his room? The one he'd only wear to the dinner?'

She gave him another quick glance then hastily looked away, nodding.

'And he's still . . . he's mostly frozen. Which means he had time to freeze basically solid before all the electrics went down . . . or else he'd be thawed by now or not frozen at all,' I continued. What I thought, but did not say, was that something as dense as a person would take a lot longer to defrost than a bag of peas. Unfortunate images of legs of lamb occurred to me and my stomach twisted. Grim.

'You're saying he was in here the whole time?' Max turned to me, his expression a mixture of incredulity and, unmistakably, fear. I understood. We'd thought we were in danger from Lars but if Lars had been dead the whole time . . . who was out there, and what did they want?

'I told you he wouldn't do those things,' Aloisia said, voice shaking. 'I told you!'

'You also said someone had seen him after he missed the briefing – when you were looking for him at the welcome dinner,' I said to Aloisia. 'Do you remember who said that?'

She slowly shook her head. 'It was so busy. I can't . . .' She made a frustrated sound in the back of her throat and turned away from the freezer, putting her head in her hands.

I frowned at her bent head, finding I didn't believe her. Not a hundred per cent. There weren't that many staff members here even before the avalanche. She was the manager, surely she'd know all of them? But why would she lie? To cover for someone? Who?

Aloisia straightened with what appeared to be great effort. She took a breath and seemed to get herself under control. 'If Lars has been here since the dinner, who killed Jan? And Nils? Who shot Lionel? And how did Lars even end up here . . .'

Max was leaning over the freezer, peering somewhat reluctantly at the body. 'Looks like he was hit in the head – from behind. There's blood . . . just like with Jan . . . and there's a big tin, wedged under his leg. Maybe they hit him with that?' I watched as he swiftly patted Lars's body down.

'What are you looking for?' I asked. Suspicion was never far from my mind; it went with the job.

Max looked at me and held up his hand, jingling the bundle of metal and plastic at me. 'His keys. Whoever killed him left them behind.'

I felt a flash of embarrassment. Still, I was glad that only Aloisia and myself knew about the notebook we'd found in Lars's room. Lionel had known, but he was dead and I supposed it was possible Jade had overheard. But even so. For some reason it felt important that Max didn't find out about it. I hadn't forgotten that he'd rushed off to the outer door from the vault room right before the shooting. Something still felt wrong about that.

I cleared my throat. 'Whoever did this . . . maybe they only realised they needed a master key later on. That's why they attacked me and took Aloisia's. Coming back here must have been too risky with everyone swarming the foyer and trying to find first-aid kits and stuff in the kitchen. Or . . . I got attacked by someone else entirely and we have two murderous bastards running around.'

Aloisia turned back to us. 'I think the important thing is if Lars was already dead, he wasn't in the foyer last night – so if he didn't shoot Lionel, whoever did was probably already out there . . . and they must have run upstairs with everyone else.'

I wasn't so sure. Yes, everyone in the foyer was a suspect, but Aloisia had left the office before the gunshot and I hadn't had eyes on Max then either. He could have left the vault room by the second door into the hallway. If he was fast, he might have been able to shoot Lionel and then run back in order to pretend he was responding to the shot. The only people who couldn't have shot Lionel were me, poor frozen Lars and Lionel himself. But for now at least I had to keep Aloisia and Max in the dark that my suspect list included them.

'Jesus.' I shut my eyes for a second to process and then shared a despairing look with Aloisia and Max. 'What do we do now? Go door-to-door and just . . . ask if anyone has a gun they'd like to surrender?'

'I . . .' Aloisia swallowed hard and tried again. 'I don't think there's anything we can do. Not now anyway. Whoever it is, we have no idea who they are or why they're doing this. If we provoke them, who knows what might happen? We should just keep everything calm until we can get out of here.'

'So what are we meant to do?' Max snapped. 'Pretend we never found Lars? Just . . . try and act like everything's normal until help comes and hope the killer's done for the time being? He's killed three security guards – that's a fucking pattern.'

Aloisia didn't look away, but her shoulders slumped a little. 'I don't see what else we can do but keep it quiet and hope whatever this was . . . it's over.'

I glanced at Roberta, still hugging herself on the floor. 'And what about her?'

The other two seemed to have forgotten Roberta entirely. To be fair she had been quiet as a mouse down there, curled into a ball.

Aloisia went and crouched down beside her. 'You heard all that, right?' she said softly.

Roberta looked up, wet-eyed and pale. She nodded.

'We need to keep everyone calm, and not give whoever did this any more opportunities to hurt people – OK? Can you keep this quiet for me?'

Roberta nodded again. I felt a knot of tension in my chest slowly release. How could Aloisia be a cold-blooded killer and be so calm and patient with Roberta? I liked Aloisia, I'd trusted her at every turn. She wasn't a bad person, of that I was sure.

As much as I didn't want to go along with the 'do nothing' plan, I couldn't see an alternative. The guests and the remaining staff had mostly scattered upstairs, going into their own suites or random rooms. Divided like that, there was at least a good chance that most people weren't holed up with a killer. Unless said killer was in the room with me right now. Either way, if we gathered everyone together again as we had before, we'd only be ensuring that the killer had more potential victims around. Better if everyone stayed where they were.

'Right . . . Let's get some food together, go door-to-door and pass it out,' Aloisia said tiredly. 'Try and encourage anyone still in the foyer to go to their rooms and . . . I'll go and check the spa, see how Paula and the casualties are getting on. Hopefully she's sobered up by now. Her and Miss Harris.'

Max had no way of objecting to the idea of serving people room service now. He sighed but there wasn't much we could do about it. I held out a hand to Roberta and helped her up. She still looked upset and pale but once Aloisia closed the freezer, she seemed to rally.

Together, Roberta, Max and I filled trays with portions of jam-covered bread, small sauce pots of dried fruit and nuts and the last of the fresh fruit. We passed Renard and Silvie on the way out of the kitchen – he'd moved her into Aloisia's office and set her up a bed on the sofa. He shot us an apologetic look but didn't come and help. He had his hands full taking care of her, I suspected. He'd already proven he was a liability around blood and gore, so it was no great loss. Silvie seemed even less stable than she had yesterday. I couldn't blame her given the open shooting.

We carried everything upstairs, and the food attracted those few people who'd lingered in the foyer overnight. As they followed us up the stairs Max leaned in to mutter to us. 'Stay together – the last thing we need is to get separated by whoever has the guns.'

I wasn't exactly filled with confidence as we started

knocking on doors. However, it soon became apparent that most people were only willing to open the door a crack anyway. Just enough to take food, ask what was going on and to snap at us that we'd better not try and come in. I understood the aggression, cornered as they were, but still it made it impossible to tell the murderer from the frightened guests and staff.

When we reached Patrick's room he refused to open the door until someone other than Roberta called through to him. As if she didn't count as reason enough. Even then he only opened the door a sliver and snatched the food Max handed over, ignoring his wife. He wasn't about to let anyone else in that room, not even her.

Beside me, Roberta stood taller and her eyes were sharp with anger. She inhaled sharply through her nose. 'Coward!' she hissed at the closed door.

I was proud of her. She finally had some steel in her spine.

We'd almost reached my room when someone came running at us down the corridor. The sound of quick footfalls had us all turning and Max took out his cleaver, ready to attack – for what good that would do against a gun.

It was Jade, and she stumbled to a halt when she saw the knife, looking at us all in bewildered panic. Then she snapped out of it.

'I need help . . . I think Carri might be dying.'

Chapter 22

'Why is she up here and not in the spa – that's where she was last night,' I said as Jade rushed us towards Carri's room.

'I have no clue, she just came up like . . . ten, twenty minutes ago?' Jade said, hardly out of breath despite her sprint down the landing. 'I ended up in her room last night after the gun went off and she nearly gave me a heart attack just stumbling in – but it's her room, so . . .' She opened the door and ushered us in.

Carri was on the floor, wearing a robe. She'd apparently come out of the bathroom as I spotted yesterday's clothes strewn on the floor. I went to her side and peered at her face. She wasn't unconscious but didn't react when I shook her. Her pupils were far too small and they didn't move when I waved a hand over her face.

'She came out and just . . . fell,' Jade said. 'I tried to pick her up but she made this sound and . . .'

Carri gurgled, a weird choking noise. Without hesitation I rolled her into the recovery position and checked her mouth but she hadn't swallowed her tongue and she wasn't being sick. At least not yet.

‘I’ll go get that doctor woman,’ Max said, and took off running.

‘If she’s awake,’ I muttered to myself, because last time I’d seen Paula she’d been drunk off her arse. I leaned close and could smell booze on Carri – not vodka this time, something with a more pronounced fruity odour. But something wasn’t right. Carri wasn’t just drunk, she was completely out of it, like she’d taken something stronger.

‘Her pupils are tiny,’ I said, looking up at Jade. ‘Did you see her take anything?’

‘Like . . . drugs? No, I didn’t see anything. She was in the bathroom right before this.’

She was still talking when I got up and rushed to the bathroom. Nothing much to see, just a normal, plain bathroom. Same as the one in my suite. I started turning it over, shaking the tissue box, opening the toilet cistern, unfolding all the towels. I finally found something in the bathroom bin – a bottle of cognac, the contents maybe an eighth gone. The same brand as the one I’d seen under Aloisia’s desk last night, only this one had a silver ribbon. I hurried back into the main suite and set it on the floor.

‘She must have taken this from Aloisia’s office at some point. It’s cognac, I can smell it on her.’

Roberta had taken my position near Carri’s limp form. She was checking her pulse, counting under her breath. ‘Her heart rate’s really slow.’

‘How would you know?’ Jade snapped, pacing anxiously.

‘I used to be a nurse – well, student nurse,’ Roberta corrected herself. ‘Her pulse is slow and weak.’

Despite my rising panic over Carri’s condition, I felt a twinge of suspicion. Aloisia had called for anyone with medical experience to help in the aftermath of the avalanche and Roberta hadn't spoken up. Had she already fled by then? I couldn't remember. That night was so jumbled. Maybe, or maybe not. Perhaps she'd cared more about scurrying after her awful husband than using her skills in that moment.

Carri was turning bluish-purple around the mouth and her skin was waxy with sweat. I knelt down and checked her fingers, where the nails were also purpling. I knew what it was. I'd seen it before. But it didn't make any sense.

I flung myself to my feet and rushed out to the mezzanine. There was no sign of Max; he must have already reached the spa.

'We need Narcan!' I screamed, as loudly as I could. 'Naloxone!' My throat felt like it was tearing. I hoped Max could hear me. That someone could. This place was a refuge for celebrities hiding from their problems, including their addictions. They had to have treatment on hand for opioid overdoses. I was betting Carri's life on it.

I rushed back into the room. 'Jade, go to the spa, we need them to bring Narcan, if they have it.' I looked at Carri. 'God, I hope they have it. And a defibrillator if they've got one and it works.'

Jade didn't wait for an explanation – she was off. Her footsteps pounded the stairs, pattering rapidly over the foyer floor.

'You think she's overdosing?' Roberta asked, and I wondered how long ago she'd left training to not see the signs. Then again, I'd probably seen more real life cases of it than she had.

'On opiates, yeah,' I said, and started to rub at Carri's

arms, trying to get her to respond to touch, to my fingers snapping in front of her glazed eyes. 'Where she got them I have no fucking idea, but she's taken a lot of them and the alcohol is just adding to the mix.'

Roberta leaned in and checked Carri again. 'She's not breathing.'

'Shit.' I flopped Carri over onto her back and opened the robe. She was wearing a camisole underneath, thankfully, easier to deal with than a bra. We could do CPR through one but the bra would have had to come off if we had to shock her. If we even could. I was hoping against hope that the spa would have a defibrillator on-site and that it would still have charge. Those things had to have really long-life batteries, right?

I started CPR on Carri, desperately trying to keep her blood oxygenated while we waited for the Narcan, which was hopefully coming. It would counter the opiates in her body and bring her round, get her breathing normally again. As I started to tire I looked to Roberta to take over and she did, leaping in seamlessly.

I could hear doors opening and people talking as other guests responded to the shouting but no one came to assist us. I couldn't really blame them, to be honest. As far as they knew we were being murdered. They were better off staying put and hiding.

Then I heard footsteps racing up the stairs and Jade burst in, followed by Aloisia, who was clutching a portable defibrillator and immediately set it on the floor and started opening the plastic case.

'Where's Paula?' I demanded, taking back over from Roberta on the CPR.

'Asleep.' Aloisia was grappling with a yellow plastic

box wrapped in cellophane. 'I couldn't wake her. But we found this.' She finally shredded the plastic and got the box open – getting at the plastic syringe inside. She passed the entire box to Roberta, who just held it helplessly.

'Give it here – take over.' I let her start compressions again and checked the box contents. An injectable version of Naloxone. My hand was shaking as I unwrapped one of the needles in the box and screwed it onto the syringe. It was marked with five doses, each one a black line. I wasn't sure if it would be enough.

'Do you know what you're doing?' Jade demanded.

'Yes,' I snapped back, trying to sound confident. I'd used Narcan spray before, up the nose on several people – but never in a syringe like this and never on someone who wasn't breathing, with no ambulance on its way. I stuck the syringe into Carri's thigh and pushed the plunger down. One dose. I took the needle out and watched as Roberta carried on administering CPR.

'It's not working,' I said and Aloisia reached for the defibrillator. 'Can't you get that on her any faster?'

'It won't turn on!' Jade slapped the plastic housing of the machine.

'That thing has a battery life of up to five fucking years – it'll turn on!' Aloisia grabbed it from her and tried but without success. 'Shit, it must be defective.'

I blocked them out. Roberta did three more rounds of compressions and breaths but Carri was still unresponsive. I was still holding the hypodermic. Should I give Carri more? Would that help or do more damage? The instruction leaflet taunted me from the yellow box, all that fine print and no time to read it.

Fuck it, it was better than doing nothing.

I gave Carri a second dose. 'Does anyone else know CPR?'

'I do.' Aloisia went to take over from Roberta, who collapsed onto her heels, sweating profusely.

'How much of that stuff is left?' Jade asked.

'Three doses,' I set the syringe carefully into the yellow plastic box for safekeeping. 'Can you read the instructions please?'

'Now?' Jade picked them up anyway and started scanning them.

'Yeah . . . we need to know how often to give it to her when . . . if she comes round. It doesn't get rid of the drugs in her system, just keeps her brain from responding – lets her keep breathing. But if the drugs don't wear off before we run out of doses, she'll go right back to crashing out.'

Jade was still reading the leaflet when Carri started spasming on the floor, lashing out at Aloisia and trying to fight her way free. Relieved tears burned my eyes and I felt my shoulders loosen from their painful knot of tension. Carri was responding. Aloisia caught a slap to the face and backed off, cursing.

'Carri!' I shot forwards and got hold of her arm, Roberta the other.

'Leggo!' Carri slurred. 'What are you doing in my room!?'

This part I was familiar with. Someone who'd overdosed and been brought round usually didn't remember what had happened. Roberta helped me hold Carri steady and prevented her from getting up.

'You ODed, we're trying to help you, you're OK,' I said, as soothingly as I could given the circumstances.

Carri shook her head. 'No I dinnt! I . . . I don't take

drugs . . . I don't . . .' she slumped, running out of energy. 'Juss had a drink, that's all.'

I leaned her against the end of the bed and let go of her to grab the bottle of cognac. 'You drank from this? Today?'

'Mmmm . . .' Carri nodded, eyelids falling shut. Roberta gave her a little shake to keep her conscious. 'Ahhhhh . . . bitch. Yes! I opened it today, OK?'

'You took this from Aloisia's office? When?' I demanded.

She scrunched up her face. 'After dinner . . .'

'Dinner . . . you mean the night of the avalanche?'

She nodded and I looked at Aloisia. 'There's still a bottle under your desk, right? I saw it.'

'Yes, my bottle – it was in this gift hamper we got – me and Lars, I mean.'

'But his hamper was in your office?' I stressed.

'Our office. He left it there so he could get at the snacks while we were working . . . Does it matter?' Aloisia asked, gesturing at Carri. 'Is she going to be OK?'

I didn't really know. Carri's system was still full of opiates and it was only the injection I'd given her that was blocking the effects of them from her brain – if it wore off she'd stop breathing for herself again. We had three doses left and then she'd be on her own.

'Hopefully,' I said. 'Roberta, I need you to watch her and keep administering the jab until it runs out. She needs it every—' I snapped my fingers at Jade.

'Twenty minutes to an hour,' she supplied, holding up the instructions.

'And we should try and find a defibrillator that actually works.' I sighed. 'Is there another one?'

My heart sank when Aloisia shook her head. 'Not that I'm aware of. That one's meant to work fine – I don't know why it's not.'

'Fantastic.' I got up and stretched, my muscles aching from giving prolonged CPR while being tense with panic. 'And, if Carri's telling the truth about not taking any drugs aside from the cognac – it means there's opiates in it. A lethal amount, given she only drank some of it. Someone poisoned Lars's bottle . . . Someone was trying to kill him before he got bludgeoned to death and stuffed in that freezer.'

'Lars is dead?' Jade gaped at me in shock, then scoffed disbelievingly. 'Weren't we just looking for him over in that other building? You know, risking our lives running around out where the wolves were? When did he turn up? Who the hell killed him?'

Great, me and my big mouth. That was unusually sloppy of me. 'He's been dead since before the avalanche. Someone bludgeoned him to death and hid the body.'

'Then why try to poison him, just to do that?' Jade asked. 'Why kill him at all – he's just the assistant manager right? I met him the first time I was here. He was a non-entity. Who tries to kill a guy like that, twice?'

A good question. 'Maybe they ran out of patience? If he wasn't a drinker and whoever was trying to kill him didn't know that, they'd be waiting forever for him to poison himself.'

Jade's reply was interrupted by a shout from outside. 'Hey, what do you think you're doing?'

As one we all turned to the door, through which Max's shout had come. It sounded like he was in the foyer somewhere. Aloisia headed for the door at the same time as I did. Jade trailed after us, still muttering about 'secrets' and 'this goddamn place' under her breath.

'Stay with Carri,' I turned back and told her. 'Roberta might need help.'

Jade sighed but apparently decided I was talking sense. That or she thought whatever was going on downstairs would be more risky than taking care of a half-conscious pop star.

'Put. That. Down!' Max sounded more than angry now – he sounded scared.

I found out why when I reached the rail around the mezzanine and looked down. Aloisia's knuckles were white on the railing beside me. I raised a hand to my mouth, smothering a cry of shock.

Max was standing in the foyer, having apparently come from the spa. He had his hands raised and was staring down the barrel of a gun.

Chapter 23

Patrick's arm wasn't steady but I wasn't sure if it was nerves or rage that made him shake as he pointed the gun at Max. His other hand supported a cardboard box that was tucked under his arm. From above I could see that it was full of food. I gritted my teeth in anger, despite my skyrocketing anxiety. He'd obviously been stealing.

'Get out of my way.' Patrick's voice was as shaky as his gun arm. He sidestepped, trying to get closer to the stairs without getting within arm's length of Max.

'Put it down,' Max said again, obviously attempting to remain calm and commanding, even though he was facing down a man with a gun. A man who had potentially already killed four people.

'I won't tell you again – move!' Patrick skirted around him and reached the stairs, backing up them. He was apparently oblivious to his audience as he unsteadily climbed the first few steps, keeping his eyes and the gun trained on Max.

Max didn't look our way. Either he hadn't seen us or he didn't want to tip Patrick off that we were up there. I tapped Aloisia's arm and motioned for her to be quiet.

The element of surprise was all we had if we wanted to separate Patrick from the gun. But what if in surprising Patrick we shocked him into pulling the trigger? Max would be right in front of him.

Patrick was still walking backwards up the stairs, finding each tread with his foot and only occasionally glancing down. The box was obviously heavy and he had to keep fumbling to keep it wedged under his arm, twitching his gun arm towards it as if he wanted to use both hands but didn't yet trust Max not to rush him if he lowered the weapon. Which was probably a safe bet as Max was tense and ready for any opportunity to do so. He looked furious.

'Is that why you killed Lionel? He caught you stealing?' Max asked, a sneer on his face. Oh, he was angry, all right, and I couldn't blame him – he'd lost several colleagues in a short space of time. Friends even.

Patrick was almost on our level now. Our best bet would be to rush him once he turned to go to his room. That way the gun wouldn't be pointed at Max if it did happen to go off. I held my palm out in front of Aloisia, holding her back while I waited for him to get into position.

'You don't know what you're talking about,' Patrick shouted, over Max's continued accusations. He'd reached the mezzanine and nearly tripped as he stepped up onto the landing. 'Just stay there and don't follow me— Ahhhhh!'

Aloisia cried out and I shrieked involuntarily as Patrick yelled.

Everything happened very quickly. Roberta had pushed Patrick hard in the back, putting both hands and her full weight into it. So much so that she nearly fell down the stairs along with him. Patrick flew forwards, still yelling.

He dropped the box and tins clattered down the staircase. The gun went off as Patrick gripped the trigger, three shots deafening us as they echoed around the foyer.

Max dove to the floor at the noise and threw both arms over his head, shouting over the din. One of the bullets must have hit the fancy light fitting overhead, because I heard a ricochet and then glass rained down on the foyer. Aloisia screamed at the noise, but despite that I heard every fleshy thump of Patrick's body on the steps. He tumbled over and over down the stairs until he landed in a crumpled heap at the bottom.

Then there was only the icicle tinkle of glass on the floor, the dull thuds of it hitting the abandoned bedding, and the whir of tins slowly rolling across the stairs and falling over the edges before eventually coming to a stop.

I looked at Roberta, still standing at the top of the stairs, looking down at her husband. Her hands out from the push that had sent him over the edge. She was pale and clasped her hands together as if she couldn't believe what they had done and was trying to keep them from acting out again.

'Are you all right?' Aloisia called down to Max in a shaky voice.

He uncurled himself and carefully got up, brushing broken glass off his clothes. He nodded, his formerly sallow colouring now very grey. 'I think so . . . not really sure about him though.'

Max jumped and whirled around as the door behind the marble desk slammed open and Renard appeared, trailing Silvie behind him. He stuck his head out, eyes wide. 'What the hell was that? Are you all right?' he asked Max.

'Yes – or I will be if people stop jumping out at me,' Max snapped.

'Oh Jesus . . .' Renard had spotted Patrick's body and appeared not to hear Max's words. 'Is he OK? Did he get shot?'

For the first time since his fall, all eyes turned to Patrick and Max slowly made his way over. I assumed he was going to check for a pulse, but that became unnecessary when Patrick groaned and started to move. I honestly couldn't tell who was more disappointed that he'd survived – Max, Roberta, or me.

Max walked over and grabbed him by the arm to drag him to his feet.

'Be careful! He might have broken bones!' Aloisia called, but it made no difference. Max was apparently beyond caring about the welfare of a man who was the number one suspect in the deaths of four of his colleagues. I couldn't exactly blame him. Patrick had the gun – even if he wasn't guilty of the murders, he had to know something.

'Get the wheelie chair from the office,' Max snapped at Renard, who vanished to do as he asked, leaving Silvie gaping in the doorway. I became aware of eyes on us and turned to find Livvy and Emmitt poking their heads out of one of the nearby rooms. I supposed it was Emmitt's room and he'd returned to it that morning to find Livvy hiding inside after last night's shooting. Apparently they were curious enough about what had happened to risk a peek at the rest of us. Seeing no obvious danger, Emmitt widened the crack in the door and half-stepped into the corridor.

'Was that Patrick? What's going on?'

'He . . . fell down the stairs,' Aloisia said, mustering

a bright customer service smile that bordered on the demented given our current situation. Emmitt didn't look like he was buying it. He frowned and moved further in to the open, despite Livvy trying to pull him back, like she was his mother and he was an overactive toddler.

Below us Renard returned with the chair. I supposed that Silvie had gone back to the safety of Aloisia's office – though 'safe' wasn't how I'd describe a room where a bottle of poisoned booze had been found. At the back of my mind I had to wonder where the drugs had come from to lace the cognac, here of all places, but that was a matter for another time. Right now I was more concerned with what was going to happen to Patrick. Guilty or not, he deserved a chance to explain what had happened. I wasn't certain that Max felt the same way.

He was still groaning and appeared only semi-conscious as Max hauled him into the office chair and then dragged the chair over to the desk. I watched as he pulled the cord out of the desk phone there and started tying Patrick to the chair with it.

'What are you doing?' Aloisia nudged Roberta away from the top of the stairs and hurried down them towards Max. Roberta appeared to snap out of her post-attempted-murder daze and she turned to look at me sharply. I nodded back towards the suite where Carri was still under Jade's care and Roberta hurried back inside.

Should I have been worried about Roberta and what she might do next? She had attempted to kill her husband right in front of me and ordinarily that would have probably made me a little wary. But having met Patrick and seen how he was with her, and given that he'd left her shut out of their room after the shooting . . . I could see where she was coming from. Though, I thought as I headed for the stairs, if Patrick had been the one to shoot Lionel, he'd have known there was no danger to Roberta in the foyer. Perhaps he'd shut her out so she wouldn't see the gun or evidence of his actions.

I reached the ground floor and went over to where Renard, Max and Aloisia were gathered around the semi-conscious Patrick. There was a large patch of grazed skin on his face and neck from the fall but otherwise he looked mostly unharmed. Though later on he'd probably be one massive bruise.

'Get me some water to throw on him,' Max ordered Renard. 'I'm not waiting around for answers anymore. I want to get to the bottom of this.'

Renard rushed off again, eager to follow orders. Aloisia looked concerned.

'What answers are you expecting?' she asked Max. 'Do you really think he's responsible for all this? He's an idiot.'

I snorted despite myself and Max frowned at me before responding to Aloisia. 'He had the gun, so he knows something. He can tell us where he got it, or from whom. And if he did kill Lionel, Nils – even Jan and Lars, then we'll get the truth out of him and deal with it.'

'You mean, wait for the police and hand them over?' Aloisia said, though like me I think she knew that wasn't what Max was suggesting. Something had shifted since Lionel's death. We were no longer people trapped and awaiting rescue from civilisation. We were separated from the real world and its rules seemed to apply less and less with each passing moment. Survival was becoming the only metric by which our actions could be judged.

I took a deep breath and frowned. I could still smell that bloody cognac. Carri must have slopped some over the bottle as she drank and it had gotten onto my hands. The rich, fruity smell filled my nose, making me feel sick with unease. Why, though? I knew Carri was conscious. She was hopefully going to be OK.

'Hey! You can't do that!' Emmitt came striding down the stairs, with Livvy following after him. 'What the fuck gives you the right to tie him up like that, huh? He's a guest!'

Emmitt tried to pass Max and grunted in surprise when Max elbowed him hard in the solar plexus. One shove later and Emmitt was sprawled on the abandoned bedding and broken glass on the floor, gasping. He looked up at Max in disbelief.

'What do you think you're doing?' Aloisia hissed, her face a mask of horror at this breach in customer service.

'I am done with these fucking people,' Max snapped, rounding on her. 'I am getting off this mountain alive – I'm not sacrificing my life for any one of these arseholes. I don't deserve to die like the others.'

'Please . . . I think we all need to calm down,' Livvy said, raising her hands to placate him. 'We all want to get out of here, but there's no need for violence.'

'Shut up,' Max said. 'Get back in your room, out of my way.'

Livvy looked to Aloisia as if expecting her to stand up for her. But she was still looking at Max and appeared to be deferring to him now. The balance of power was shifting and I didn't like it. There was still something bothering me as well, and the smell of the alcohol on my hands had my mind spinning its wheels in the mud, trying to get to the answer. Something about Carri. About the cognac. That smell.

'Help me up,' Emmitt croaked and Livvy bent to do just that, the two of them staggering back as she struggled with Emmitt's weight.

'Wait.' I'd finally found the right gear and my thoughts were on the move again. It wasn't just the cognac that was niggling at me. It was where the drugs Carri was on had even come from.

'Aloisia, how many addicts are here right now? Specifically opiates, like heroin or morphine?' If anyone would know, it would be her.

Aloisia glanced automatically in Emmitt's direction and then quickly looked away. 'Um . . . I don't know that I can give out that information. Legally.'

'Is it just Emmitt?' I pressed.

'Hey! She can't tell you that – don't you dare tell her that,' Emmitt snapped at Aloisia, confirming my suspicions.

'And Emmitt – did you smuggle opiates in here?'

His thin, anxious face immediately stiffened. 'I . . . No, why would I . . . you can't prove . . .'

I waved his denials away. 'Look, I don't care if you did, I just need to know if you still have them,' I said, cutting him off as he tried to deny it again. 'It's important . . . someone might die if we don't find out.'

A small exaggeration on my part since knowing wouldn't actually help save Carri, but urgency was often key in extracting secrets from someone who might otherwise lie to save their own skin. A fictional illness to get someone to admit to fathering a love-child, and a life-or-death situation to find out what someone had or hadn't taken.

Emmitt glanced at Aloisia as if she were his headmistress and he was worried about being expelled. But she just nodded, giving him permission to speak the truth freely. As if it mattered now.

'I . . . fine. I brought some just . . . just in case I . . . in case I needed it. But I didn't get them through security here,' Emmitt muttered, then he snorted bitterly. 'They're prescription but they were confiscated anyway.'

'What does any of that matter?' Max demanded, as Renard returned with the water, a two-litre bottle of the stuff, as the taps were still frozen.

'Carri's overdosing on opiates. My guess is that whoever wanted to poison Lars doctored that bottle of cognac the day we arrived here, right before Carri stole it – and Emmitt's drugs would have been perfect for that. Carri was poisoned and it was meant for Lars from someone here who had access to the guest's contraband.' I turned to Aloisia. 'When does that stuff get taken from the luggage, and what happens to it?'

She blinked at me, obviously still trying to catch up with what I was talking about. 'Uh . . . at the lower aerial tram station. Anything illegal is removed and destroyed, and the rest is sealed into plastic bags then transported in the luggage compartment with the actual bags. At this end it goes straight to the vault deposit hatch with the personal effects surrendered on arrival, overseen by management.' She saw the accusation in my eyes and answered it by squaring her shoulders in defiance. 'I was there when the cart was taken from the upper station to the vault, accompanied by Renard. Neither of us was ever alone with it.'

That ticked the pair of them off in the 'no opportunity' column. But everything was coming together in my head, that cloying smell leading me towards the only possible conclusion.

'So whoever took Emmitt's drugs would have done so before we all arrived at the upper station?' I said, just to make sure.

'I . . . suppose?' Aloisia said hesitantly. 'Only one member of staff checks the bags since we only have a few arrivals at a time.'

I was still thinking, trying to remember back before the avalanche sent everything into chaos. 'Carri wasn't with us then, so she couldn't have taken it for herself at the lower station but . . . anyone else at the station could have, if they snuck away for a second and got into the bags. Or if they were the person checking them.'

'No, that's . . .' Renard set the bottle down and the half-frozen water inside sloshed with an odd crunching noise. 'Silvie was on duty that day – she'd never . . .'

'I think she would,' I said and Aloisia looked at me incredulously. Even Max seemed shocked. 'I don't know why . . . but the day we arrived I know I smelt cognac on her. I thought it was some weird perfume until I got a whiff of it in Carri's room. Silvie had cognac on her that day we arrived, the same day she had access to Emmitt's drugs. I think she poisoned that bottle.'

'How dare you?' Renard sputtered. 'Silvie would never . . . Aloisia, you can't believe this!'

'Where is she?' Aloisia said, cutting him off, apparently noticing Silvie's absence for the first time.

Max moved around behind Renard, smoothly cutting off his exit. Even Emmitt and Livvy were watching him, waiting to see what would happen next.

'I don't know . . . back in your office?' Renard stammered.

My skin prickled with cold. 'Hey, where did the gun go?'

Chapter 24

I couldn't blame Livvy and Emmitt for immediately bolting for the comparative safety of their room, or rooms. If I trusted anyone else to resolve the current situation without me I'd have likely done the same. Instead I rushed over to where Patrick had landed and checked the shadows of the stair treads, while Max searched around the staircase. Our eyes met through the banisters – neither of us had found anything.

'Shit,' Max struck the railing and it reverberated with the force of his hand. 'Where the hell did it go?'

Aloisia was turning over the bedding near the stairs, scattering broken glass as she did so. I could see her starting to panic as she moved faster and faster, throwing pillows and blankets every which way.

'Did he definitely still have it when he fell?' Max was looking towards the top of the stairs.

I nodded. 'I saw him fire as he went down, so he definitely had it with him . . . Where the fuck is Renard?'

We all turned to see that he'd rushed off and there were really no points for guessing where. He'd gone to Silvie to warn her, to protect her. Still trying to play the white knight even now he knew his damsel was a suspect in at least one attempted murder. But what if he'd also picked up the gun? There were so many duvets and cushions that it could have been anywhere and we'd all been focused on Patrick – and then, I realised guiltily, on me and my theories about drugs and cognac. Renard could easily have found and picked up the gun while we ignored him, thinking he was just fetching water or a chair. Just as Silvie could have done it while none of us were watching her.

Damn it. We'd let our guards down while we thought Patrick was a viable suspect and now the gun was back in play.

Patrick groaned and wriggled against his bindings. Max looked between him, me and Aloisia. Like a dog desperate to be let off lead. Finally he took off towards the reception doors at a run without waiting for Aloisia's OK.

'Stay with him! I'll get the other two back here!' he called back.

'But what if they have . . . the gun . . .' I trailed off as the door banged shut and Max disappeared. Had he heard me? Had he understood?

'You think Renard took it?' Aloisia said, frowning. 'To help Silvie?'

'Maybe . . . or Silvie grabbed it. I wasn't keeping an eye on her. And we still don't know where the rifle is.' I sighed, considering Patrick. 'But there is one way to find out, and he's the only lead we have right now.'

I picked up the bottle of water, and struggled to get the cap undone. Then I upended it over Patrick. The spatters that hit me were icy cold, more slush than liquid and, judging from the way he shrieked, horribly unpleasant to be doused in. I'll admit, even in all the tension and fear, that gave me a small twinge of satisfaction. It was the least he deserved after threatening us with a gun.

'What the f-f-f-fuck?' he got out, through chattering teeth. 'You b-b-b-bitch!'

I dropped the bucket and grabbed his wet shoulders. 'Where did you get the gun?'

'I could've had a heart attack, you stupid c-c-cow!' Patrick continued to struggle against the cords that bound him, turning puce with rage. 'Let me up! And where the fuck is Bertie? Don't think I don't know it was you that shoved me, you crazy bitch!' His roar filled the foyer and hot spittle hit my cheek.

'The gun – where did you get it?' I snapped, shoving the wheelie chair back a few inches until it hit the marble desk. But Patrick continued to snarl and swear and threaten until he was practically foaming at the mouth. Aloisia was no help, just hovering by my side limply, probably thinking about lawsuits and bad reviews and her P45.

I slapped him, hard across the face. Just once. The sort of slap I'd once had to give to a hysterical singer-songwriter-klepto when she'd got caught with a Gucci bag up her skirt two days before the Brit Awards. Sometimes in a crisis you had to give people a hard reset to get them to hear a word you had to say.

Patrick's mouth gaped in silent outrage – but the silent part was really all I needed. I took two fistfuls of his wet shirt and leaned into his face. 'Tell me where you got the gun, or I am going to push you right outside that door and let the wolves enjoy a new enrichment game called

"Twat on a chair".' It was an empty threat, really – I'd never wish that death on anyone, not even Patrick. Also, I'd rather chew off my own fingers than risk luring the wolves any closer to the hotel. But he didn't need to know that.

His breathing had slowed slightly, the slap and the threat forcing him to work on keeping himself calm. Though his eyes were dark and murderous. 'You wouldn't kill me,' he seethed.

'You could have killed any of us with that stupid stunt with the gun, so don't try me,' I snapped back. 'Where did you get it from? That's all you have to tell us, and maybe when we explain all this to the police, we'll forget to mention you threatening to shoot Max.'

The empty promise worked where the threat hadn't. Patrick seized his chance. 'I found it,' he spat, straining forward against the plastic cord. 'On the floor when everyone was running around after the gunshot. I took it for protection, because it's not as if anyone here gives the faintest fuck about what happens to the paying guests anymore!'

It was such a ridiculous story that I actually believed it. The equivalent to a child with a fifty-pound note claiming they 'found it in the playground'. A cover story so pathetic that it almost sounded true.

'You just found it? Right. So, did you see who dropped it?' I demanded.

'No, I didn't see anyone,' he admitted, sullenly. 'It was dark. I thought it was his – the dead bloke – that he'd dropped it when he went down. Didn't realise it was the one that was used on him.'

The story was paper thin but the fact that Patrick

wasn't trying to make himself look the hero lent it weight. I hadn't fully thought him capable of all the murders even when he'd appeared with the gun. Like Aloisia said, he was an idiot.

'But why take it?' Aloisia hissed. 'You had to know it would make you look guilty, that you'd be putting people in danger by withholding evidence and protection.'

I managed not to roll my eyes. Maybe Aloisia wasn't the kind of person who'd see a gun in the middle of a post-murder stampede and immediately grab it for protection, but I certainly was, and while I didn't like that Patrick and I shared this trait, I understood it. I mean, if I had found the gun first I wouldn't have used it to steal food. But it struck the right chord with me. He was telling the truth.

'Did you see what happened to it when you fell?' I asked.

'I didn't fucking fall – that bitch pushed me. I'm going to get her put away for that – hear that, Bertie!' His voice rose again until he was bellowing up at the mezzanine, the tendons in his neck standing out against his livid purple skin. 'You're going away for life and I'm going to get on every talk show going! You just resurrected my entire career!'

The worst part, the part that made my skin crawl and my throat burn with acid, was that he was right. This would get him sympathy and attention galore. It would mean every comment on every platform that called out his racism would be immediately rebutted with a convenient 'Can't believe you're bullying a victim of abuse'. Patrick had his 'get out of jail free' card in his pocket and if he got off this mountain, he wouldn't hesitate to use it.

There were a whole host of people who'd either genuinely sympathise with him, or pretend they did to 'own the feminists' with a comparatively rare and well-publicised case of a woman trying to kill her husband. 'But what about Patrick Keegan?' was about to become the most popular sentence in the manosphere.

I thought of Roberta tearing up, desperate to return to her family cottage to be free of a man who had so transparently been grinding her under his heel for years. She might have pushed him for selfish reasons but she'd also been disarming a threat to all of us. She'd have to sell her escape cottage for legal costs, most likely. I could only imagine the kind of prenup she'd signed and how aggressively Patrick would fight her for every penny. All while he rehabilitated himself in the public eye, did press opportunities for domestic violence and men's mental health. He'd probably get on the honours list off the back of it too.

And if he was my client, I'd be advising him to do just that.

All my hatred of Patrick turned inwards, an iron maiden of disgust that instantly drew blood. I had no one to blame but myself, of course. I'd had a rough start in life but so did many people. I was the one who'd chosen to use my skills for people like him, against people like her. People who just wanted the truth to come out. Who just wanted the world to be the tiniest bit fairer.

Not anymore.

'Listen, you,' I said, channelling the kind of authoritative aggression I usually used to keep journalists in line. 'As soon as I can get to a working phone line your career will be so dead, it'll make the performance you gave in your last film look vibrant and interesting. You stole a gun and used it to hoard food in a survival situation. You shut your wife out of your suite when, as far as anyone knew, there was an active shooter in here.'

'She pushed me down the stairs,' Patrick growled.

'Did she?' I tilted my head to the side. 'I didn't see that – did you, Aloisia?'

I turned to her and she blinked at me, apparently so caught up in watching us that she was lost for words. Slowly, under the pressure of my gaze, she shook her head.

'I . . . um . . . I think you may have tripped, Mr Keegan,' she said apologetically. 'But then, you were walking backwards and pointing a gun at my employee.'

His eyes were furious slits. 'He saw – the security bloke.'

'Yeah . . . and he hates you,' I stage-whispered. 'Even your wife hates you. And I bet I can find other people who hate you as well – probably people with good reason to. Like every woman you've ever worked with. I bet there were affairs too . . . maybe some kids of yours somewhere, hmm?'

A better actor could have hidden the slight tic of alarm as his eyes widened. But Patrick wasn't a good actor. I'd thrown out a few random shots and already scored a hit on his battleship. He was mine. I pressed that advantage, taking him down the rest of the way.

'If the words "She pushed me" ever come out of your mouth again, I will bury you – in child support, sexual misconduct allegations and your own disgusting words. And make no mistake – I really, really want to. So you'd just be doing me a favour.'

I straightened up and caught my breath. I felt alive and

alert, buzzing with righteous anger. The sick, slimy feeling that usually accompanied my 'professional victories' was completely absent. I felt . . . good.

Patrick sputtered furious denials but I ignored him and turned to Aloisia. All this adrenaline had given me new focus and with it came a creeping sense that something wasn't right. I'd had half an ear out for the sound of the gun going off but even though everything had remained silent, I didn't feel great about what that meant.

'Shouldn't Max be back by now?' I said to Aloisia and watched her turn pale.

'Maybe he's talking to them – trying to get their side of the story?' she hedged, but we both knew Max wasn't in the mood for that. He wanted to know who'd killed his colleagues and he didn't seem willing to be diplomatic about it. I was actually starting to worry about Silvie as well – what would Max do to her if he suspected she hadn't just tried to poison Lars, but had killed Jan, Nils and Lionel? Their deaths had been so brutal and bloody, I was having a hard time imagining Silvie as the sole perpetrator. What if Max had gone after her because they were in it together?

'We should check on him – on them,' I said. As much as the idea of going back into the tight hallway beyond the reception area made the back of my neck prickle with fear.

'Let me go first,' Patrick hissed, still not having ramped back up to full fury. 'If you bitches get yourselves killed I don't want to be stuck here.'

'Your concern is heart-warming,' I muttered, stepping away from him and approaching the reception door.

'Shouldn't we—' Aloisia said but I could hear her following me. She wasn't worried about Patrick either.

We were maybe a few feet down the corridor when he started shouting. 'Hey! They're after you! Guy with the gun! Ambush!'

'That fucking idiot son-of-a . . .' We'd lost the element of surprise and I sprinted down the corridor before I could think better of it. I turned the corner, my body tensing in expectation of attack. But there was no one there.

Aloisia shot out of the vault room door, having taken the route through the office. I jumped slightly but she didn't seem to notice. 'No one,' she panted. 'Where . . .'

I pointed to the external door, which was flapping open in the icy breeze. My stomach flipped to see a way in for the wolves, for danger. Even as I considered that the danger might have just left us for parts unknown.

'They're . . . gone? Out there?' Aloisia slowly approached the door and peered out at the snow-covered landscape. 'But there's wolves . . .'

'Not such a big problem if one of them has the gun, or both guns,' I said, joining her at the door and pulling it closed for my own sake.

'What are you doing – we need to follow them!' Aloisia grabbed for the push bar on the door and I held it firmly shut.

'We don't have a gun,' I pointed out. 'We don't even know who to be afraid of.'

'What does that mean?' Aloisia gaped at me. 'You think Max . . .'

'I think every other security guard is dead, except Max – and maybe we need to stop and think about why that is before we go running out there after him. We might only have a one-in-three chance of picking the right killer and we do not get a do-over if we get it wrong.'

I didn't say, but certainly felt, that we weren't in a good place to make that gamble. I'd been around all three of them for days now and couldn't honestly say I had any intuitive sense one way or the other. Maybe they were all in it together, maybe they weren't. But I certainly couldn't tell and I wasn't about to risk Aloisia's life on it. Or, quite frankly, my own.

'But Max couldn't have shot Lionel, right? He wasn't out there when the gun went off,' Aloisia argued.

'Maybe. But what about Jan, and Nils? What if Lionel was in on it and he accidentally shot himself in the leg, or Patrick's lying about when he got the gun and he did it. All I'm saying is . . . there are three people out there right now and we don't know which one of them has the gun. Or where the rifle even is and who might have access to it. We need to strategise. Because so far we haven't been in control of anything.'

Aloisia was still looking at me like I was speaking gibberish but she slowly let go of the outer door push bar and eventually nodded. 'OK . . . what do we do?'

'Can we find out where they're going? See the full grounds from somewhere? Or contact Max somehow and try to get the information out of him? What about the radio?'

She fumbled for her radio but nothing happened. 'Batteries are dead . . . but we could try and spot them from the roof? That would give a full 360-degree view of the surrounding area.'

'OK, see, good plan,' I waved her back down the

corridor and we turned the corner towards reception. 'I still can't work out what the hell to believe about that poisoned cognac. If Silvie did do it she must have had a reason, even if it was one that only made sense to . . . What?'

Aloisia had paused and suddenly grabbed my arm. 'She did! She – I can't believe I didn't remember this sooner – she was the one I asked about where Lars was at dinner. The person who told me he was around somewhere.'

My mind was reeling. 'But Lars was already in the freezer then. He had to be . . . and if she lied about that she'd be covering up for the murder,' I said slowly. Something didn't feel right. 'But you said you didn't remember who told you they'd seen him?'

'She was filling in last minute – for Lilli after I sent her away right before service. I forgot she was even in the dining room that night. That's not normally her job,' Aloisia said. 'And, you know, there was an avalanche right after that. It slipped my mind!'

I wanted to believe her. She'd been nothing but helpful and trusting of me. Still, something didn't ring true here. How could she have forgotten that it was Silvie she'd spoken to? Especially as Silvie was one of only a few surviving staff members and she'd been right with us the entire time – wouldn't seeing her have reminded Aloisia of that night? But that didn't negate the evidence of the cognac on Silvie, and that she'd had access to Emmitt's drugs when Aloisia didn't.

Unsure what to think, I pretended to take her words at face value. 'You think Silvie poisoned the bottle and then realised she couldn't wait for Lars to drink it, so she decided to, what, bludgeon him instead? Why?'

'I don't know, but . . . I think at the time I just assumed she was covering for him because they were seeing each other,' Aloisia said uncomfortably. 'Then with everything that happened afterwards it just didn't seem important.'

'Silvie and Lars?' I couldn't quite believe what she was telling me. Silvie, quite possibly one of the most beautiful women I'd ever met, not to mention young, was with . . . Lars? A greying middle manager who looked like he ate plain porridge for every meal and ironed his socks? I wasn't exactly an expert on straight relationships, but even to me that seemed very off.

'I know, it sounds a little bizarre – and it's not allowed for management to fraternise either but . . . I saw them together, in the sauna one night.' Aloisia pulled a face and shrugged. 'I spoke to him about it and told him it wasn't appropriate but he seemed so embarrassed I didn't take it any further. Only now I'm wondering if . . .'

'. . . If maybe a girl like Silvie really saw something she liked in Lars or . . . if she was trying to get something out of him. Like the vault code only he and you know,' I finished. 'Which would explain why the vault hasn't been raided yet – they knew we were guarding it. We need to get to the roof. Whatever the plan was, it's obviously falling apart. We have no idea what she might do next. Or who else she's working with.'

'What if it's both of them?' Aloisia asked as we hurried into the foyer, ignoring Patrick's renewed cries for freedom. 'Renard and Max, helping her?'

'Then we thank our lucky stars they all left the building and stop them coming back in. Either they leave or the cold and wolves take care of them.'

'And . . . if one of them's innocent?'

I didn't say anything, just focused on climbing the stairs as quickly as possible. I didn't want to think about that scenario, because the likelihood was it wouldn't end well for the innocent party involved.

Chapter 25

We'd just reached the mezzanine when Jade came out of Carri's room. She'd cast off her running top and was just in a black vest and leggings now, looking sweaty despite the cold. I guessed it was the stress of the situation but between armed robbers and taking care of Carri, I knew which problem I'd rather be facing. Or at least I thought I did until Jade opened her mouth.

'We're out of that stuff – the Narcan or whatever? It's all gone.'

I stumbled to a halt. 'Shit . . . is she still breathing on her own? Is Roberta with her?'

Jade nodded. 'Yeah, but we had to give her more just now and she's starting to make those noises again, like she's struggling to breathe . . . is there any more we can give her?'

'I don't know – did you see any when you were in the medical bay?' I asked, looking between her and Aloisia.

'No, but it was pretty messed up in there,' Jade said. 'Like that doctor woman was just grabbing stuff without keeping track. Or it was all slung in there to start with. Maybe it got moved or mixed in with the rest of the supplies?'

'I don't know how much we actually had on hand,' Aloisia put in. 'Our doctor did all the ordering and kept his own inventory on his computer, which obviously we can't check.'

I groaned through gritted teeth. 'Fuck! OK . . . Aloisia – you go up and see if you can spot the others. I will go to the medical bay and try to wake Paula or find the stuff myself. At least I know what it looks like and the different names for it.'

'I could go?' Jade pointed out.

'No – we need two people with Carri in case she needs CPR again and you're a lot fitter than me so, you'll be able to keep it up for longer if needs be,' I said. 'Move it!' I added, when Aloisia just stood there looking at me. She started like a frightened rabbit and bolted off down the corridor past the guest rooms. Surely she couldn't get into trouble on the flat roof of this stupidly modern building?

'Go back to Carri,' I told Jade as I turned around and ran down the stairs. 'I'll be right back.'

It felt like forever since I'd last been to the spa side of The Sorgente. Had it really only been last night that I'd escorted Paula there and then helped put Lionel's body in the tiny morgue? So much had happened since then. I felt like I'd aged five years in a single day. The idea that I'd come to this place because my life was stressful seemed ridiculous. The freedom to go anywhere, buy anything, and not get shot or eaten by wolves sounded pretty good to me just then. As much as I loathed my job, now I'd had some distance from it, I never wanted to take the rest of my life for granted again. It might be small and lonely and stressful, but it was still a life. One I wanted to return to.

I stuck my head round the door of a few treatment

rooms. The lack of lights on the heart monitor worried me but I realised it too had run out of battery and the chest of the person hooked up to it was still rising and falling under a blanket.

Paula was still out for the count where I'd left her. If nothing else she needed to get up and take care of her patients. I shook her and, when that didn't work, I pinched her nose and mouth shut until she sputtered back to consciousness. Her slaps and swats barely hurt and I stepped back out of reach before she could hit out any harder.

'The hell are you doing?' she groaned, rubbing at her face. 'Oh God, I feel like death.'

'I'm not surprised. You had a lot of vodka yesterday – have you seen any yellow plastic boxes of meds around? Or a nasal spray? Anything with Naloxone in it?' I was already pulling drawers out and checking them. Jade hadn't been kidding, the place was a mess. Organisation was clearly not Paula's strong suit. Then again, she was probably used to having nurses around to take care of that sort of thing and last time I'd been in here it hadn't exactly been well organised. I dumped stuff on the floor and went through it all, then moved onto another drawer, growing desperate.

'Naloxone? Someone's on . . . heroin?' Paula swung her legs off the bed and clutched at her head as if it might fall off and bounce across the floor if she didn't. 'Ah, shit.'

'Prescription opiate overdose to be exact. But yeah. We used all the doses in the syringe we had but she's still ODing and we need more.' I dropped an empty drawer on the floor and pulled out another. 'Defibrillator doesn't work either. Won't turn on.'

‘Not surprised . . . Whoever ran this place was a moron,’ Paula groaned. ‘Like, a barely qualified idiot. Probably let the battery expire . . . There’s more in there.’

I looked up and saw her waving at a corner cabinet. Inside I found two chunky orange rectangles. They looked like reusable icepacks but had stickers on them with dates and installation instructions. Spare batteries for the defibrillator.

Hallelujah. I grabbed them and started hunting through the rest of the cupboard.

‘Any idea where the Naloxone is?’ I demanded, crushing packets and tossing them aside to reach further back.

Paula sighed but levered herself off the bed and slumped towards the desk. She dug through several drawers next to it. Not nearly urgently enough for my liking. Once I was done with the cupboard I elbowed her out of the way and hauled the drawers out, throwing out folders and pens and boxes of gloves until my fingers clasped a pink box.

‘Yes! Fucking get in!’ I brandished the box of Narcan nasal spray, already angling myself towards the door. ‘If you find any more, take it up to the top floor and shout for Jade,’ I said, my heart soaring at this victory. ‘You should check on your patients. And if you find half a bottle of cognac upstairs? Don’t drink it. It’s poisoned. Don’t ask.’

I rushed back towards the foyer, clutching the Narcan. My pulse was wild with panic that I’d taken too long. That it was already too late. I could see Jade at the end of the hallway. She was poised as if in a relay race – ready to sprint back upstairs or towards the medical bay as the need arose.

‘Jade!’ I pulled my arm back and threw the box as hard

as I could. It flew down the hallway, dropped to the floor and rolled towards her. I slid the batteries along the floor like they were curling stones. She was on them before they stopped moving, turning and sprinting away like a champion cricketer, clutching them and the spray.

I staggered to a stop, a stitch in my side, heaving air into my burning lungs. I'd done all I could. My legs were like rubber and I couldn't run any more. There were instructions on the battery; she'd know what to do with it. I just needed to catch my breath.

For a few moments all I could hear was the pounding of my own pulse. Then a shout broke my fragile sense of relief and everything came rushing back. I turned towards the sound, which had come from the floor-to-ceiling glass doors to the outdoor spa area. Where the plunge pools, hot tubs and saunas were blanketed in snow. It had started to snow again, I realised, the fat flakes whirling from a grey sky, billowing through the air. Still, I could see the figures outside, struggling over the gun – solid black against the white and grey.

The gun went off and I threw myself sideways away from the window. Outside, a heating lamp shattered and Silvie screamed, ducking for cover. For a moment I couldn't see the gun, then Renard raised it. He'd won the struggle.

I moved automatically to the side of the glass doors, hiding. I eased the sliding door open a crack so I could hear what was happening outside. Not that anyone out there seemed to have noticed me. Silvie was watching Max as he backed away, hands up. His palms were reddened with cold, his cheeks too. Silvie was shivering, neither of them dressed for the weather out there. It had to have been a rash decision that had made them go outside. There was no way they'd get far without coats at least.

Renard held the gun steadily, despite the snow and the wind. He was stiff and robotic as he took a step forwards, forcing Max to step back once more. I watched in silent horror as Max's boot disappeared into the snow and kept going, his weight crashing through the covering on one of the pools. His hand flailed for the chrome railing but missed and I heard ice crack and water splash as he landed. After all this time without heating, that water had to be freezing, but he didn't yell. I realised he was probably too shocked by it to make a sound. That, or he was underwater still.

Renard stepped forwards and stopped a foot or so from the edge of the pool, where water had pitted the ice, and pointed the gun down at Max. Silvie scuttled towards him and I heard her voice as she held a hand out to him.

'Renard, don't! Just come with me – we can leave – get away before . . .'

Renard was already shaking his head and she trailed off. He turned his head slightly towards her, gun still trained on Max. 'There's no getting away with this. Not now . . . all we can do is finish it. Once and for all.'

So Silvie wasn't the main aggressor here. It was Renard. Had it always been or had things shifted? Was I witnessing a betrayal – Renard taking out a co-conspirator, or was Max innocent and even now potentially drowning in the icy water?

Maybe at some point in the future, I'll understand why I did it. After all, I'd just told Aloisia that we had to start planning things, stop reacting and rushing around. I'd built an entire career managing other people's crises, without becoming part of them. I was an outsider, moving between catastrophes and seldom appearing as part of the story. I was behind the cameras, on a burner phone, not turning up at the media circus outside my clients' homes. I did a lot, but one thing I never did was put myself on the line. Not for anyone. Not for any amount of money in the world.

But, for some reason – maybe a guilty conscience, maybe idiotic instinct, certainly nothing so worthy as bravery or heroism – I slid the glass door open and stepped out into the buffeting wind.

Chapter 26

If I'd thought the cold was bracing before under a heap of outdoor gear, it was practically lethal now. The wind stole my breath as I stepped out onto the snow, soundless in my sheepskin slippers. The icy air felt like needles penetrating me to the bone and injecting ice water into my marrow. My heart actually skipped a beat at the shock of it. The whirling snowflakes stung at my cheeks and I blinked rapidly, terrified that they'd blind me and leave me even more defenceless than I already was.

Silvie noticed me first. Renard was too focused on the pool and Max to glance sideways, but she was face on to the door. I didn't hear her make a sound as her eyes widened but she must have gasped or said something because Renard glanced her way and then turned to look at me.

For a second he didn't move, as if he was weighing his options, trying to come to a decision. Then he turned the gun on me. 'Go back inside – this has nothing to do with you.'

He sounded tired, resigned. Not angry at me – not yet. I held my hands up automatically. 'I know, believe me, but . . . I thought maybe I could help.'

'Help?' Renard repeated, his voice edged with a bitter laugh. 'No one can help me. Not now. It'll all come out and that'll be it. I'm fucked and I know it.'

'You'd be surprised,' I said, as he turned away back towards Max who I could hear thrashing in the water, probably trying to reach the side. I sidestepped to keep myself in his line of sight. 'Whatever it is, I can almost guarantee I've dealt with worse. That's my job by the way – crisis manager. I can't remember if I told you that before, but I'm good at it. Really good. So . . . maybe I can help?'

'Crisis manager, Jesus . . .' Renard's eyes were red I realised. As if he'd been crying, out here in the icy air. 'This isn't a "crisis" – it's justice,' he said firmly, glaring down at Max, who I could now see a little of, enough to tell he was still alive, for now. He was by the edge of the pool, hands on the side but obviously too afraid to climb out and make himself a target.

'Justice for what?' I asked, keeping my voice curious rather than judgemental or incredulous. The same way I'd handle a stressed-out client who was being cagey about the details of whatever career-ending blunder they'd called me in to handle. 'Must be something pretty awful . . . You can tell me. I've heard it all.'

'Go back inside,' Renard said again, sounding more annoyed than tired this time. 'I won't tell you again. This isn't your business and if you stay out here, you're going to get hurt. Go. Back. Inside.'

I didn't even consider it, not for a second. Again, I don't think it was bravery so much as . . . pride. I'd come out here to handle this and that was exactly what I was going to do. Chloe Wallace did not back down from a crisis, even if it involved a gun in my face.

I licked my chapped lips and they immediately started to burn in the cold. 'I can't do that. I'm sorry. I really am . . . but I'm out here now and I think that you could use my help. See . . . I don't think you wanted to hurt anyone,' I said, though I knew no such thing, but it was an educated guess. I'd known Renard a few days now and seen him in the room where we'd found Jan's body. He didn't seem the type to relish violence; he'd hardly been able to handle looking at the blood. He wasn't the type to enjoy the suffering of others – that was a type I'd met many times, a great example of which was currently tied to a chair in the foyer. Renard was different.

'You don't know me,' Renard snapped. 'You have no idea what I've been . . . what's been happening here.'

'OK . . . why don't you tell me?' I said gently. 'I want to know. We've spent a bit of time together, haven't we? You know what a nosy piece of work I am so . . . tell me. I might not know much but I know hurting Max isn't going to make things better for you. Or for Silvie.'

That seemed to hit home with him. He did care about her, I was right on that front. But it also seemed to rile him up more. He twisted to glare at me while keeping the gun on Max, who was shivering, disturbing the water. He glared at Renard but didn't dare speak. The snow was still coming down, occasionally blowing into my eyes, making me blink.

Maybe it was the loss of eye contact that gave Renard his spark back. 'You don't care about Silvie, or me. You're only out for yourself like the rest of the pricks that come here – like this waste of space.' He waved the gun in Max's direction. 'You all think you've got actual problems but you're just rich and awful. No cure needed except a dose of reality. You'll say or do anything to take care of yourself. No matter who gets hurt.'

He was sort of right, I had to give him that. OK, sympathy wasn't working – time to try shock. Riskier but it might have the desired effect. I wasn't about to give up now.

'Was that what you were doing, when you blocked the equipment room door?' I said, and Renard's shoulders slumped a little bit. 'Was that "doing anything it takes, no matter who gets hurt"? You shut us out, knowing we might be killed by wolves, or freeze. Was that to protect yourself, and Silvie?'

'. . . Yes,' Renard said, but the pause told me more than the single-word answer.

Silvie moved then, stepping forwards to confirm my suspicion. 'I blocked the door.'

'Silvie!' Renard snapped. 'Don't.'

'I did,' she insisted. 'I brought the doctor some tea after Renard told me a group had gone out to the lodge . . . I wasn't thinking about anything other than getting rid of Lionel . . . I'm sorry. I never wanted to hurt anybody else. Anybody innocent, but I wasn't thinking straight. I just wanted him gone, and Renard . . . he was panicking.'

I had both of them talking. What I was going to do now I didn't really know. This was not something I'd been trained for or encountered outside of cheesy films. Talking down a man with a gun wasn't in my repertoire, so there was going to be an unfortunate amount of trial and error at work in my approach. I tried not to think about what 'error' would mean in this case. I didn't plan to fail and if I did, well . . . it wasn't as if I'd have long to dwell on it.

'Tell me about Lionel,' I prompted, trying to keep

her talking and not let Renard regain control over the situation. 'Tell me what had you so scared of him? What made Renard panic?'

Nothing. Silvie's eyes were all over the place but she didn't offer a single word in her defence. She'd receded into herself again, whether out of guilt or fear I couldn't tell.

'Or, maybe we should start with Lars?' I pushed. 'He was the first, right? The one you really wanted dead? So much so you tried to kill him twice in one day. That's a pretty big risk.'

She looked to Renard and he shook his head slightly. The cold was in my bones now. I could only imagine how the two of them felt, having been out in it for a while now without so much as a glove between them.

'Why don't we move inside where it's warmer?' I tried. 'You both look frozen, why don't we—'

I sucked in a painfully cold breath as Renard's arm moved suddenly, pointing up at the grey sky. The shot made me jump, and it echoed around us, carrying through the mountains. Renard slowly lowered the gun, training it on me.

'You go, we'll stay,' he said. 'I'm not leaving until he's dead like the rest of them. That's all I've got now. I'm not going away for the rest of my life and leaving him free. You let me kill him and I promise, everyone else will be safe.'

I was shaking with more than the cold now. Out of the corner of my eye I saw Max lying on the side of the pool. He must have pulled himself up when the gun went off, taking his chance while everyone was distracted. My teeth chattered in fear as I tried to force words off my tongue. I had to keep talking – it was all I could do to keep Renard looking at me.

'What's the plan after that then?' I asked. 'You shoot Max and then . . . try and walk off this mountain without so much as a woolly hat on and a half-loaded gun to protect you from the wolves?'

Renard's eyes flickered and I didn't dare look away to see how Silvie was reacting. He had doubts, I could see that. Buried, but very much there. He knew he wasn't some kind of wild-mountain man capable of pulling off a great escape like that. If he left the retreat in a storm like this he was as good as dead.

Max was on his feet now, crouching. I couldn't tell without turning my head and giving him away, but I thought he was watching Renard. Waiting for an opening. I didn't trust him any more than I did Renard, but I didn't want to be the reason he got shot either. If he went for the gun that would at least get it off me. Maybe give me a chance to get it away from both of them and calm this situation down.

'If you do make it – without coats or food and only the one gun – where would you go?' I asked, and didn't give him a chance to respond before ploughing onward. 'Up here there might be no CCTV, but the real world is out there, with cameras and licence plate recognition and bank records. You can't hide, not in this day and age – not without practice or some idea of the traps you need to avoid.'

'And what, you want to help us with that?' Renard interrupted. 'After Silvie just admitted to trying to kill you . . . why would you help us?'

Max was further into my field of vision now – creeping

towards Renard and ready to strike. Just a few more moments. I had to keep Renard and Silvie from noticing him.

I slowly lowered my hands, keeping them well away from my pockets. But I had to show a little trust. This moment was crucial, I could feel it. For the first time I was close to having him. I just had to give him a reason to believe me. If he wouldn't accept altruism, how about something a little baser? I had to keep him distracted.

'The same reason I help anyone . . . money,' I said. 'If you can give me the vault code . . . I can give you some tips, help you evade capture and get out of the country.'

I knew I'd fucked up before the words were completely out. Renard's expression went stiff and his lip curled into a sneer. For the first time he looked like he hated me.

'Money – just like the rest of them, you . . . argh!' he kicked at the snow, furiously waving the gun about in a way that seemed to unnerve even Silvie. 'This is not about fucking money – it's about right and wrong! He needs to be punished!'

My hands had crept back up as the gun steadied on me and I nodded, hoping to appease him. 'OK . . . OK . . . You obviously have a cause, a reason for doing all this . . . so why not tell me? Hmm? Tell me so it gets out there, so people know. Because this place will never let the real story get out – you know that. They'll say you went nuts and killed a load of people for no reason, just to cover their own arses. I see it every day – they will bury the truth so deep no one else will ever know to even look for it. So tell me. Let me help you.'

He wavered. But my advantage would be fleeting. I needed to hook him, get him to listen to me, to keep engaging, but how? My mind was working overtime, fuelled by fear and desperation. What did I know about the security guards, about Lars? What would lift the lid on whatever it was that had caused Renard to back himself into this corner? What could convince him that I was on his side? What could I offer him that he didn't already have?

And then I had it.

'I have Lars's notebook,' I said and saw immediately that I was on the right track. Renard's attention was fully on me as soon as the words escaped my lips. The gun stayed where it was, pointing at me. Max was poised on the ground, waiting for his chance.

'I found it hidden in his room,' I continued. 'A list of initials, dates, amounts of money. He was up to something – I just don't know what . . . But you do, don't you? That's how all this started, right? With Lars? With his notebook you can prove it. You can prove you had a reason to do what you've done here. Mitigating circumstances. Whatever it was that made you choose to kill him . . .'

'We didn't have a choice . . .' Silvie whimpered, interrupting me.

Renard instantly tried to silence her. 'Shut up, Silvie – you can't—'

But she cut him off by laying a hand lightly on his arm. 'We're not getting away from here, Renard,' she said softly. 'She's right, even if we made it off the mountain, we'd be caught soon enough. We don't have any idea how to avoid the police, and our fingerprints and DNA are all over the place here. Once they can get through the snow, it's over for us.'

'Then we go out together.' Renard held up the gun, but there was doubt all over his face now. Desperation. He didn't believe what he was saying and both Silvie and I knew it.

Silvie slowly shook her head. 'I don't want to die . . . I don't think you do, either.'

'You'd rather go to prison?' Renard pressed. 'You'd rather I end up in prison?'

'I can't decide for you . . . but I'd rather live. At least prison would be better than what we lived with here,' Silvie said, and finally turned to me, a determined crease to her brow. 'I tried to kill Lars. OK? I'll admit that. I read in the guest paperwork that we had someone coming in from a rehab centre and those clients always seem to only want to score when they get out. So I stole his pills and I put it in Lars's cognac, because I couldn't take it anymore. I couldn't live with what he was doing to me, to us. What they were all doing.'

'Shut your mouth, bitch.' Max's voice was unsteady, his teeth chattering from the extreme cold. 'You've got no proof.'

Renard immediately rounded on him, shocking he'd crawled so close. I could have killed Max myself for ruining the advantage he'd had. Renard pointed the gun at him and I fought to keep my voice calm as frustration threatened to take over.

'They'll have the notebook,' I said, trying to force Max to shut up as I fixed Renard with my eyes. 'You have my word – you can have it. And if you had good reason – self-defence, maybe? – I can make that work. I can try and spin this for you, if you tell me what happened.'

'You're both going away,' Max was shivering badly

but no less furious because of it. 'She can't help you. You might as well blow your brains out right here, right now. Because no one is going to believe you.'

I was willing him to shut up. Did he not see that I was trying to save his life as well as mine? Even if, as I now suspected, he'd been involved in something criminal here, surely being prosecuted had to be better than being shot out here.

'If it was a blackmail ring or attempted robbery – anything – trust me, I can explain your side,' I said, talking over him, directly to Renard. 'But you have to promise not to kill him, or anyone else. That's my only term. All right? I don't need anything else from you. I don't want money, I just want the killing to stop. Right now.'

Silvie looked to Renard and he looked helplessly back. I could see the resignation in them both. But she'd found her voice now and I could feel the story ready to come out. She was going to talk, finally, after days of secrecy.

'. . . I tried to poison Lars,' Silvie began, wrapping her arms around herself in a futile attempt to keep warm. 'Because he was keeping us prisoner here. Both of us. All of us.'

Chapter 27

'A few years ago I got kicked out of the house by my mother, because my stepdad didn't want to live with "someone else's kid",' Silvie said, sounding resigned and flat. The snow dusted her hair and I could see her tears making tracks over her wind-reddened face. She looked so much younger now than she had when we'd first met. All that professional sparkle stripped away to reveal the broken woman beneath.

'I was homeless for a few months, going from sofa to sofa, friend to friend until there was no one left to give me a bed for the night,' Silvie continued. 'I couldn't get a real job with no address, couldn't do anything. So I started working for cash, just what little work I could get. And also stealing – hanging around cafés and train stations, going through bags people left unattended, taking wallets out of coats. I ended up getting arrested a few times and once quite seriously charged, after using a stolen credit card. Not the first time I'd been caught but the first time it stuck. And with a criminal record I wasn't going to get a job and even finding a place to stay was harder. It all seemed completely hopeless . . . and then I met Lars.

'He posted an advert in this sketchy online group I was using to find work, looking for live-in staff. No need for references. Seemed like the solution to all my problems – somewhere to live, heating and food, and money of course – so I applied and he immediately got back to me. He'd already checked my name out and he knew I had a record but he said that didn't matter. He'd give me a chance. I was absolutely thrilled, and so grateful. You have no idea how desperate I was.'

I had a fair idea actually. Having been raised in care I didn't have a support system once I aged out. Not really. I'd taken my share of sketchy jobs that promised the bare bones of living conditions – housemaid, night carer, overnight hotel receptionist. There was one universal truth about all live-in jobs that I'd learned the hard way: once you were in, they thought they owned you. Because they did. They controlled your access to housing, to your wages, everything. Looking at Silvie now, it was clear she'd learned the same lesson. I wasn't focusing on the gun in Renard's hand now, or on Max. I was caught up in her story and needed to know how it had ended here.

'I couldn't believe my luck when I saw this place.' Silvie's smile was sad and twisted by tears. 'It was like a paradise and I got my own room, hot meals three times a day, a uniform instead of my old clothes . . . I felt like a person again. I thought I could save some money and after a year or so maybe get some qualifications, start building a career in hospitality. That my life was going to be back on track now. And then I found out what Lars was really doing and by then it was too late to get out.'

I could imagine. We were, after all, halfway up a

mountain in the middle of nowhere. If Silvie decided she wanted out, where would she go? All right, so she could get down to the lower station and maybe get a ride out to the airport in one of The Sorgente guest cars, but it wasn't as easy as just leaving and walking to the train station. Lars was management – if he said 'no lifts' she wasn't going to get one. Even her clothes weren't hers, for crying out loud.

'He hired all of us that way,' Renard said, when Silvie had been silent for long enough that it was clear she couldn't go on. 'I think he just went by the pictures online – picked people who'd fit in here but with "problems" he could offer to fix. I had a conviction for drug possession and for dealing from when I was a teenager. I needed a job and no one would hire me, no one that was willing to pay good money, anyway.'

'Because you were a fucking criminal,' Max spat. 'Both of you. Jesus, you were lucky to get a job here! And now you're crying because it was hard? Because you couldn't run away again? Pssht.' He shook his head. 'You were ungrateful brats.'

'We were prisoners!' Renard snapped back, brandishing the gun again. Max just glared at him. Renard resumed his tale. 'Then I saw the advert. Lars said he'd take me on. Give me a chance – paid for me to get the train out here, picked me up, drove me to The Sorgente. Showed me my room, made it all sound so great and then . . .' He shook his head bitterly. 'I should have known, really, that he wasn't just giving people like me a chance. He just looked so boring, so . . . normal. I thought he was a religious do-gooder, you know? That he wanted to save people. But no, he wanted money. Just like the bastards who got me to deal for them when I was a kid. That's why he hired us, to make money for him.'

'He faked your security checks,' I said slowly, remembering what Aloisia had told me about Lars's responsibilities in that area. Easy for him to falsify a clean record – who would question Lars's word? He was so dull, so predictable looking. The furthest thing from a human trafficker you could imagine, yet that was exactly what he'd been.

'He gave you a job, convinced Aloisia that you were all good candidates and then I'm guessing . . . he demanded part of your salary?' I said.

'You owed him,' Max hissed.

Renard ignored him. 'He let us keep ten per cent, I guess so it would look like we still had spending money, even if it was barely enough for a few snacks and the casual clothes and toiletries he sold us. He called the rest his "finder's fee", and of course I threatened to go over his head, out him and his little scheme, but no one was going to believe me. He knew it. I knew it. And he had security helping him keep us here. We didn't even have money for a train fare – we were trapped. We all were and he knew it. We needed him for everything. Couldn't so much as get a new toothbrush without going through him. He even opened our mail.'

'It wasn't that bad, to start with,' Silvie interrupted. 'I mean, we had somewhere to live and we were earning something at least. We were all in the same situation mostly, and the work wasn't hard. I wasn't going hungry or trying to sleep in cinemas and stations . . . but it got worse. He started wanting things. Favours. They all did.'

I thought of Aloisia telling me she'd seen Silvie and

Lars together in the sauna and I shuddered. Apparently exploiting their labour hadn't been enough; Lars had wanted Silvie's body as well. I could see from her expression that she knew I'd worked it out. Had Aloisia known, or at least suspected? Was that why she'd pretended to forget that Silvie was the one who lied about Lars's whereabouts? Was she trying to cover up what had happened here? Had she been part of it?

'You wanted it,' Max said, apparently unable to keep from defending himself, even though he was being held at gunpoint. 'You sold yourself for a little extra cash.'

'You shut your mouth!' Renard said as Silvie again receded into herself. 'He had us stealing for him too,' he continued sharply, driving each word into Max like nails. 'If we got caught, Lars would fire us, keep his hands clean. Again, if we tried to defend ourselves, tell the truth, no one was going to believe a thief with a criminal record he'd be able to expose. He had the whole security team on his side. Watching us on camera all day every day, monitoring any calls we made on the phone system, checking our internet activity. A few people tried to just walk out but they got their stuff searched and anything of value confiscated – even money they'd saved. He paid us into accounts he controlled, handed out our share in cash. We'd be leaving with nothing. Not even a fucking snack for the road. His thugs took everything.'

'He was using us too,' Max spat. Was he getting desperate now? Realising he was running out of time to defend himself or taunt Renard into making a mistake. 'I've got stuff in my past, you know – he brought me in and held that over me. I didn't have a say.'

'But he paid you,' Renard snapped. 'We know it – you

got your salary, you got the same "perks" he did. He was stealing from us and buying your silence – that's not the same.'

Max scoffed. 'I'm not going to be lectured by a fucking drug dealer. A murderer, no less. You got treated like scum because that's what you are – look what you did here!'

Renard flinched at the word 'murderer' and tried to hide it. But I could see the regret in his face. He hadn't wanted any of this. I could see that now. But like a rat in a trap he'd grown feral and frenzied, ready to lash out at anyone or anything that he thought stood between him and freedom. It must have been unbearable, knowing just how trapped he was, that Lars had tricked him.

I breathed in air so cold it felt sharp and tucked my hands further into my armpits. I wasn't about to suggest we go inside again. Not while Renard still had the gun. I had to stay and listen and then maybe he'd be satisfied. Maybe he'd trust me enough to hand Max over to the police instead of killing him in front of me. As deplorable as what security and Lars had been doing was, it didn't warrant a death sentence and certainly wasn't worth Renard getting in even worse trouble and possibly hurting someone innocent into the bargain. This had to end.

'I couldn't live like that anymore,' Silvie said, turning sad eyes on me. 'I'd just started to suspect that I was . . . I was pregnant and I wasn't willing to have his baby or get kicked back onto the street with it. There aren't many places without cameras, but the office is one of them. I was desperate – I had to get away from here with some money, some way to get myself help, but he was never going to let me go.'

So she'd poisoned Lars. But hadn't waited for him to drink it before bashing his skull in? Something didn't make sense, and apparently it showed on my face because Renard stepped in.

'I didn't know she'd done it. Maybe if I had, none of this would have happened. But, the day of the avalanche, Lars took me aside and told me he wanted me to help him blackmail that politician's wife – that I was good-looking and she was pissed off with her husband, so it'd be easy for me to seduce her and get it on video. That she'd pay to keep it quiet, or her husband would buy it as evidence for the divorce. It made me sick. He wanted me to get her drunk and . . . Anyway, I said no and he told me about . . . about Silvie.' He paused and shook his head, face contorted with disgust. 'She never told me about . . . that. None of the girls did.'

'Because it's a lie,' Max growled. 'That's what she is – a liar! Just like you.'

'I couldn't,' Silvie muttered and Renard reached over and took her hand in his, gently, as if she was made of ice and might crack.

'I was horrified and it made me . . . so angry. I just . . . lost it,' Renard said quietly. 'I hit him with a catering can and he went down. One hit and he was dead! I didn't mean to do it, for him to die, but after that I didn't have a choice! I knew I had to get out of here before he was found. Before it all came out and I was sent to prison. So I stuffed him in the freezer with the can and locked it, tried to make sure no one would find him until later. The plan was to wait until after the welcome dinner and then get myself fired, like Lilli just had. I thought I could get out of here before anyone found out what I'd done. I wasn't even planning on what to do once I got out of here. I just had to be gone before anyone knew what had happened.'

'And then the avalanche happened,' I said.

'Yeah.' Renard's face took on a humourless smile. 'Of all the luck, right? Suddenly I was stuck here – even more trapped than before – and everything was going crazy. There wasn't any way out and Aloisia was looking for Lars. I knew she'd find him eventually. The food situation was pretty dire and that freezer was going to get opened.'

'But you lied about Lars during dinner,' I said to Silvie. 'Did you know he was dead, that Renard had killed him already?'

She shook her head. 'I thought he'd taken the bottle back to his room – he sometimes drank before work, not much, but the odd glass. He said it made it easier to tolerate the guests. When he didn't show up to the briefing I thought he'd been poisoned and I just wanted to keep Aloisia from finding him until he was beyond help,' she said. 'That's why I shut you out. I thought that way it wouldn't get out that Lars was poisoned. It wasn't until you came back from the lodge and said you hadn't found him that I realised he wasn't dead in there. Later, I started to put together what was happening with Jan and Nils and . . . I thought maybe it was one of the other security guards, that they were trying to take over from Lars or they wanted out and were destroying the evidence. After Lionel, I thought it was Max trying to shut everyone up about what had been happening here. I didn't know it was Renard until he pulled the gun on Max.'

'Not so easy is it, to kill someone face to face?' Max

said. 'I should have guessed it was you that killed the others. Cowardly – striking from behind.'

'I didn't mean to kill anyone,' Renard insisted. 'I just . . . Lars was a mistake. A . . . I was angry and it just happened. But then the avalanche hit and I realised I was stuck here and that as soon as someone found Lars they'd check the cameras in the storeroom and I'd be caught. I just wanted to destroy the system, get rid of any proof that I'd done it.'

'You're the one who attacked me,' I said, as neutrally as possible, despite the fact that he could have easily killed me by accident. 'For the keys.'

He nodded miserably. 'I wasn't thinking when I stashed Lars, or I'd have taken his set. But I had to get into the security room and I thought Jan was checking on the utility building. He came back and surprised me. I panicked. He saw me messing with the system, he tried to grab me and I grabbed the hole punch . . . I just . . . I hit him. I kept hitting him.'

'You can't pretend it was an accident,' Max snarled, bristling with the cold and fury. 'You murdered Lars, you killed Jan, then you took a gun and went after Nils. You wanted revenge from the start.'

'That's not true!' Renard pointed the gun at him emphatically and then wavered, lowering it as if horrified at himself. 'I took the rifle for protection – from the wolves. I had to get to the lodge and grab my stuff and whatever valuables Lars hadn't sold yet, then try and get away on foot. With the rifle I stood a chance, at least.'

'But Nils saw you packing up,' I supplied.

Renard's shoulders slumped. 'He knew Lars was missing by then – Aloisia was asking everyone if he'd been seen. I was in Lars's room, stealing back what he'd taken from me. Nils came upstairs and I panicked, tried to get away, dropped my bag and he pulled his gun . . .' He looked on the verge of tears. 'I've never used a gun before. The rifle just went off. I was just holding it with my finger on the trigger and I didn't mean to . . .' He trailed off and looked down at the ground. Silvie was still holding his hand and she rested her cheek on his shoulder. I wondered if she truly believed he was innocent or if it didn't matter to her. If she just understood what had made him do all this, because she'd felt the same thing.

'And Lionel?' Max asked mercilessly, his face hard as ice. 'Did your finger slip then too?'

Slowly, Renard shook his head. 'He saw the handgun I'd taken from Nils. I hid the rifle once I got back to the main building, away from the wolves. But I kept the other one, in case I got cornered. It was tucked into the back of my trousers and he saw it when he came out of the reception door to check on us. Even in the dark, he must've seen it against my shirt. He knew I had to have taken it from Nils. He was going to tell everyone what I'd done . . . and I shot him before he could. I killed him, on purpose. Are you happy now?' he spat at Max. 'I'm a murderer! I admit it. Why don't you admit what you've done?'

Max's mouth set into a thin, hard line, but he didn't move or speak. Renard scoffed under his breath and I shared his contempt in that moment. Max was far from innocent. If Renard and Silvie were telling the truth, all of them – the security guards and Lars – had been at the very least guilty of human trafficking and enslavement. Not to mention the sexual assault and coercion.

But that didn't mean I was going to let Renard kill again.

I held out my hand.

'Give me the gun, please, Renard,' I said, as calmly as I could. 'You can end this, right now. Just give me the gun.'

Chapter 28

I held my breath, waiting. This was the moment I'd know if I'd irrevocably messed up – if I'd managed to get Renard to trust me, or if I'd just provoked a killer. My hand hovered in the empty air, fingers numb with cold. I was hit with the mad thought that this would be such an embarrassing way to die.

There were no more moves to make though. Nothing more that I could say. I held my hand out and waited, hoping that it was enough. That, after everything I'd been through, I wasn't about to get shot dead on a frozen patio.

'Renard,' Silvie breathed. 'Please. End this now.'

Renard looked at the gun in his hand. Then his eyes met mine. Slowly, so slowly I thought at first that I was imagining it out of hysterical hope, he held the gun out, offering me the grip.

Without daring to breathe, I took it. It was heavier than I thought it would be and cold as ice. I let out a slow breath as I pointed it down at the ground. If I'd known how, I'd have taken out the bullets or put the safety on, something, but that would just have to do for now. At least it was in my hand and no longer pointed at my face.

Renard seemed to slump inwards with relief and resignation. Silvie wrapped her arms around him protectively, her eyes finding mine. 'What happens now?' she asked.

I opened my mouth to answer and Max barrelled into me from the side. We hit the snow-covered ground together in a tangle of arms and legs. Silvie screamed and Renard was cursing but I couldn't see what he was doing. I was face down in the snow and I could feel Max's fingers tearing at mine. I clung to the gun until it felt like he was going to break my bones to get it, but it wasn't enough.

A moment later I was alone on the ground and struggling over onto my back. Above me, Max had scrambled to his feet and was pointing the gun at the three of us in turn. Keeping us at bay while he caught his breath.

'Right . . . now, this is how it's going to go,' he said, dark eyes darting between us. 'You – Chloe, are going to give me that notebook, and then maybe I'll let you live, once I've killed these two in self-defence.'

'You bastard!' Silvie screamed, wild in panic, and I flinched in fear for her. Max could kill any one of us with the squeeze of a trigger. He wouldn't need any more provocation. He was already looking at a very long prison sentence. Renard seemed to realise this as well – he caught Silvie's arm and held her in place as she moved as if to run at Max. She collapsed into sobs.

'The book,' Max said, holding out his free hand and circling around, coming closer to me but keeping the others in his eyeline. 'Or I take it from your body.'

'I don't have it on me,' I lied. It came out so smoothly – that's what a lifetime of practice had earned me. 'I hid it after Lionel died. I didn't know who to trust.'

'Where is it?' Max asked immediately, his face twitching with impatience.

'I'll tell you, once I know I'm getting out of here,' I said. 'Without it they have no proof. You don't need to kill them.'

He smiled slightly then and I saw the man behind the mask. The man who'd held Silvie and Renard prisoner here for Lars. For money. 'I know I don't have to . . . but I owe them, for coming after me.'

I glanced sideways at Silvie, who was holding onto Renard tightly with her eyes screwed shut. Renard was looking at the gun, mouth quivering as he realised he was going to die right here. I looked back at Max and my heart went still. I opened my mouth but no sound would come out. I couldn't so much as twitch a finger to point.

'What the fuck are you . . . ?' Max began to turn, then stopped himself. He was too afraid to look away from us.

I was too afraid to look away from the wolf.

It must have crept onto the patio while I was distracted, fighting over the gun and watching Max to see what he'd do with it. It wasn't moving, but was tense with the promise of sudden action. Its mouth hung open, foggy breath rising into the cold air. My own breath caught in my throat, which felt like it was closing up. A choked-off wheezing noise escaped me.

'Stop that!' Max pointed the gun squarely at my chest. 'The fuck are you doing?'

'Oh, shit.' Renard had seen the wolf and his tongue wasn't shrivelled by fear. He looked my way at the door to the spa, calculating the distance. I heard Silvie whimper as his fingers dug into her arm. He was getting ready to drag her to safety.

The wolf began to move and picked up speed so quickly that everything else seemed to slow down. My heart punched painfully at my ribs. Renard moved and Max shouted a warning, turning the gun on him. But Renard wasn't stopping for anything.

The wolf leaped and caught Max in the back, bringing him to the ground. I screamed as the gun went off, and that broke my trance of fear. Silvie was screaming too as Renard dragged her to the spa door.

A horrible gurgling sound made the hair on my body stand on end. Blood steamed on the snow. Splashes and gouts of it as the wolf clamped its jaws around Max's neck and shook him like a terrier would a limp rat.

Bile stung my throat. I couldn't will my limbs to move. My mind was working again, but the rest of me was frozen to the spot in terror.

'Chloe!' Renard yelled from a crack in the spa door. 'Run!'

But I couldn't.

Max's arm flailed in the bloody snow. Was he still alive or was it some muscle tic, the force of the wolf's continued mauling? I couldn't tell – my eyes were full of tears, stung raw by the snowy wind.

Something skidded across the ground into my foot. I looked down and saw a blur of black in the white and red. The gun.

A growl had my head snapping up again, eyes fixed on those of the wolf. Its face was smeared with blood and it bore its teeth at me. The scar on my arm felt like it was on fire with the memory of fangs tearing into my flesh.

'Chloe!' Renard yelled.

My whole life I'd struggled, lied and thought only

of myself – to survive. To keep going. All that instinct streamed through me then, contorting my muscles, fighting the terrified paralysis that had come over me. It forced me down and my hand found the icy weight of the gun.

I felt hot breath on my face. Heard the thud of paws on snow.

I screamed and brought the gun up, pulling the trigger. My finger spasmed on it, over and over, until clicking replaced the deafening blasts.

A mess of grey had joined the dark shape of Max's body on the ground. I collapsed onto all fours, the gun still clutched tightly in my hand, and vomited into the snow. Acid burned my throat and my eyes swam with tears. I didn't resist when someone grabbed me and pulled me upright.

Renard half dragged, half carried me to the spa door and helped me through it, closing it tightly behind us. My body was wracked with shivers and I clutched at my arms and torso where the snow on my clothes was melting.

Silvie barrelled into me and I automatically grabbed her. Renard wrapped his arms around us both. I felt as if we'd just survived a car crash. All that noise and sudden bloody violence. I had to force myself to breathe.

Renard pulled back first. 'He's dead. It's . . . It's over.'

'We're still trapped here,' I said in a voice that sounded strange to my own ears. As if I was hearing myself on a recording underwater. 'But help will come – police will come.'

We separated and I saw Silvie and Renard exchange a look. One that said they had briefly forgotten about the weight of their crimes. The fact that I knew about them. We'd been brought together by the relief of surviving that awful moment outside. Now, though, they were once again the criminals and I was the witness.

'We all need to get warm,' I said. 'We wait and then . . . when help comes, I'll be there with you. To explain.'

'And if they won't listen?' Renard said.

'I can make them listen.' The shock was fading and my confidence returning on a wave of adrenaline. 'We have the notebook to back up your story. I expect it's records of how much Lars was making off every staff member – he couldn't risk that being digital. But there'll be evidence of the criminal record checks he falsified somewhere, and the police will find it. I bet the guards got sloppy – maybe there are messages between them that can be recovered. Trust me, we did not survive that just for you two to end up serving life.'

They exchanged looks, and Silvie slowly nodded. Renard took her hand. 'All right . . . I suppose we just have to trust you. There's been too much death here. I don't want anyone else to get hurt.'

'All right, let's go find the others,' I said, waving them towards the corridor and following on wobbly legs.

I fell behind them a little as we trailed along the corridor. My body was still flooded with fear and relief and so much stress that I could hardly believe that I was alive and uninjured. The numbness of my frozen body just added to my sense of unreality. I was OK. The last of Lars's little gang was dead and gone. For the first time since the avalanche I felt safe.

We'd just reached the bottom of the foyer stairs when I heard shouting from above. I rushed to catch up with Silvie and Renard and turned to see Aloisia standing halfway down the stairs, pointing a rifle at the three of us.

The sight of another gun made my heart start hammering. But I told myself that it was Aloisia – she was on my side. I swallowed a bitter gulp of saliva and managed to speak up.

'Aloisia! It's OK . . . I've got things under control.' I held the empty gun up in as non-threatening a way as I could. 'It's over. Silvie and Renard confessed. They're not going to hurt anyone else.'

Patrick, forgotten on his chair across the foyer – began to yell. 'Where's that guard? Who was shooting? Let me go, now!'

Aloisia ignored Patrick but her wide eyes moved over the three of us. Her face was tense with suspicion and fear.

'Confessed? To what? Did they kill Lars? The security guards? What is going on?' Aloisia demanded, her voice growing shrill with panic. 'I found this—' she looked down at the gun in her hands '—just outside the roof door. How did it get there?'

'I hid it,' Renard admitted, somewhat sheepishly. 'It was the only place I thought no one would go . . . and where I could hide if and when the police came.'

'So it's true – you killed Lars and everyone else?' Aloisia asked him, tightening her hold on the rifle. 'Why? Jesus, Renard, why would you do that?'

'Because he was keeping us prisoner here,' Renard cried. 'No one would have listened to me, I didn't have a choice!'

'You could have come to me, I'd have believed you . . . Oh my God . . .' She lowered the gun slightly. 'All this insanity . . . Jesus, where's Max?'

I wet my paper-dry lips. 'Max is dead. I confronted them outside, he got hold of the gun and tried to kill these two, and probably would have killed me if a wolf hadn't got to him first.'

'A . . . Oh my God, Max. He didn't deserve . . .' Aloisia's voice trailed off and she turned slightly grey with shock.

Silvie spoke up, her voice tight and full of unshed tears. 'He was a rapist. Just like Lars. He hurt me, hurt Lilli.'

Lilli? The girl who'd narrowly escaped being trapped here by the avalanche because Aloisia had fired her just hours before? Because, in Aloisia's own words, she was a thief. And a liar.

'That . . . can't be true,' Aloisia whispered.

'You see – you wouldn't have believed us!' Renard cried. 'They were doing it right under your nose and you never even knew.'

Aloisia looked between us all again and then slowly lowered the rifle, looking stunned. 'If it is true, then it needs to come out . . . but right now you both need to be kept away from the others. You must see that?'

'I thought we could put these two in the storeroom – for their safety as much as ours. The other guests might not take kindly to them being allowed to walk free,' I said.

'If that's what it takes for everyone to feel safe, we'll do it,' Silvie said with an air of resignation. 'Please, just let us stay together.'

'That's . . . doable,' Aloisia said. 'OK – I'll come with you.'

She joined me in steering the pair of them towards the reception door. We all ignored Patrick's continued demands for freedom and soon we had Silvie and Renard shut in the storeroom. They seemed to relax a little once they were in an enclosed space, even with the presence of

Lars's body in there, shut in the freezer. They could easily ignore him in there. I think they just wanted to be alone now that the weight of deception was off them.

Aloisia locked the door with a master key. With Renard and Silvie no longer on a murder spree and the last crooked guard dead outside, I felt as if I could breathe again for the first time since I saw the three of them on the terrace. I leaned heavily against the wall outside and looked at Aloisia, who seemed to be just as done in as I was.

'How's Carri?' I asked, my anxiety spiking again as I remembered what had sent me rushing to the spa in the first place. 'Is the nasal spray working?'

'For now,' she said. 'I don't know how long it'll keep her conscious for. But we got a new battery into the defibrillator, it's working now if we need it . . . Can you please explain to me what the hell is going on with my staff?'

I heaved a sigh. 'I still don't know all the details but . . . it seems as if Lars was falsifying security checks in order to hire people with past convictions or legal trouble, and once he got them here he was pocketing most of their salary and using them to steal from guests. It seems he and the guards he was paying off took advantage of Silvie and who knows who else . . . That's what you saw when they were in the sauna.'

Aloisia covered her mouth and silently closed her eyes. It couldn't have been easy to hear. I was still trying to wrap my head around it after everything else that had happened since Renard's and Silvie's revelations.

'Renard insists the killings were out of desperation, that they were trapped here with no way out in sight.

Which, now I've experienced it, I can say would make you do some crazy things.'

'Jesus,' Aloisia whispered. 'How . . . I can't believe I didn't see this. Didn't realise . . .'

I was having a hard time with that as well. I kept thinking about how vehemently Aloisia had defended Lars's character. I'd thought she was being protective of her staff, but she'd called Lilli a thief and a liar easily enough. Was that because Lilli had been caught red-handed, or was there more to it?

More importantly, did I have it in me to keep turning over rocks after everything that had happened today? If anything, I needed to focus on myself and getting out of this place in one piece. I'd lived my life by the code that I could only ever depend on myself. Trying to help other people here had only put me in danger and had nearly ended with me crushed in the jaws of a wolf.

'What do we do now?' Aloisia asked.

'We wait and let the police handle it.' I sighed. 'I just want to go home. But I think Silvie has a pretty strong case for self-defence. She's also pregnant, she seems certain it's Lars's baby.'

Aloisia looked sick. 'And Renard?'

'. . . He killed four people. Maybe he can claim Lars was manslaughter, that he didn't mean to kill him. But I don't think he's going to get away without prison time. He seems fairly resigned to it. All he wants now is for the truth to come out.'

'This is such a mess,' Aloisia whispered. 'And . . . what about these?'

She held up the rifle and I realised I was still holding the now empty gun.

'The vault?' I suggested. 'There are probably more bullets for this somewhere. Better if it's out of play entirely. We can stick them in the deposit hatch.'

'What if they change their minds about going quietly and try to attack us?' Aloisia said.

'Better that there are no guns for them to get their hands on then,' I pointed out.

She opened her mouth to argue, but just then a tinny trill started up, sounding in two quick bursts, then silence, then sounding again. I tried to work out where it was coming from.

'Is that . . . an alarm?' I asked, but Aloisia was already running, clattering down the corridor in her heeled pumps.

'It's a phone!'

Chapter 29

As we raced towards Aloisia's and Lars's office, my mind was a blur of conflicting thoughts. We still had no power from the utility building so it had to be a landline phone, but it hadn't been working before. Had whatever damage the avalanche had done been repaired elsewhere, giving us a link to the outside world? Or was it an internal call from another part of the retreat?

Aloisia reached the desk before I could and snatched the phone from its cradle. Our eyes met as she brought it to her ear and I saw my own confusion reflected back at me. As I set my gun down on the desk a bubble of hope swelled painfully inside my chest. We were getting out of here.

'Hello?' she said, then some sort of ingrained response must have kicked in, because she continued, 'This is Aloisia at The Sorgente speaking, how may I assist you?'

I couldn't hear the other side of the conversation, just a general buzz as someone spoke on the line. Slowly, Aloisia settled into her desk chair and started to nod. 'Thank God. OK . . . I see . . . Just wait a moment, please.' She covered the receiver with her hand. 'It's our parent company – the landline is the only thing that doesn't use our generators. Apparently the line was down but it's been repaired. I need to explain everything to them – can you go and check on Carri and the people in the spa? Just so I can give a full report?'

'Of course,' I said, but my suspicion was piqued. I didn't much like the idea of leaving the room now that we finally had a way to contact those outside The Sorgente, especially as I wasn't entirely sure about Aloisia's motives. But there wasn't much I could do without causing a scene and losing her trust.

Still, I wasn't above a little eavesdropping.

I left the room and shut the door but didn't immediately leave. After a few moments of cautious silence I heard Aloisia speak again.

'We've been without power since the avalanche. Heavy casualties, and we need immediate medical help for several of the guests – one has overdosed but we're trying to keep her stable, and a few of the guests and staff are injured and require attention for broken bones . . . No, I don't think we'll be able to last much longer on the supplies we currently have . . . When do you think the ploughs will break through? OK . . . we can make it to tomorrow morning, I think that's doable. Yes, thank you.'

Ploughs. So they were working to clear the snow blocking the road. From the sounds of it, by tomorrow morning they'd be through to us and we'd have the police and ambulances arriving. That was good. Satisfied with this little update and knowing I ought not to push my luck by delaying further in case Aloisia came out after me, I rushed off to check on Carri.

'What're you doing?' Patrick growled as I passed him,

like a chained dog. 'Let me out of here now or I swear I'm going to sue you into the ground!'

I was already at the stairs, hurrying up them. 'Go nuts. Gives me an excuse to ruin you.'

He went silent, thankfully. After the past hour or so I was drained. I didn't have anything else to give. The only thing I wanted was to get off this mountain and back to my life. Nearly losing it entirely had given me a new appreciation for what I had. I wasn't about to give this place another chance at killing me.

In Carri's room I found Jade and Roberta sitting on the same side of Carri's unconscious body. They were close together and there was a definite air of camaraderie that hadn't been there before. I wasn't entirely surprised. After all, they'd been stuck together in this room for a few hours now, caring for Carri. That sort of thing formed bonds quickly – I remembered how Silvie, Renard and I had embraced after our narrow escape. Trauma really did a number on people and I was no exception.

Roberta seemed more relaxed, less anxious and mousy. There was a determined and resilient stiffness to her spine. For the first time I could see how she would have been a good nurse had she finished her training. She had a sort of quiet strength that made me feel as though Carri was in good hands with her.

'How's she doing?' I asked.

'Mostly the same,' Roberta answered. 'Good thing you found the Narcan though, a while ago she started breathing abnormally, but she's settled now. I hope the extra doses can help her overcome the drugs in her system . . . Did I hear gunshots just now?' She looked at me as if she wasn't sure whether to be worried or not.

'Oh yeah, sorry – we caught the people responsible and both guns are in Aloisia's office now. Renard and Silvie are in custody, as it were. It was Renard who killed the security guards and Lars. Silvie . . . helped a bit.'

'Why?' Jade asked, looking at me like she wasn't quite sure whether I was talking sense or not.

'Honestly, it'd take too long to get into it but . . . Renard doesn't want to hurt anyone else. It was about them and what they were doing here,' I said. 'We should just focus on making sure we all stay safe and wait for help to come. Which'll be soon.'

I didn't want to give an exact timeline because if they mentioned it to Aloisia later it'd become obvious I'd been spying on her. But Jade and Roberta both deserved a little bit of hope under the circumstances.

'I need to go check on things in the spa – do you need anything else? Aside from more Narcan, which I don't think is happening,' I said.

'If they have an intubation kit, that might be necessary if she stops breathing,' Roberta sighed. 'I'd prefer oxygen, but . . .'

'Not likely,' I said regretfully. 'Think whatever oxygen they had on-site got used right after the avalanche, but I'll see what I can find.'

I hurried off to the spa to check on Paula and found her mostly awake and shuffling around. She'd obviously heard the gunshots but had stayed put, probably more to save her own skin than for her patients' sake. Still, I could understand that. In her position I'd have probably done the same. With an update on her remaining patients and a promise from her to locate an intubation kit and get it upstairs, I returned to Aloisia's office.

She wasn't on the phone when I arrived, just sitting in her chair staring at the black plastic handset with a subdued expression, her hands in her lap beneath the desk. I felt a twinge of foreboding deep down in my belly. Why did she look so worried when rescue was meant to be on its way? She looked up as I came in and cleared her expression with what appeared to be a concentrated effort. I recognised the look of someone putting on their customer service smile.

'They had to go – lots to organise,' she said. 'I said I'd give them the update in an hour. What do you have for me to tell them?'

I retook my seat from earlier. 'Carri's stable for now, hopefully won't run out of Narcan before help comes, whenever that is. Paula's lost two of her five patients – the one who was impaled and the broken leg. But she thinks the two with concussions are past the worst of it and she's set the broken finger so . . . looking fairly hopeful. Considering.'

'Still . . . a lot of people whose families are going to be getting bad news shortly,' Aloisia sighed and sank back in her chair. 'They think they're going to break through the snow wall to us in the morning. So . . . I'm sure ambulances will be the first to arrive. I took your advice and put the guns into the vault's deposit hatch. They've done enough damage for now.' She took a shaky breath and looked around her office, at the pictures on the walls and the certificates in her and Lars's names. 'They're worried – my bosses – about how this is going to play out once the media gets involved.'

'I can imagine,' I said, though I was still considering what she'd said about the guns and the expression on her face before she'd seen me. One of worry and conflict. I rested my hands on the desk, trying to get her to mirror me – but she didn't.

Was she holding a gun under there? Even now she could be pointing it at me, under the desk. Waiting for me to force her hand, to make myself someone she had to get rid of for her employers.

I was being paranoid, I told myself. Seeing threats where there were none after so long being on edge. I cleared my throat and continued, as easily as possible. 'I wouldn't want to be the person stuck doing that press conference. I mean, the avalanche is bad enough, the lack of food, the ill-equipped infirmary with the out-of-date defibrillator. That all looks pretty bad even before you add in the human trafficking and the murders.'

Aloisia shut her eyes for a moment, her body going limp and hopeless in her chair. Still her hands remained hidden. 'What would you do?'

'If it was me or if it was my client?' I asked.

'Your client – if this was your crisis to manage . . . what would you be telling them to do? Telling me to do?' She fixed me with a helpless look and lifted one hand to push her hair out of her face. 'Because I don't know anymore, what I should be trying to do here.'

Relieved to see her move at last, exposing an empty hand, I considered for a moment. It felt good to be back in my element, where I knew the rules and could take control. I'd missed it, I realised. It was as reassuringly familiar as the rustle of cellophane on a packet of cigarettes. The same thrill every time.

I leaned back in my chair and gave Aloisia a considering look. 'If The Sorgente was my client then . . . I'd be telling them to cover up as much as possible. The avalanche isn't anyone's fault, not exactly. That can be overcome with a good PR campaign, some nominal precautions put in place. You could definitely get people up here again. Couple of little planning issues wouldn't take much to bury – having the backup power in the same place as the main was a bad idea, but we could shift that blame onto one or two people during the construction and planning process. Your doctor's dead and only a few people know about the lack of supplies and the state the medical bay was in, so pretty easy to pay them off or pressure them to keep quiet.' I shrugged. 'All in all, could be worse.'

Aloisia was watching me carefully, taking it all in. I liked how that felt, being listened to. Being respected for what I could do. She was soaking up my every word. A far cry from how I'd felt practically begging Renard and then Max for my life. Still there was a lingering prickle of unease at the back of my neck. Only one of her hands was visible, now resting on the desk. The other was out of view.

I kept going. 'The other stuff . . . well, quite a few people here know some of it – that would be harder to keep out of the press.'

'But not impossible?' Aloisia asked, quickly. She shifted in her chair. Was that the creak of castors on carpet, or her hand tightening on the gun's plastic grip? 'We could pay them, or . . .'

I forced my eyes away from the surface of the desk, where I'd been staring as if I could see through the wood. 'Oh, absolutely – money would work on most of them. Paula definitely, since she's boozing her way to being struck off. Roberta's going through a divorce and could use it, plus you have the attempted murder of her husband to hold over her. Patrick's greedy enough to buy off, maybe use him in some press ops, give him some victim status he can exploit to keep his career going. Jade would definitely take a sponsorship with a place this high profile, and linked to health . . . very good for her brand. Carri probably won't remember much of anything that happened anyway. And, unfortunately, a lot of the other people Lars victimised are dead already, but you could find anyone who left or was fired before now, like Lilli, and hush them up. Make sure they never point the finger your way. Sounds like most of them wouldn't turn down a settlement off the books.'

'But Renard and Silvie . . . they'd be the main problem?' Aloisia said. 'They wouldn't just take a pay-off, not after what happened.'

Still trying to push my nerves down in favour of clear thinking, I clicked my tongue thoughtfully to buy time. 'Mmmm . . . you'd be surprised. If Silvie is pregnant and she keeps it, well, kids are expensive and people will make all kinds of sacrifices to give their children a good life. Including moral ones. And even if she chooses not to carry to term she's still going to be homeless and any lawsuit about this place will take years to pay her anything . . . she might go for a reasonable amount of hush money in perpetuity. Renard, on the other hand, he's got an agenda and if he doesn't love Silvie enough to keep quiet for her sake, you can bet he won't let you buy his silence. No, him you'd have to threaten and he doesn't really have anything to lose so . . . not sure how well that would work.'

'But it could be done?' Aloisia pressed, eyes alight with hope. 'If he would keep quiet, it would be for Silvie?'

'I can see that happening,' I confirmed, willing her to show me her hands. 'And, trust me, I've done this dance so many times . . . honestly, I could walk you through it with my eyes closed. But that doesn't come for free.'

'Of course.' Aloisia's face took on a more relaxed expression. 'Well, I'm sure my employers would pay very well for your expertise. Plus a generous remuneration for your personal experience here.'

I smiled a small half-smile. She was relaxed and calm, I wasn't in danger as long as she didn't panic. 'It would have to be very generous, you realise.'

'I'm sure whatever number you're thinking of would sit well with them,' Aloisia assured me. Then finally, finally, she laid both her hands on the desk and laced her fingers together. I almost let out a sigh of relief. The panicked hamster wheel in my brain slowed down and I could finally think properly. Finally remember something that almost made me laugh aloud.

I stopped worrying about Aloisia and whether or not she'd put the gun in her lap or a shelf under the desk. That didn't matter. There was only one thing I could do right now to ensure everyone got out of this in one piece.

My job.

'Hmm . . . well that is reassuring,' I said thoughtfully, crossing my legs and tapping a foot in the air. 'I can take care of everything I've already outlined. But that doesn't account for your biggest problem.'

'But if that's not Renard . . .' Aloisia blinked at me, confused. 'What is it?'

'Who,' I corrected.

'Who is it then?' she said, clearly on the edge of losing her patience.

'Me,' I shrugged.

'You?' Aloisia gaped at me.

'Like I said. I can take care of everything . . . but I don't want to. I don't want to cover up for another shitty company run by morally bankrupt arseholes. And that includes you, I'm sorry to say. Because I liked you, Aloisia, I really did . . . and it's quite upsetting that after everything that we've been through together in the past few days, you would choose to lie to me.'

'I haven't,' she said, too quickly. 'I'm just asking for your help because I'm scared, OK? Scared they're going to scapegoat me or force me to quit. I've worked so hard to make The Sorgente what it is and if it goes under then I never get the recognition for that, and that recognition is what'll get me another job at this level, or higher. This is my life I'm talking about.'

'It's not though – it's your job,' I said sharply, feeling the jittery way I usually did when working hard on a stubborn client. 'Your life is what's going to be over if and when everyone else finds out that you lied.'

Her eyes were wide and her voice climbed in pitch. 'I'm not lying! I am in the same boat as you with all this – it's been an awful, horrendous few days and I never saw any of this coming. Any of it.'

I watched her for a moment, her expression so pleading and desperate. So adamant and perfectly trustworthy. She was a good liar when it really counted, I'd give her that. And I really did like her, which had blinded me to what she was really capable of.

'I believe you didn't know about Lars . . .' I began, and watched her shoulders slump slightly in relief. '. . . until you fired Lilli.'

Aloisia stiffened and I knew I was right. That what had been at the back of my mind ever since Silvie mentioned the name 'Lilli' in connection with Lars's crimes earlier was true.

'I don't know what you're talking about.' Aloisia's tone was careful and flat now; I'd caught her off guard and she was struggling to remain believable.

'You caught Lilli stealing the day of the avalanche and you sent her away – lucky for her, right?' I sat casually, but kept my eyes on her, watching her every move and expression. 'It seemed weird to me that you would defend Lars so faithfully and then call Lilli a thief right to my face. Not just a thief – a liar. You wanted to paint her as a liar, because there was a possibility that when everything else came to light, she might talk. And what would she say? That once you caught her, she spilled the beans on Lars and his whole scheme. She was only young, probably still young enough to believe that if she told the truth, to you – another woman, no less, and Lars's superior – you'd believe her. That you'd help.'

Her eyes flickered with something like shame. 'She . . . I thought it was a lie, to get herself out of trouble.'

'Now that, I don't believe. Sorry,' I said, anger making my voice more strident as I continued. 'I think she told you and suddenly what you'd seen between Silvie and Lars at the sauna started making a lot more sense. You might even have gone looking for the criminal record checks and done a little digging. That's why you were so desperate to find Lars that night.' I bulldozed over her stuttering denials, unwilling to stop now I was building steam. 'You wanted to stop this before it went further and ruined the good thing you had going here. And then the avalanche happened and . . . everything got a lot more complicated.'

She was mute now, staring at me as if I was Medusa – turning her to stone in her sleek leather chair. I took a quick breath and ploughed on.

'Maybe you even believed at first that it was Lars killing off his accomplices, that somehow he'd got wind that you knew about his scheme and he was going to loot the vault and disappear. You were hoping that once he was caught, the buck would stop with him. But then you found out he was dead all along – another lie you told me, by the way. You knew it was Silvie who'd told you he was alive and well all along. You lied to me. You were keeping all your cards close, trying to work it all out for yourself.'

'I . . .' Aloisia choked, but no other words were forthcoming.

'You must have been so relieved that he was dead. You can pin a lot on a dead man. Did you decide then, to make a deal with whoever survived and keep everything under wraps? You didn't want to take a problem to your bosses, but an oven-ready solution? They'd be really happy with that. And you'd just be the poor innocent manager who was duped by her deputy, and not the self-serving cow who found out her colleague was a rapist and an extortionist . . . and covered it up for him.'

Aloisia didn't move, didn't blink. I could see the calculations behind her eyes, the variables spinning like the dials of a fruit machine. There was no way out, she and I both knew it. She'd lied to me and I'd caught her. I still had the notebook, Lilli was out there somewhere and would validate my theory. Aloisia was done.

And whether she had it or not, the gun wasn't loaded.

I'd emptied it into a wolf only a short while ago and I was willing to bet my life – literally – that Aloisia hadn't had bullets lying around in her office.

'You asked what I would do,' I continued, gentling my tone with a great deal of effort. 'Well, if I were you, I'd remember that no one knows that I – meaning you – had any knowledge of what Lars was doing, aside from Lilli, who only told you about it right before the avalanche. And obviously since then you've been preoccupied, cut off from the outside world. I'm guessing you told her you'd investigate – just to get her to go quietly – so, as far as she knows that's what you fully intended to do. And now you know it was all true.' I held up my hands. 'You might look a little naive but you haven't done anything wrong, not that anyone can prove. That is, unless you try to cover this up – that's when things get a bit dicey for you. Because you're going to be the one making the threats and writing the cheques, so your boss and his boss and everyone else up the chain can say it was all your fault when this inevitably comes out. And it will come out, because I'm going to make sure it does.'

'I'll lose my job,' she whispered. 'If I don't help them . . . they said they'll fire me.'

I wrinkled my nose. 'I doubt it. They'll offer you redundancy, because that way you can't sue them for firing you. You'll find another job – you're the hero manager who coped with an avalanche; don't tell me you can't spin that. Look—' I sighed and leaned forwards in my chair '—I know what happened on that call. They put someone like me on – a poisonous bitch who told you it's just a little lie, it's not that bad. It's just . . . not saying something. But the thing about lies that they don't tell you is that they're sort of like credit cards. You can wait and wait, but the debt doesn't go away. It grows. It keeps spiralling out of control, until you wonder why you didn't just pay up front. Believe me, the truth is a lot easier to sell when it's the first thing out of your mouth.'

Aloisia appeared to think about this for a moment, then her eyes narrowed slightly. 'Why are you helping me?'

'Because I think you're generally a good person who made a mistake, and I've recently had a bit of a personal awakening in that regard.' I shrugged. 'That and . . . I'm not doing it for nothing.'

'What do you want?' she said, quietly.

'As soon as that vault opens?' I sat back in my chair, legs crossed. 'I want my vape, and a cup of coffee. In that order.' I sighed. 'And then I want to go home.'

Chapter 30

Aloisia and I had brokered a certain kind of peace and understanding. It had helped to restore some of my faith in myself to be honest. I'd been sorely tempted to slip back into the comfy, terrible old me. But I'd resisted and, because of me, she was doing the right thing. Or at least trying to.

I still checked under her desk the second she got up and went to call the others down. I'm not entirely sold on working purely on trust. There was no gun. But that didn't mean she hadn't been tempted. Maybe she'd checked and found it empty. Maybe if it hadn't been, we'd have had a very different conversation.

Still, "maybe" wasn't worth anything. What happened had happened and that would just have to be good enough for me. At the end of the day I could only judge people by what they did, not what they thought about doing. My thoughts wouldn't pass muster either.

Jade returned with Aloisia as Paula had turned up to assist Roberta, bringing the intubation stuff with her. With three of us we alternated guard duty over the store cupboard with distributing food and news among the survivors upstairs. They were relieved to know that the person responsible for the deaths had been shut away, but more so to find out that we'd soon all be leaving the mountain.

Word spread and I had to be very firm that valuables were to be collected after midnight and couldn't be accessed before. By the time the vault opened there was a queue down the hallway and into the foyer and people were getting antsy. Thankfully we'd wheeled Patrick into Aloisia's office to keep him out of the way so as not to start a riot.

I was one of the last people to get my valuables back. The only things I was really excited about were the coffee pot, grounds and my vape. Even though it wasn't the same as a real cigarette.

We boiled water and made as much real and instant coffee as we could from what had been confiscated. That actually seemed to go down well and for the first time since the avalanche I saw guests talking to one another in a way that suggested friendliness and not imminent mutiny. With my coffee in hand I went up to the roof access door and waited, watching the dark skyline for signs that we were saved.

The lights came first – flickering blue and amber in a long string along the road. The sound of engines came next and then I heard people below rushing to windows so they could watch the approaching vehicles. I set my empty cup down and retreated to the stairs, hurrying down to join the rest of the mob.

'Everyone back up from the doors!' Aloisia was saying, corralling guests and the few remaining staff away. 'We need to let the ambulance crews through!'

Most listened; those who didn't were quickly shoved or elbowed into line by Jade or myself. An ambulance appeared, slowly mulching its way over the pristine flowerbeds and paths that had been narrowly spared when the avalanche destroyed the aerial tram, just to be mangled by our rescuers. The sight of all the faces of my fellow survivors, lit by blue flashing lights, was somehow both heartening and sad. It was finally all over and the reality of how many lives had been lost was sitting heavily with me. Talking Renard down, convincing Aloisia to do the right thing, saving Carri, those were all wins. But in between those we had lost a lot.

Aloisia opened the front doors and the paramedics came through, apparently stunned to be with us, to see so many people. I quickly stepped in.

'The overdose patient, she's upstairs, this way. The others are that way, in the spa – Jade?'

'Follow me.' Jade waved them onwards, commanding their attention as the rest of the gathered crowd asked questions about the avalanche and when we could leave. As the paramedics followed me up to the mezzanine a general cry went round the crowd.

More vehicles were coming, reported by someone who was peering out through the kitchen windows. Cars with white lights – a whole stream of them, maybe twenty, all identical. The intent was clear: they were coming for us, for the guests. To take us away from this place.

I looked down at Aloisia and caught her eye. She shrugged helplessly and I understood. The cars had been sent by her higher-ups, in defiance of the fact that the police would want to talk to everyone at The Sorgente in the wake of the disaster and subsequent murders. They knew, as I did, that the trapped guests would be frothing at the mouth to get off the mountain and that it would take a lot of effort for the police to stop them. They were banking on it not being enough. Sure the police would eventually manage to get statements from everyone but it would take days of tracking them down to different countries, different airports. Meanwhile The Sorgente would get credit for being so helpful in getting their guests to safety, even if they'd had to share a ride to civilisation.

Unfortunately, I would have to stay. One of the downsides of being well-informed. At least they'd probably put me up somewhere else – though no doubt it would be far from the luxurious retreat I'd booked. Right then I didn't care. In fact, as long as whichever cheap hellhole the police put me up in had coffee, hot water and Wi-Fi I could use to order a filthy pizza, I'd be more than happy. Wellness wasn't all it was cracked up to be.

I watched as Carri was loaded onto a stretcher and carried downstairs. She was pale, sticky with sweat but still alive. I wondered how much she'd really taken in over the past day or so. If she'd even remember what happened to her or if it would all feel like a nightmare. Likewise the three casualties, two staff members and one guest, who had been stuck in their respective treatment rooms, totally unaware of all that had occurred. I wondered if they'd even identified the noises they'd heard as gunshots.

The paramedics hadn't long departed when the cars began to arrive. All of them black and sleek, hired from some high-end rental firm, no doubt. There was a stampede as guests rushed for their luggage and valuables, shouting for assistance from staff who either wouldn't or couldn't help them. Bags were thrown from the mezzanine by those who couldn't face the stairs and some burst open, sending silk underwear and cashmere jumpers through the air.

One of the last people to leave was Livvy. I spotted her as she came scurrying along the mezzanine, huge handbag clenched under her arm. As she reached the top of the stairs I saw her stumble a little bit. A shower of gold and silver items fell from the bag, catching the light as they tumbled down the steps. She looked around quickly as if checking for witnesses, then gathered up what she could and hurried along. If I had to guess I'd suppose she'd been darting into unsupervised rooms and taking a few bits and pieces from people's reclaimed valuables. After all, her husband had managed to get most of their accounts frozen and investigated. After stumping up for her escape to this place, she had to need a little extra cash. Anyone who noticed things missing would probably blame the hotel.

I suppose I could have said something. Possibly should have. But a little petty theft, even if it was of thousands of pounds' worth of jewellery and knick-knacks, felt exactly that – petty. Especially in the face of everything else that had happened. As far as I knew, my red lacquer S.T. Dupont lighter was shoved in her bra or something and I couldn't bring myself to care. As much as I was apparently making saving souls my new calling, there were limits. Renard and Aloisia could be saved. I doubted very much if anything I could say would bring Livvy round to a new, less selfish way of thinking. No, airport security could sort her out when she turned up with all that suspicious baggage. That or when she tried to sell what were likely to be one-of-a-kind items, the police could handle it. I was tired.

Halfway through the chaos the police started to arrive and attempted to block the doors, to reason with the guests. But short of placing them under arrest there was nothing they could do. Like swarming ants carrying designer luggage instead of leaves, the guests poured out of The Sorgente and piled into the cars, leaving quiet in their wake.

The police gathered in the foyer, negotiating the bedding that hadn't yet been kicked aside and the spilled clothing alongside abandoned bags. Aloisia was waiting for them by the reception desk and I was surprised to see that Jade still remained, as did Roberta. Aside from Patrick, still tied up in the office, and Paula, sitting at the bottom of the stairs with a coffee and her patient notes, none of the other guests had stuck around.

'Officers, if you'd like to come this way, I'll explain everything to you in the kitchen,' Aloisia said. 'We have several . . . um . . . suspects? In custody. I don't know how much has already been shared with you by my managers.'

The assembled police looked doubtfully at those of us still there as if worried we might escape as well. I glanced around at everyone and then cleared my throat. 'They'll be here till the coffee runs out, don't worry about it.'

They still seemed reluctant but went with Aloisia. I followed after them, as I wasn't about to leave it to her to set the record straight. I didn't trust her a hundred per cent even after everything. Two officers stayed in the foyer, presumably to watch the door.

Patrick started yelling from the office as we passed and Aloisia waved a hand at the door. 'One of the guests tried to hold us at gunpoint, so we had to tie him up.'

The police exchanged looks and I guessed that little

nugget of information hadn't made it into the call that brought them here. They'd probably only been told about the avalanche and that some deaths had occurred afterwards. Aloisia's bosses were leaving her to spin the really big lies herself, in person. The best way to ensure plausible deniability.

In the kitchen Aloisia hopped up onto a counter and wrapped her arms around herself. The six officers who'd accompanied us there arranged themselves around the room and the most senior-looking one – certainly the one with the busiest and most decorated uniform – cleared his throat.

'Can you tell us what happened, after the avalanche?' he asked Aloisia. 'And why you have detained people here?'

She took a deep breath and seemed to let go of something, as her spine straightened and her expression smoothed out. Our eyes met and I gave her a reassuring nod, the kind I'd usually give to a client about to lie their arse off. This time, I was letting her know it was all right to tell the truth.

'It actually starts before then . . . with a member of staff called Lilli, who made some very serious allegations prior to the avalanche.'

I fought the urge to give her an encouraging thumbs up and took a seat on a stainless steel counter, while she told our story, unedited.

The truth had never sounded so good.

Epilogue

'That'll be £7.75, please.' The woman on the checkout smiled at me and I smiled back, handing over a tenner and waiting for my change.

'I like your bracelet,' I said, nodding at the braided leather on her wrist. It was very intricate, a seven-strand woven design in different shades of brown. It avoided being unfortunately hippyish thanks to the industrial-looking clasp on it, which appeared to be handmade as well.

'Thanks – I made it actually.' She handed back my change and I tucked it away in my purse.

'That's amazing – do you have a storefront online or something? I'd love one.'

'Jesus Christ,' I heard someone behind me hiss.

I didn't have to turn to know that it was the man who'd been tapping his foot in line behind me for the entire five minutes I'd been queuing. The back of my neck was hot from his irritated and faintly stale coffee-scented sighs. I rolled my eyes at the girl on the checkout and she hid a guilty smile.

'I'll give you my Instagram, if that's OK. I don't really

sell them but I can always make you one just because.' She shrugged, jotting her account down on my receipt. 'And I'll give you a follow back.'

'Cheers . . . have a good rest of your day,' I said and picked up the receipt and my nicotine gum before shooting her a parting smile and walking away.

On my way out of the supermarket I stopped at the café kiosk outside and got myself a latte. While waiting in line beside the newspapers I picked one up and flicked through. Patrick's sentencing hadn't made the front page, nor indeed the first twenty. But it was there. Five years, for possessing a firearm with intent to cause fear or violence. I imagined Roberta reading the same paper in her cottage garden and smiled.

Livvy was still on a suspended sentence herself for being caught selling stolen engraved jewellery. I wasn't sure if she'd turn her life around but, there was always hope. I hadn't heard much of anything about Emmitt – but there were rumours of a reunion tour for him and the band. Time would tell if his sobriety could handle that or not. I'd dropped his agent a recommendation for a new wellness retreat in Spain, managed by Aloisia. I could probably get her to offer him a discount.

I took my coffee back to my car and settled in. I found the cashier's Instagram account in moments and followed her. She had a few scattered photos of her bracelets in there, but it was mostly the usual selfies, sunsets and seascapes. They were lovely bracelets though. I took a screenshot of her account and added it to my folder of potential candidates for pro bono PR services. It was something I'd started doing to give Brie more experience and, to be honest, to clean up our company reputation.

After helping to do so much bad, getting people to trust us to do good was a process. But hey, nothing worth having was built overnight.

Our biggest project so far had been a crowdfunding campaign for Renard's legal fees. While the authorities had declined to prosecute Silvie, he was very much still facing manslaughter charges at the very least. We'd done a lot of PR for him and got his story out there. Landing Silvie some exclusive interviews and a book deal had helped create public sympathy for him. She was doing well the last time we spoke, a week or so ago. It looked like her mother had ditched her awful stepdad and had welcomed her back. I wasn't sure if it would last, but Silvie would find her feet again even if it didn't, I was sure of it.

My phone rang as I was taking my first sip of coffee – one of the two I allowed myself daily. I saw Brie's number and answered, putting her on speakerphone.

'Morning – how're things at the office? I'll be in later, I'm just on my way back from that place in Hitchin you recommended? It was a great shout actually – such a relaxing weekend and I think the lavender farm might be interested in our rebranding package. How was your weekend?'

'Pretty good, thank you.' I could hear Brie stirring her tea at her desk. 'Went wedding cake tasting which was lush. Glad you had a good rest because . . . I'm calling about M. Shale Limited?'

I sighed, yet another ghost coming back to haunt me. Montgomery Shale. In the year and a half since I'd returned from my 'wellness' break in Switzerland I'd turned Wallace Consulting around, made it into something I could be proud of. Something that let me sleep at night without pharmacological intervention. But that change also now meant we'd ended up on the opposite side of things to our former clients. Situations that could be tricky both legally and professionally.

'OK, let me have it,' I said, leaning back in my seat. 'What're they coming after us with?'

'Well . . . Thanks to the pressure we've been putting on them via socials, they're prepared to offer all four of our clients a generous severance package in exchange for a signed non-disclosure about why they were fired. In exchange they want them to take down any social media posts about the company . . . and retract their "unfair assertion" that they were fired because of their LGBTQ+ identities.'

I rolled my eyes. Amanda Shale had turned out to be just as much of a bigot as her father, she just didn't rant about it on Twitter. But she had made a big problem for herself by firing her office's only queer employees for trumped-up reasons and barely concealed rhetoric about 'not fitting in with the culture'. Of course I'd taken on the whistle-blowers as clients – using social pressure to circumvent the efforts of very expensive solicitors, and had got them interviews, planned a social media campaign and even got them on national radio. All to push the company into a payout that would cushion the blow of sudden unemployment, faster than any wrongful dismissal case. During all of that I'd kept what I knew about Montgomery Shale's previous issues secret. I wasn't about to be accused of being indiscreet with client information. Even if my company was no longer the same one that had helped them cover up their founder's bigotry with a fake boyfriend – who was now playing a bit-part in a soap opera off the back of his 'fame'.

'Well, it's up to our clients but I'd definitely push back on that last point. We have the leaked email that proves it was a matter of their identities being an issue so they can't claim it was all a big misunderstanding. Releasing that to the public would really put a dent in them.'

'Right,' Brie said, 'but . . . the thing is they've brought in Richard Weaver? And he's saying that if we don't convince our clients to take the deal as offered, he's going to go public with the fact we . . . you . . . orchestrated the Montgomery Shale cover-up? He said, and I quote, "Let's see how many clients the high and mighty Chloe Wallace can get once everyone knows what a Judas she is".'

'Judas seems a bit too clever for Richard.' I sighed. Richard Weaver had once been one of my competitors. Now he was my replacement – slithering to the top of the food chain in my absence.

'Well, he said "Jupitus",' but I think that's what he meant,' Brie said, a smirk evident in her voice. 'But this could be really bad for us, right? I mean, we've rehabilitated our image a lot since then but, all anyone's going to see is that a queer woman helped a homophobe fake a coming out story to get out of trouble. Sorry,' she added.

'No, that's fair. Honestly I didn't feel good about it then and I feel even shittier about it now.' I set my coffee down and meditatively unwrapped some gum. 'Fuck it . . . take it to the clients and tell them that last point is bullshit. Let Richard do whatever he wants. It'll look just as bad for Shale as it does for us, if not worse. Either he's bluffing or he's stupid enough to do it, but I think we need to take that gamble.'

'You're sure?' Brie asked doubtfully. 'It's pretty

damning, and you were so excited about "finally being able to justify going to Pride".'

I was, but I'd rather go with my head held high than because of another lie. I actually had a date lined up at one of the after parties, miracle of miracles.

'But it's the truth. Might as well face it now rather than putting it off until later.' I popped the gum into my mouth and looked out of my windscreen, watching a pair of ravens hop around the almost deserted car park. 'Honesty is the best policy, and all that jazz.'

'A few years ago you'd have slapped those words out of my mouth, metaphorically speaking. Or not.' Brie laughed uncertainly. 'This really isn't just a bit, is it? You're really serious about what we're doing?'

'I am, yeah,' I said, and turned the key in the ignition. The satnav blinked to life, guiding me towards the office. We weren't in central London anymore, morals weren't profitable enough for Soho real estate. But we had a nice place in a commuter town with views over a canal and a balcony garden. I'd be there in less than an hour, on clear roads, with sunshine blazing overhead. Just another thing to be grateful for. 'See you in a bit, yeah? Don't do anything I wouldn't do.'

Acknowledgements

First thanks as always go to my family for being there for me while I wrote this book. The coffees and sympathy were much appreciated. I was also on a diet at the time of writing, so can't imagine that made me any more fun to be around! Shout out to my Auntie Mel for asking 'How does my lovely niece know so much about drugs???' of my last book, this one will probably be just as concerning to you!

I owe everyone at Avon for their support, the fantastic cover art and copy that have gone along with this and all my other books. Thank you to Rachel Hart, who got me started with this one – you are a wonderful editor and I'm sad to see you go. But I'm also thrilled to be working with Anna Nightingale in the editing stages of this novel – your humour and imagination brought so much to the re-draft. I had a blast working on this with you.

Apologies to Cat Phipps – when I saw your copy-edit I promised myself I would learn more about hyphens and how to put ellipses in properly. I can't say it'll happen quickly, but bless you for not burning my house down. All joking aside, your steer on the final confrontation with Aloisia was inspired. Thank you.

Thanks go to Dandy Smith, a brilliant author who begged me not to kill a dog in any of my books. Do wolves count? Bit late to ask now.

Thanks as always to Laura Williams at Greene & Heaton, my incredible agent. For every three crackpot ideas I send you, there's usually at least one you can see the potential in. A great skill. Without you I would probably still be writing up reports on broken guttering or the flammability of upholstery, so thank you.

Lastly, thank you to everyone who has bought, borrowed and read *The Alpine Retreat*. I hope you enjoyed the book and would love to hear about it on Instagram @sarah_goodwin_author.

You'll want to stay. Until you can't leave . . .

A group of strangers arrive on a beautiful but remote island, ready for the challenge of a lifetime: to live there for one year, without contact with the outside world.

But twelve months later, on the day when the boat is due to return for them, no one arrives.

Eight people stepped foot on the island. How many will make it off alive?

A gripping, twisty page-turner about secrets, lies and survival at all costs. Perfect for fans of *The Castaways, The Sanatorium* and *One by One*.

'Because he chose you. Out of thirteen girls. You were the one. The last one.'

Lucy Townsend lives a normal life. She has a husband she loves, in-laws she can't stand and she's just found out she's going to be a mother.

But Lucy has a dark and dangerous secret.

She is not who she says she is.

Lucy is not even her real name.

A totally gripping, edge-of-your-seat thriller with twists and turns you just won't see coming. Perfect for fans of *Girl A* and *The Family Upstairs*.

It was a safe haven . . . until it became a trap.

Mila and her husband Ethan are on their way to her sister's wedding at a luxurious ski resort, when the car engine suddenly stops and won't start again.

Stranded, with night closing in, they make their way on foot back to where they saw a sign for some cabins. They find the windows boarded up and the buildings in disrepair.

They have the eerie sense they shouldn't be there. With snow falling more heavily, they have no choice but to break into one to spend the night.

In the morning when Mila wakes, Ethan is gone.
Now she is all alone.
Or is she?

A totally gripping and spine-tingling psychological thriller. Perfect for fans of *The Hunting Party* and *The Castaways*.

You can't outrun the past . . .
. . . for what's done in the dark will come to light . . .

Summer, 2022. When Meg and Cat are forced to take a dangerous shortcut home one night, they notice two men silently following them. Suddenly running for their lives, they scramble into an abandoned building to hide and wait for help.

One year later. Attempting to escape the horrors of that fateful night, Meg barricades herself into a safehouse at the edge of a crumbling sea cliff. As a storm rages outside, a blackout plunges the house into darkness. But Meg's not alone.

A totally addictive psychological thriller with bombshell twists that will leave you stunned. Fans of *The Sanatorium, The Paris Apartment* and *One of the Girls* will be hooked from the very first page.

When the truth surfaces

. . . who will sink . . .

. . . and who will swim?

New Year's Eve, 2023. When Hannah and her friends rent a luxury yacht in an Italian marina, they party in style under the stars until they pass out.

The next morning, they are horrified to find they have been cut adrift into the open ocean, with no sight of land and no fuel in the engine. And that's when the first person goes missing . . .

A twisty locked-room thriller that will have fans of *The White Lotus*, Lucy Foley and Amy McCulloch addicted from the very first page!

'It's the hottest ticket in town. But once you're in, there's no getting out.'

Jody, Ari and Carla have won golden tickets to the summer's hottest music festival, which promises to be full of glamour, mystique and lots of freebies.

But, arriving on the sun-drenched shores of a private Greek island among influencers and celebrities, the trio are dismayed to find the small festival site far from the beacon of music, art and 'immersive experiences' they were promised. Disappointed but not deterred, they vow to make the most of the trip.

But when a shocking discovery on day three turns the festival into a nightmare, the girls find themselves trapped on the island with no escape . . .

Fyre Festival meets *One of the Girls* in this psychological thriller with twists you'll never see coming.

**Some parties are unforgettable . . .
this one might be deadly.**

In the dazzling lights of Thailand, socialite Lila Wilde is set for the night of her life. When her fame-hungry DJ boyfriend proposes at an exclusive nightclub, Lila makes a spur-of-the-moment decision: she invites a mix of strangers to keep the party going back at her luxurious villa – just a short flight over the Thai jungle.

But when disaster strikes mid-flight, the dream turns into a nightmare and the group are stranded in an unforgiving jungle, far from the world of luxury they know. What begins as a desperate fight for survival quickly descends into something darker as the stranded passengers realise the greatest threat might not be the jungle – but each other.

Fans of *The Castaways*, *The Hunting Party* and *The White Lotus* will be totally gripped from the very first page until the final, breath-taking conclusion.